The Back
Of The Tiger

By the same author

The Whitehall Sanction

The Back
Of The Tiger

A NOVEL

Jack Gerson

BEAUFORT BOOKS
Publishers
New York

Copyright © 1984 by Jack Gerson

Library of Congress Cataloging in Publication Data
Gerson, Jack.
   The back of the tiger.
   1. Kennedy, John F. (John Fitzgerald), 1917-1963 –
Assassination – Fiction.   I. Title.
TR6057.E72B3   1984   823'.914   84-20326
ISBN 0-8253-0261-7

Published in the United States by Beaufort Books

Printed in the U.S.A.   First American Edition

10 9 8 7 6 5 4 3 2 1

For Joe Stirling, without whom . . .

'In the past, those who foolishly
sought power by riding on the back
of the tiger ended up inside.'

JOHN F. KENNEDY
Inaugural Address
20 January 1961

Prologue

1979

His footsteps, echoing on the marble floor, resounding back from the high curved ceiling. That was the first impression. Second, phoney Greek architecture, period, late nineteenth century. An architect's disease of the time throughout the District of Columbia. Something, too, had been engraved on the stone above the entrance. He couldn't make it out. Thought it should be *E Pluribus Unum*.

The brass plaque on the wall had said 'Department of Justice' so he could be sure he was in the right place. But he was not at all sure it was the right place. Yet it was possibly the only place left.

He approached the reception desk. The young woman behind it was synthetically pretty, no hair out of place, no minute smear of lipstick. Some distance from her, leaning against a wall with easy confidence, a security guard. And to his right, a row of hard little seats on which sat a broken row of hard small ushers – youths with clear, unacned skin, and diamond chips for eyes. All of them, hell bent on being senators, secretaries of state or perhaps, modestly, upgraded ushers in the nearby Capitol Building.

'Good morning, can I help you?' The synthetic secretary said, and her smile brought her alive, not necessarily in an advantageous manner. Her teeth were crooked.

'McBride,' he said. 'Alexander McBride. Senator Newberry told me to come here.'

Eyes down, consulting a large appointments book. 'Oh, yes, Mr McBride. Room twenty-six.' Voice rose in pitch. 'Usher!'

A small aging youth came over.

'Take Mr McBride to Room twenty-six.'

'Thank you,' McBride said.

'Have a nice day.' An evocation, a prayer, surely more than good wishes. McBride knew it was a doubtful proposition. It seemed he hadn't had a nice day for a long time.

He was led up the stairway which could have come from the Tara set in *Gone With The Wind*. Past a great window from which he could see the exterior caryatides from close up. They might have been based on the founding fathers bearing justice on their shoulders; or a number of Hollywood character actors of the thirties who specialised in playing crooked politicians. There was Edward Arnold there, Robert Warwick and Guy Kibbee further on.

Room twenty-six was nondescript. A room. Four walls. A small desk, one upright chair and two armchairs. An ashtray on a side table and beside it copies of *Fortune*, the *Reader's Digest* and *Time*. No windows. No apparent purpose for the room unless the desk made it an office. Except that the desk was obviously unused. And the room was empty.

'Please wait,' said the boy usher with the casual manner of those accustomed to wealth, condescending to carry out a menial job. Were the ushers here like those in the senate, the siblings of powerful families? Or were they simply imitating those families?

He was ten minutes alone in the room. Time to fall asleep, dream of other times or read in *Fortune* about the state of the union from the viewpoint of General Motors.

At the end of ten minutes a tall man came in. He was in his middle forties, fair hair turning to grey, eyes blue but watery. He was dressed in immaculate grey flannel, Brooks Brothers conception. He carried a small folder under his arm. He was approximately six foot two in height and towered intimidatingly over McBride's five foot ten.

The intimidation of height was dispelled by an outstretched hand.

'McBride!' The handshake was firm, strong, deliberately so.

'Hello.'

No name was given in return. The tall man sat down easily in one of the armchairs, smiled and beckoned McBride to sit.

'Senator Newberry has asked me to see you,' the man said affably. 'You'll understand, we get so many cranks wanting to testify before the Senate Committee. My job is to interrogate you, take a statement and then we ascertain whether you are or are not one of the cranks. Which I am sure you're not.' The last words were added with an understanding smile.

'I understand. I want to testify quickly . . .'

'Of course you do. This shouldn't take longer than a day or so. At the end we'll prepare the statement, a deposition if you like. And the Senator will see that and decide to call you . . . or otherwise. Fine?'

'Fine.' McBride said, not feeling fine at all.

'Right. I've ordered coffee. Should be here in a moment. Then we can get right down to it.'

The coffee arrived on cue. McBride sipped his, trying to determine from his interrogator's voice where he came from. The man's tones were overladen with educated Boston but there were indications that it had been acquired. Underneath were hints of a mid-western origin. McBride knew well the mid-western shadings of speech.

11

Coffee being sipped.

'Your first time in Washington, Mr McBride?'

'Second. I was here in early '64.'

'Busy place. But exciting. I find it so.'

McBride thought, you have to find it so. You live and work here. Your very being is here. Where the hell is mine?

Then the coffee cups were put aside.

'If you'd care to begin, sir?'

Where do I begin, McBride asked himself. So much to say, over so many years. So many incidents. A long narrow tunnel of years.

The fair man seemed to read his thoughts. 'The beginning is always a good place to start. The beginning for you . . .'

McBride started. 'It was nothing to do with me, of course. I mean I wasn't even an American. I was from another country. From Scotland. I just happened to be there. In Dallas, that is.'

'What were you doing in Dallas?'

'I was working,' McBride said, trying to remember exactly what he had been working on. It wasn't going to come easily. 'You see I'd been in Los Angeles. Trying to get work. Writing for the movies I . . . I always was a writer, you see. And I'd got a work permit and a resident's permit . . . to work on a short story of mine this producer had read. Paid for my trip out from the U.K. Very generous at first. A feature film to be made from the story. It never happened. Like so many others. So I tried to get other work. I . . . I did get a couple of television credits. And I was doing newspaper articles. Bread and butter. A couple were syndicated.'

'It must be interesting to be a writer,' the interrogator said irrelevantly.

McBride went on. 'Anyway this editor in Dallas wrote me. Liked my style or something. Would I come to Dallas, do the Britisher's view of Texas? The Texans seem to like to hear about themselves. Anyway this editor, Charlie Neaman, offered me work. And I needed it. So I went to Dallas.'

'Dallas.' the interrogator repeated.

'I went in late September '63.'

'You were then twenty-four years of age?'

Was I? McBride asked himself. I must have been. Hadn't thought. Age, I never thought about. I am always the age I am now. So it seems. Anyway not relevant.

'Yes, I think I was. Twenty-four . . . twenty-five. Anyway I was in Dallas. And I was in Dallas, 23rd November 1963. Not a good time to be in Dallas. Not for Lee Harvey Oswald. Not for a lot of people.'

'You saw the assassination?'

'No. I was at home. An apartment I'd rented on the other side of town, almost on the other side of the tracks. Two up, two rooms, cold water. I was working at the apartment when the news came on TV. I . . . I felt like everybody else, I suppose. Shocked. Horrified. Also removed. Not my country, not my President. But shocked.'

'So what happened that you were involved?'

Memory stirring. A dinosaur coming alive. Beginnings that he had wanted to forget. He wished the fair man would go away now, leave him to read *Fortune* magazine. Then there would be no need to remember. And no way, too, of purging himself, which was why he was here. Not of guilt, he had no guilt. It was memory and the need to hold the memory that he wanted to purge himself of, for good and all.

'You were born in Paisley, Scotland, Mr McBride?'

'Yes.'

'And although you worked here for seventeen, eighteen years you never actually took out American citizenship papers? Any reason why not?'

Plenty of reasons. All coming back to that night in

13

Dallas. But not to be said here and now. Later, perhaps after he'd been before the Senate Committee.

'Just . . . just never got around to it.' A small easy lie.

'Go on about Dallas.'

'It was the day after the assassination, 23rd November. In the evening. I'd been working and I was a bit low. Sad. Everybody was, that day. I shouldn't have been. I'd just sold a short story to . . . I think it was to *Playboy*. They pay pretty well. I should have been happy. But nobody was, in Dallas, that night. Maybe not in the world. Anyway I went out looking for something. Amusement, entertainment. I still didn't know many people in the city, apart from Charlie Neaman, the paper's editor, and . . . and a couple of the boys on the paper. But they were all home with their families. Still, I went out. Downtown Dallas. Dead. As if people were ashamed to be about after what had happened. Places were closed. Or just empty. Then I went into this bar. I'd been there a couple of times before. So I went in . . .'

It was coming back easily now. Everything that night falling into place. He settled back in the armchair. It was going to be easy. No, not easy, but easier. The fair-haired man was listening, making an occasional note on a sheet of paper within the now opened file. It was going to be all right, McBride told himself.

14

PART ONE

Billy Sandrup

1

1963

The furnishings of hell must approximate to a bar in a downtown American city that called itself a cocktail lounge. Dark red neon strip lighting cast the roseate glow of much imagined regions of Hades over all. Narrow tables in narrow cubicles around the walls provided instant claustrophobia. Garish abstracts on the walls hid themselves in the low-key lighting.

The bar was empty when Alec McBride came in. Empty seats, empty tables, even the atmosphere was lacking the customary cigarette smoke and the sound of voices. Behind the bar, a solitary barman polished one glass over and over again with lacklustre enthusiasm. He stared straight ahead into a middle distance that expressed an infinity of boredom.

This was Dallas, downtown, one day after the event in Dealey Plaza which caused the city to hide in shame. Streets, usually busy, were deserted, cinemas were empty, neon poured its multi-coloured illumination into concrete canyons almost devoid of life. Even the whores had vanished from their regular beats, in mourning for the fractured innocence of the people.

McBride sat alone in the deserted bar, the general depression gripping him. He should, he told himself, be reasonably happy. He had sold a story, received a decent cheque, and this on top of a small but adequate income from regular newspaper articles. Yet the miasma that hung over the city had reached him, seeped into his brain, taken over.

The barman presented him with the ordered Scotch-on-the-rocks in silence and he sat in one of the cubicles facing the entrance as if to will the arrival of some fellow drinkers. Not that he wanted company for himself but merely the sight and sound of strangers close by proving that life still existed on earth and particularly in Dallas.

The big man entered some ten minutes later. He was dressed in denims – blue jacket and matching blue trousers, both slightly grubby. Working clothes at once comfortable and practical. Cowboy boots and two-inch heels added to his height and the broad-brimmed stetson indicated the true Texan – the hat well-worn, almost a caricature of itself.

McBride reckoned he was in his thirties but with a boyish look many Americans seemed to retain well into middle life. The man glanced around the empty bar, a bleak look, finally settling on McBride. He swayed over, a cowboy or an oilworker on the loose, looking for company and already juiced-up with liquor.

'Okay if I sit here?' The voice was slightly hoarse.

'Yes, sure, if you want to.'

The man sat, facing McBride. 'Billy,' he said. 'Billy Sandrup. My name.'

McBride felt the need to be noncommittal. 'Oh, aye.'

'You going to give me your name?' A kind of amiable aggression.

'McBride. Alec McBride.'

'Foreigner?'

''Fraid so.' Why so damned apologetic? He was glad he wasn't an American. Certainly at this time and place.

'Limey?'

'Scots.'

A grin appeared on Billy Sandrup's face. The child

had found a new and unusual toy. 'Yeah? For real? Scotch, eh? From Scotland?'

'Scots,' McBride emphasised. 'Scotch is for drinking.'

'Good thinking.' A shout to the barman. 'Hey, Joe, two Scotches for me and my buddy.'

The barman acknowledged the order with a flicker of his eyes.

'Really there's no need,' McBride felt the need to say.

'There's always need to drink, man. You don't wanna drink with me?'

'Yes, sure but . . .'

'Then you drink with me. See, I didn't have to sit here with you, did I? Place is like the prairie in winter. Plenty of room. Everything in Dallas is like that. Dead. Three, four shots kill a man and a whole city goes into hiding. Crazy.'

'It's true.'

'Sure, it's true. But it ain't going to kill me. Not yet. Not Billy Sandrup. See, I don't even drink alone. You don't drink alone. You drink alone, you hear everything you're thinking echoing in an empty glass.'

Homespun philosophy already, McBride thought. But he said nothing. The barman arrived and placed two Scotches on the table. Billy Sandrup became even more expansive.

'There's twenty bucks. Keep 'em coming until we've killed it!'

'It's your liver,' the barman said mournfully and departed.

Billy Sandrup drank quickly and with enthusiasm. When the $20 had run out another twenty followed. After three drinks, Alec McBride took to sipping slowly and negating the arrival of any more glasses with a discreet shaking of the head at the barman. Sandrup did not appear to notice this but went on talking as he drank.

'You get to thinking, in a couple of hundred years

19

the world's going to be filled with plastic drinking cups. You know, with those goddam cups the plastic never wears out. Whole surface of the planet covered in plastic drinking cups. That's how it's going to be.'

'Yes, indeed.' There was the need to make noises to encourage him, McBride felt.

'The day the world caves in, they're going to find the centre, the core of it, is solid plastic. You gotta believe me, man. Because I'm bigger than you. And drunker, Mr Alec McBride. Only thing to do in this great big, fancy, plastic town is get drunk. Which we are doing.'

After a time Alec looked at his wristwatch. 'It's getting late,' he said, feeling he had been companionable enough.

'The hell with late! Late is earlier than you think. See that guy behind the bar?' A large hand indicated the barman. 'He worships me. Because I'm one of the few guys in Dallas keeping the wheels of commerce running. I'm spending money.'

'Can I buy you a drink then?' McBride asked tentatively.

'You're stuck with me. Least I can do is pay for the booze. Anyway I'm making with the words. And dough is something I don't need to worry about.'

'Nice for you.'

'You gotta understand . . . outside this town . . . just outside, there's a million oil wells. They're not producing oil, they're pumping up money. Spewing up dollar bills. Like there's no tomorrow.' He paused and frowned. Billy Sandrup wrinkling his brow, trying to grasp a thought. 'Anyway, there is no tomorrow for me. It's been cancelled. Pressure of money.'

'You're in oil?'

'Heck, no! I spit on oil men. Rape the prairie, they do. Maybe indirectly they pay me, those wells, but I spit on the kinda guys that own them.'

'What business are you in?'

20

'I kill people.'

Somewhere in the distance a police siren sounded, echoing through the canyons. Billy Sandrup grinned. 'Your mouth's open, son.'

'I thought you said . . .'

Billy cut in fast, 'I did. I said it. As that guy on the radio used to say, that's what the man said, he said that.'

Rubbing his nose Billy took a deep breath. 'That's why there's no tomorrow for me.'

'You kill people?'

'All kinds. Black white, yellow. Started with the yellow. Korea. Kill the little yellow guys, that's what they trained us for.'

McBride felt a sense of relief. 'You mean, you're a soldier?'

'Used to be. Not now. Told you. Just kill people. Hired gun. Or knife or bomb. Whatever you say. Funny. Now some other guy is going to come along and do it to me.'

Shifting uneasily in his seat, McBride thought, I've got a crazy on my hands. Probably just a drunk crazy but a crazy nonetheless.

'What do you mean?' he asked, partly to fill up the silence.

'What do I mean, what do I mean? I said it. No tomorrow. I'll miss all those plastic cups taking over the world. You want me to make no tomorrow for you? I could do that. Just ask me. Easy. Ask me to wipe out tomorrow for you.'

Alec felt like laughing. A crazy comedian, a fantasy merchant, there were plenty of them in Scotland. Glasgow was a city full of fantasy merchants. Billy Sandrup was just the Texan variety.

'Okay, do it,' Alec said.

The big Texan's mouth curved in a crooked grin. 'I killed John F Kennedy,' he said. 'There! It's done.'

21

'You're really crazy!' The minute he said it, Alec regretted it. Sandrup flushed and leaned forward. Alec could smell the whisky on his breath, a sour smell, nauseous, unpleasant.

'Don't say that, son. Don't call a man you don't know crazy. Especially when he ain't. I told you something now and that's just included you in my death sentence. Because now you know what you shouldn't know. You get it?'

'They've got a character in jail for killing Kennedy. Oswald something or other.'

'Sure they have. Lee Harvey Oswald. Couldn't shoot his way out of a shit house. But he'll be the marksman of the year. Ole Lee Harvey, the fall guy. The original biological detergent. Like soap powder only he's blacker than black. Packaged in the good ole USA to keep the American conscience nice and shiny. So every Joe in the street can say, it wasn't me.'

'Oh, come on!' Alec protested.

'Come on, nuthin'! Oswald's the big zero. Be dead in a week. That's all fixed. Like they'll get me too. Any time. Like they'll get you if they know I told you. You heard me. You asked for it.'

McBride glanced across at the barman. The man was out of earshot. He was studying the sports section of a newspaper. More silence. Billy Sandrup grinning now.

'You gonna ask me more?'

'Who are *they*?' Alec asked. 'The *they* who'll get us?'

'That's the sixty-four billion dollar question. Who *are* they?' Sandrup turned in his seat and called to the barman. 'Hey, my glass is empty. Spiders are building webs in my glass.'

'Your dough just ran out,' the barman replied.

'I got more. Keep pouring.'

'One more you got, then I close.'

Billy glowered. 'Heck, it's only five after ten! The

22

happy hour's hardly over. Since when you shut so early?'

The barman sighed wearily. 'It's my tribute to the President. Tonight we shut early.'

'Lyndon Johnson's the President. He ain't done nothing to be tributed to yet.'

'So I live in hope,' the barman replied with a shrug. 'But, until then I shut in five minutes. Have a nice night.'

Billy turned back to McBride scowling. 'Guy's a bum! So nobody's drinking but us, so he shuts up. What's the country coming to? No service no more.'

He hesitated then, searching his mind for the subject of their conversation. Then it came back to him. 'You were asking who "they" were, Scottie. Look in the mirror. Just over your shoulder any time you'll see them waiting. Look in a store window. They'll be reflected behind you. Waiting. You're on one side of the street, they'll be on the other. The dark side. I know 'em. They pay me, they'll finish me.'

The silence was broken only by the barman noisily selecting a new bottle from behind the bar.

Then McBride spoke, 'Why don't you run?' Not that he believed what the man was saying, but he knew the man believed it.

Sandrup ran a large hand through thinning hair. 'Nowhere to run. Go down a gopher hole, they'll be sitting at the end of the hole. They don't miss a shot. They just appear once and it's bang, bang, have a nice day.'

The barman put full glasses in front of them. 'That's your last.'

'Somebody's always counting,' Sandrup said, paying him from a thick wad of bills.

McBride stared with distaste at his glass. The taste of whisky had soured his throat. He wanted away from

23

here, away from the empty, unpleasant bar with its unsubtle neon and its vacant tables.

'Look, I think I should be moving . . .'

'I gotta couple of quarts back in my hotel room. You come back with me.' Sandrup was starting to slur his speech now.

'Sorry, but I have to go.' The statement was ineffective. Sandrup ignored or did not hear it.

'You come back with me. Don't get me wrong, I'm no faggot. But I like you, McBride. You listen well and I got to have someone to listen.'

'Really, I'm sorry . . .'

'You married or something?'

'No.'

'Then you ain't in a goddam hurry. Anyway . . .' The Texan swayed slightly in his seat. 'Reckon I need a little help gettin' back to the hotel. Even guys like me need help from friends. You help me, mebbe I kin help you.'

'I don't think . . .'

'That's right. Don't think. Take me back and drink with me. Maybe I can tell you a little more . . . help you get out.'

There was some kind of a story here, McBride thought. The man might live in a fantasy but there might be a story in that fantasy. Collective guilt manifesting itself in personal guilt.

Sandrup went on, 'Mebbe you ain't been noticed yet. Mebbe they ain't seen you with me. See, that's how these bums work. You're with me, you're dead. I'm not kidding you, mister. Once they notice you with me you're one of the walking dead. Just like me. So you just let me finish this drink and we'll move. Say, what do you work at?'

McBride told him.

'Makes you dangerous to them. But mebbe, jest mebbe you could tell my story. Frighten the livin' shit out of them. So you better come back and listen to me.'

24

The canyons were warm in the yellow street lights. Somewhere above and around was darkness, the great city surrounded by blackness. The streets were deserted. An occasional figure in the distance seemed to dissolve in yellow night. Everything was receding from them as they walked; the streets stretching to some infinitely distant point, the buildings, glassy-eyed, shut, doors locked, barred, neon-lit but seemingly empty. One car drove by quickly, the driver invisible behind dark glass. A block later a police car cruised by slowly, examined them and moved on. Dallas was a ghost town and their two figures must seem like phantoms.

'Sure, I got a great respect for writers,' Billy Sandrup said, weaving gently across the sidewalk. 'You gotta have. They tell it like it is. Not that I'm a great reader. Too busy living. But that Mickey Spillane, now he knows what it's all about.'

What am I doing here, McBride said to himself, wandering along a street in Dallas, Texas with a drunk cowboy who claims he is a killer? In a foreign country, in a foreign environment – how had I arrived here? He'd asked himself the question before, asked it in California, wondered why he had ever left Scotland. Now it came to him again, the question which he could not answer. He'd come to America, filled with hope and determination and found nothing to which hope could be attached, no way in which determination alone could provide a direction. The land of promise had gone into history; only money provided direction and those with money clung to it with greedy desperation.

'You hear that?' Sandrup broke into his thoughts, stopping, listening. McBride stopped obediently and listened.

Something, a solitary footfall behind them. They turned. The street was empty.

'Footsteps,' Sandrup said. 'You hear them? Walking behind. Like a goddam echo. That'll be them.'

25

'Again?' McBride smiled. Paranoia. Simple, uncluttered, paranoia. So easily definable.

'Yeah. Again.' Sandrup grinned without humour. 'They're coming for me. And they'll know you.' He started to walk again making McBride trot to keep up with him. 'They killed Buncey tonight,' the Texan went on.

'Who's Buncey?' The question came out breathlessly. Couldn't the man walk at a normal pace?

'One of my partners. One of three. We fired the guns in Dealey Plaza.' A determined paranoiac.

'Yeah, they took Buncey out first. He wouldn't listen to what I told him. Wouldn't believe they'd pay us off and let us go. Not for this job. Picked him up, into a car and one shot behind the ear. That's how they do it. He'll never be found.'

A zephyr of warm air brushed their faces.

'What will happen to him?'

'Buried deep in the lone prairie. Or the desert. Who's going to find him? Who's going to look? Who's going to dig up the desert?' Sandrup shrugged, large shoulders moving like a minor earthquake. 'I don't feel bad about Buncey. Skinny little guy with a mean temper. And a moustache, Mexican style. Always looks . . . looked as if he needed a bath. Trouble was, he did. Also he liked killing people. Enjoyed it.'

'You didn't?'

'Nobody says you got to like it. I did it. For a living. Didn't like it though. Buncey liked it. I never took to a man that liked that kind of a job.'

'I could see that.' Humor him. There might be some kind of a story. The collective guilt of America surfacing in one man.

One street light flickered, danced, making shadows dance across the street. McBride hadn't realised how many dark corners, doorways, alleys there were in the streets, at the corners, at the edges of the eye.

'Where do you live?' Sandrup asked.

Don't give him your address. Might never get rid of the man, might find him on the doorstep anytime.

'South. Eight, nine blocks,' McBride informed him carefully.

'Too far. Too far to walk alone. I'll get you a room for the night.'

'No, thanks. I can walk.'

'You wouldn't make it. Anyway we can have a drink. Don't look so worried. Told you, I'm no fag. I'll get you a room on me. Oh, I got money to burn. And that's what'll happen to it. Be burned. Like me.'

McBride told himself, go along with him. Humour him, he'd said it before, keep it up now. Later he can just take off. But now play it the big Texan's way.

Another block and they turned right. The streets seemed identical. Tall buildings broken by patches of grass. Along on the right, a big open area, over-lit, a car showroom and rows of parked cars under lights. Each chained to the stonework of the yard. Never trust anyone. 'Buy your used car from Happy Harry . . . he's practically giving them away.' All you have to have is money. McBride should have had a car. No man was a whole man in the USA without wheels. He'd had a car in California but it had gone to pay his fare to Dallas. Never enough cash yet to buy a car here. Made a man some kind of freak without wheels in Dallas. That or dirt poor. It occurred to him that Billy Sandrup should have a car.

'You got a car?' he asked the big man.

'Thunderbird. Back of the hotel.'

'Why don't you get in and drive then? They . . . whoever they are . . . they wouldn't get you if you kept moving.'

Billy Sandrup laughed hoarsely. 'Where to? I'd never get out of Dallas. They'd be watching. They are watching. Even if I got out they'd find me. You have to sleep sometime. That's when they'd get me. Oh, mebbe not tomorrow, or next week or next year. But in time. They could take years but they'd get me. I don't want to live like that.'

He hesitated for a moment then turned to stare down at McBride. 'I'm tired, son. And I'm too tired to keep looking over my shoulder.'

They turned left now and there was the hotel across the road – the Prairie Traveller Hotel, part of a small block. The entrance was dimly lit, a small awning throwing darkness onto the sidewalk. The double glass doors were locked but a ring on a bell brought a porter scurrying, a little old man in crumpled slacks and an open-necked shirt. The neck was thin, wrinkled like a turkey. He glared through the glass at them, seemed to recognise Sandrup and, unlocking the door, stared up at him. 'Yeah?'

'I'm stayin' here,' Sandrup said.

'Jest as well I reckernised yuh. Else I wouldn't open no door.'

The foyer was small, shabby, a threadbare carpet in front of the reception desk. The old man went behind the desk and stared at a box of key hooks, most of which were decorated with keys. Business, thought McBride, wasn't good.

'Room number?' the porter asked.

'How do I know what number?' Billy slurred. 'Who knows room numbers?'

The old man frowned. 'Well . . . name, then?'

'Billy! Billy Sandrup.'

Thin fingers rifled through a tattered registry book. 'Sandrup, William. Room 300.'

He handed Sandrup a key and stared, watery-eyed at McBride.

'And a room for my friend,' Billy said.

'I can still walk to my . . .' McBride's last protest was cut off.

'A room for him. Next door to mine. We got some drinking to do. Don't want him getting lost in this dump.'

The turkey neck curved, the beak pointing at the register. 'Rooms on either side of you are occupied. I could do 306. At the end of the corridor.'

Where do they get those numbers from, McBride asked himself. Probably wasn't more than twenty rooms in the entire place. Yet he was getting Room 306.

Sandrup took the second key and tossed it at McBride. 'Put his room on my bill,' he instructed the old man. 'Come on, I'm getting thirsty.'

Three flights up a narrow staircase with a strip of matting in the center, torn and worn in places. Then a corridor lit by one bare bulb at the far end. The corridor was also narrow, walls whitewashed years before and now grey with time. From one room came the sound of snoring. The rest was silence.

Room 300. A bed, a chair, a washbasin, a wardrobe and a set of rules framed behind the door. Also a television set. The walls had once had a leaf pattern wallpaper but many autumns had come and gone and leaves had fallen or faded. There was a spreading damp patch on the ceiling.

Billy Sandrup waved McBride in and sat heavily on the bed. 'The pits,' he said. 'This place is the pits. Not that I couldn't afford the Hyatt or the Hilton. But when you're working, the pits is the place to be.'

McBride agreed it was the pits. Knowing places like this he guessed his room would be exactly the same as this one. He was to find out he was right. Sandrup nodded towards the corridor. 'Fire escape next to your room. If you have to get out, that's the way.'

'So you would run?' McBride asked.

'If it was the cops, sure. But then . . . I told you, nowhere to go.'

Unscrewing the top from a quart bottle of rye,

29

Sandrup rose and went to the washhand basin. Two dusty glasses he rinsed expertly and filled with liquor. McBride paled when handed his glass and made a pretence of gulping while actually sipping. Again the thought, what am I doing here? The man's crazy and I'm feeding his mania by listening. A nut case, he is, with the kind of imagination that turns the world upside down. And now he was getting Sandrup's life story.

'Master Sergeant, I was. US Marines. If they don't kill you in training you're a gyrene. You make Master Sergeant you know you're good. So I made it. Sharpshooter. Like, you join the marines, you see the world, make friends, play games, kill people. Korea to Katmandu and . . . and the shores of fucking Tripoli. Never did know what the marines were doing in fucking Tripoli anyway. Not that I ever got there. Or a hall of Montezuma. Korea, I got to.'

'Pretty rough, eh?' McBride felt he had to say something.

'Rough. But they taught us . . . taught me everything I know. How to kill. Loudly or quietly. Silently. Very specialised profession, killing. But afterwards they took care of me. Me and my mates. Buncey and Hayward. Hayward was different from Buncey. A real pro. They took care of us.'

'Pension?'

Sandrup laughed. He laughed loudly. 'We weren't pensioned off. We were too good. They told us, leave the marines, we can use you. So we did and we worked for them. And they took care of us. They did. Dough, like it was raining dollar bills. We were in business, see?'

'You must have known who they were then.'

Billy Sandrup swallowed a mouthful of whisky. He grinned crookedly and the liquor spilled out of the corners of his mouth. 'You'll never know,' he replied. 'I'm not sure I did. A voice at the end of the telephone.

A signature on a monthly cheque. Never the same signature. Bonus at the end of every job. Except yesterday's. That was special. Terminal. We should have known. Mebbe we did but we'd got beyond caring.'

A yawn fractured Sandrup's face. 'Aw, the hell with it. I'm gonna close my eyes for a few minutes. You find your room and then come back.'

He lay back on the counterpane. The whisky glass slipped from his hand, amber fluid spilling over the carpet. A heavy sigh became a snore. McBride went over and stared down at him. He was asleep – a drunken, exhausted sleep.

Now he could go. Into the dark city and back to his cold-water apartment. But now he himself was weary; and more than that, there was something about Sandrup, something beyond the loud voice and the drink, something close to a kind of truth. Oh, the things the man said were wild, fantastic, but with a kind of belief. McBride wanted to hear more, perhaps talk to the Texan when he was sober. When the morning came, then perhaps he could winnow out the grains of truth from the fantasy.

McBride closed Sandrup's door, heard the lock click behind him, and stumbled along the dim corridor. There was something in the lack of light and the heaviness of the air that made him feel he was walking through a giant spider's web. Somewhere along the way he heard a woman laugh behind one of the doors – a harsh sound, coarse and throaty. Reaching the door of Room 306, he fumbled noisily with the room key and finally opened the door.

The room was, as he had suspected, almost identical to Sandrup's. The only difference was an off-white papered ceiling, the paper in one corner peeling and sagging. The solitary window looked out onto the contorted shapes of strange rooftops, all highlighted in

31

a glow from the distant neon of the unseen streets. A dry heat filled the night.

The bed linen was at least clean. McBride stretched out on top of the bed staring at the wrinkled ceiling. He hadn't bothered to switch on the light and he could lie watching patterns form on the ceiling, shadowed by the dim illumination from the window. After a time he slept.

And there were dreams.

Dealey Plaza, vast under the blaze of a midday sun. Not Kennedy riding in the open car, but he, himself, Alec McBride, sitting alone acknowledging the cheers of crowds, smiling, gesturing, and all the time wondering why he was there, a foreigner, hailed as if he were the President. Knowing, too, that he was not only the President but also the target.

Figures running behind the crowds. Three figures carrying rifles. One was Sandrup, recognisable by his bulk. Then they were kneeling, rifles aimed, a three man firing squad with the guns pointing at him. Then he was out of the car and it was night and he was running along the wide avenues of the city, deserted but for himself and, somewhere behind, the three kneeling figures.

Then suddenly he was facing them and from the muzzles of the rifles came three puffs of smoke, silent at first, then followed by a number of muffled explosions.

Sandrup in the bar again, enormous face peering into his. 'That's how it's done. That's how we killed people. How we'll kill you. Of course I'll be first . . .'

He sat upright on the bed, covered in perspiration, trying to rid himself of the dream. He had to make a conscious effort and seemed to take long, long seconds. And even as the dream faded he could still hear the sound of the shots, muffled as before but distinct.

He rose from the bed to ensure that he would shake off the dream. He rose and stood shaking, afraid; and at the same time reassuring himself he'd merely had a nightmare. Yet, as he stood he imagined he heard footsteps running down the corridor outside the room and a fragment of the dream recurred – the three men carrying rifles running behind the crowds.

Fear now, and not simply from the traces of the dream. Something had happened, he knew with some kind of certainty. Shaking his head he rubbed his eyes, as if to reassure himself he was now awake. Then he went into the corridor.

The movement was automatic, a reflex action without reason. Afterwards he might swear he had heard the running footsteps and gone out of the room to investigate. Yet it was not a conscious action.

The corridor was dark as before except for a wedge of light shining from an open bedroom door some yards along. He knew at once it was Sandrup's door. And he knew he'd heard gunshots, muffled certainly, perhaps subdued by silencers. Not that gunshots meant much. This was Dallas. Magnum City. Everybody carried a gun. Now and then fired a gun.

He moved to Sandrup's door. The light was on, the door ajar. Sandrup was there alone.

He was lying across the bed, head on the pillow at an angle. There were three bullets holes in his forehead. The pillow was a damp scarlet color and the back of his head wasn't there.

2

Alec McBride should have called the police, he was to tell himself that often in the years ahead. Whether it would have made any difference was something else. Perhaps it might have expedited his own death. Or perhaps he might have been charged with Sandrup's murder, neatly framed and out of the way. That's how it might have been played. And, there and then, he was convinced that would happen. An intimidating thought. More, a frightening one. The alien in a strange land makes an ideal culprit.

Stepping out of Sandrup's room into the corridor, McBride shut the door quietly. Any sound in the pervading silence was earsplitting. He stood in the darkness now thinking only of getting out, away from the body, away from the hotel. But how to get out without the desk clerk seeing him?

Fire escapes. There were always fire escapes.

The window at the far end of the other wing of the corridor opened onto a metal escape. It took some minutes for McBride to find it, padding along in blackness, stopping now and then to light a match and assess his position. Finally he reached the escape window and heaved a great gulping sigh of relief as he found it opened easily. Then he was climbing downwards, the steel creaking and protesting under his feet.

The fire escape descended to a narrow alley leading to the main road. McBride moved fast, terrified that the noise of his footsteps on the metal would wake someone in the hotel. But when he reached the ground there was no sound from behind him. Two minutes later he was three blocks away, walking fast.

Despite his comparative youth, Alec McBride, with the confidence of that youth, had always considered himself a worldly wise man. He had been born next door to a tough cynical city, Glasgow, had worked on newspapers in that city and, as a working reporter, had seen sights of consummate horror. Violence was a hobby for certain denizens of Glasgow, murder a sideline of the violence, not to be too concerned about. McBride had seen perverse crimes, reported on them but always with the detachment of the outside observer. He'd viewed the bodies of children, battered to death because of some seemingly trivial frustration; he'd seen the results of street warfare, youths slashed and bleeding. He'd reported on all of this, more than that, used all he had seen as material for fiction. But ever and always the outsider.

He'd travelled, seen Californian violence – the only difference being the advantages of a better climate in which to observe urban nightmare. He'd known a few women, been fortunate in that they had made few demands on him but had taught him, conveyed their expertise to the young man. They had avoided commitment; why be committed to a youth without money in a land where sex was a saleable commodity and the going-rate was high.

Yet for all his experience and the confidence it had brought, he had never been one of the characters in the dramas. He'd considered himself detached, the watcher. But now he was no longer outside. He'd been with Billy Sandrup in that bar this night and all that Sandrup had told him involved him. And the involvement, according to the big Texan was complete. In

36

telling him Sandrup had made him a participant and a target.

The streets were still deserted although, in the distance, through the skyscraper towers the coming dawn streaked the sky. Another block and a cruising police car appeared, slowed down to take a look at him and moved on as he simulated an amiable drunken smile in the direction of the car. He was reasonably well dressed and, while pedestrians were always viewed with suspicion in the great automobile economy of the USA, his appearance and the affectation of drunkenness stood him in good stead with the police officers. They dismissed him as an all-night reveller conducting a wake on the recent death of the President, and as such, sensible enough not to drive.

His apartment was heavy, warm with its imperfect air-conditioning. He lay, for the second time that night, on top of a bed, a sense of relief at having reached familiar surroundings taking him over. He knew that he would have to do something about the killing of Billy Sandrup but what, exactly, he had no idea. After a time, like Scarlett O'Hara in *Gone With The Wind* he determined to put it out of his mind until tomorrow. He would think about it tomorrow, determine a course of action, do something decisive. Now was a time for sleep – the alcohol and the events of the evening were taking their toll.

Sleep . . .

He woke at ten o'clock the next morning and his mind was again flooded with all that had taken place. Or had it? Could it not have been one simple horrendous dream? For a short time, over coffee he indulged the wishful thought. And then inevitably dismissed it.

The question was, when Billy Sandrup's body was discovered would the night clerk associate him with the Texan? Would he remember what Alec McBride looked like; would the police at this very moment be circulating a description?

He telephoned the newspaper to which he contributed.

'Is Mr Neaman available?'

'Mr Neaman is in conference.' The girl's voice was nasal, a comic American accent for real.

'Look, this is Alec McBride. Mr Neaman is having his coffee. But he'll speak to me.'

A long silence. Then the click of the connection.

'That you, Alec? Look, I've had an idea. How about you doing the Englishman's view of Dallas after the assassination?'

'Charlie, I'm a Scot . . .'

'Okay, the Britisher's idea. I think we could get it all over. Decent syndication. Keep you in bread for months.'

'Charlie, I'll think about it. But that's not why I phoned . . .'

Neaman's voice became strained. 'What's this, think about it? I'm your meal ticket, kid. And I'm your friend. Without me, you know . . .'

'I know. I would have starved in LA. You know I'll do it, Charlie. But this is something else. And it could be important.'

'So tell me.'

'Murders, Charlie. Killings. Last night. Tell me . . .'

Charlie Neaman laughed. 'You sound sick. You're not on crime. I got a good man on the crime beat. From you I want a little touch of class. Harry Schuyler, I got for crime.'

Just enough desperation in the voice, that should do it.

'I don't want Harry's job, I just want to know . . . there's a good reason.'

'A story reason?'

'Maybe. I think so.'

38

'I'll put you through to Schuyler.'

Harry Schuyler's voice was tired. He was an old man to McBride, nearly sixty and he'd been on the Dallas crime beat for over thirty years.

'What do you want to know about murders, kid? You're features, but not crime features. That's Daddy's territory.'

'It's a long story,' McBride said, frustration rising. Wouldn't anybody tell him anything? 'Just tell me, Harry. When I come in, I'll tell you all about it.'

Schuyler sighed. 'Look, I been haunting night court. I'm a tired, beat, old man. Do I get to sleep? No! I gotta go down to the court house to see them move Lee Harvey Oswald. He kills the President so they have to give the little bastard a comfortable cell somewheres.'

'Harry, just tell me what's on your desk. Killings last night.'

Papers were shuffled at the other end of the line. McBride could hear them.

'It was a quiet night for homicide. Guess you kill a President that counts for more than one. Let's see, two cowboys shot each other up in a downtown bar. One died. Won't be murder one. More like manslaughter. Kid killed by an uncle. Very nasty. Rape and child murder . . .'

McBride mentioned the name of the hotel. 'The Prairie Traveller? Anything there?'

'I know it,' Schuyler replied. 'Nasty and not too cheap. Were you in that dump? You've gone and roughed up a hooker, McBride? For God's sake . . .'

'I haven't roughed up a hooker. I just want to know if a killing's been reported in the Prairie Traveller.'

More shuffling of papers. 'Nothing, kid. You belted the hooker, she came to, and went home. Keep away from hookers. Plenty of blooming Texas roses willing and able to put out for free . . .'

'Harry, do me a favor. Phone the Prairie Traveller

39

and find out if a man called Billy Sandrup was found dead there this morning.'

'And I miss Oswald being brought out,' Schuyler groaned. 'And he confesses to killing JFK in order to further the cause of Communism or Capitalism and I miss the story of the century. Drop dead, kid. You got pals get killed in hotels, I don't want to know today. Tomorrow maybe, but today we're on the big screen . . .'

A pause. Schuyler was thinking. If the young bastard had come across something? There *was* tomorrow and there could be copy.

'So maybe I got a few minutes, I'll give them a ring. The Prairie Traveller. But if there's a story, it's mine.'

McBride agreed quickly. 'Of course. Your story. But Harry, don't say who you are . . .'

'What do you mean, don't say who I am? Power of the press. Right to know. Best way to get told.'

McBride insisted. 'Please. Do it my way. Ask about a Billy Sandrup.'

Five minutes later Schuyler phoned him back.

'So you're wasting my time, McBride. I don't like that. I'm too tired. I don't like it.'

'Harry just tell me, please.'

'So I phone the Prairie Traveller. I tell them I'm Sam Houston. I want to know about Billy Sandrup. He's an old friend. Billy Sandrup, huh! There's no Billy Sandrup dead in that dump. There's no Billy Sandrup alive in that dump. No Mr Sandrup has registered at the Prairie Traveller in the last week, if ever. You owe me one, kid.'

McBride replaced the receiver and stared at the phone. What had Sandrup said? Take you away and bury you on the lone prairiee.

They'd taken him.

They'd taken him and they'd removed every piece of evidence that he'd ever been there. No body, no killing,

40

no Billy Sandrup. Just as he'd predicted. And if he'd predicted that, was there not a possibility, an outside chance, that all he'd told McBride might just be the truth? Now the problem was what to do about it. And how to make somebody believe. Or at least investigate.

He lifted the phone and dialled the newspaper again.

'What now?' Charlie Neaman said with infinite weariness. 'Schuyler's gone and I'm busy.'

'I have to see you.'

'Have to? Kid, you're a feature writer. I got a newspaper to get out. Today, the word is news,' Neaman paused, drew a breath. 'But I'll take that feature on your view of Kennedy's assassination.' Another pause. 'You haven't done it already?'

'This is something else. About the assassination. Honestly, Charlie, I've got something important.'

Another breath. 'I'm having a glass of lunch at the desk here. Come in. I'll get two glasses. Beer or milk?'

Charlie Neaman drank milk. Ulcer food, he called it. He talked about his ulcer as if it was a decoration, a medal given for long and valiant service.

'Milk,' McBride said. In this, he thought there could be an incipient ulcer for him. He caught a taxi downtown.

Charlie Neaman had a large section of the second floor partitioned off. The rest of the floor was the newsroom. He was the news editor and the managing editor, a rare combination. But he scorned the office on the executive floor. He liked to be beside his newsroom.

They sipped milk and Neaman sat back in silence while McBride told him the whole story. In between sips of milk he smoked several cigarettes, occasionally coughing – his only reaction to McBride's story. When McBride had finished, there was a long silence. Alec stared at Neaman expectantly.

Then Neaman stretched in his chair, reached for his

41

jacket from the back of the chair and produced another pack of cigarettes which he threw down on the desk in front.

Finally he spoke. 'That's it?'

McBride nodded. 'That's the whole story.'

Neaman looked towards the door and the newsroom beyond. 'Did you see the wire when you came in?'

The machine McBride had noticed stood in a corner of the newsroom chattering away, a demented mechanism spewing out print.

'Came straight in. Should I have . . . ?'

'Lee Harvey Oswald was shot dead by a Dallas night club owner just over an hour ago.'

The sounds from the newsroom filled the editorial office. Yet to McBride the noise was silence, background sounds that became meaningless and therefore nonexistent. He sat, trying to assess the meaning of what Neaman had just told him. And, at once, he realised that it might simply confirm the story he had just related to Neaman. Oswald's death was an underlining of all that Billy Sandrup, in his alcoholic ramblings, had said. Oswald's death was predictable and necessary.

'It's on the wire,' Neaman went on. 'Schuyler phoned in. He was there. Guy called Ruby did it. Hung around with the newspapermen. Says he's a kind of patriot. Schuyler said Bert Sturrock from AP knew Ruby.'

'So Oswald's a dead man. Billy Sandrup said it . . . said something like that.'

The editor's mouth twisted. Charlie Neaman's version of a dry smile. 'So you met a good fortune teller.'

McBride had to protest. 'But Sandrup knew. And if he knew what was going to happen to Oswald, the rest of what he said could be true.'

'Might be, might be. That's the story of my life. If all the might-be's were, God, I'd have some real Pulitzer prize stories.'

42

'You don't believe it?'

Neaman coughed. 'Young Mr McBride, have you any idea how many cranks went into police stations in the USA the other day and confessed to killing the President?'

McBride shifted in his seat. The room was warm and the sunlight almost blinded him. A daytime nightmare. 'No, I haven't . . .'

'Well, neither have I, but I'll bet it was a helluva lot. Killing a President, man, that's the psycho's dream. Every crazy dumb bastard can have a day out, a moment of glory by the act of confession. They love it . . .'

'Did they all predict Oswald would be killed? Did they all end up dead in a cheap Dallas hotel?'

Neaman was quick. 'Only got your word for that.'

McBride felt anger rise. His integrity was being questioned and he resented the questioning. 'You think I made it up?'

Neaman wriggled awkwardly in his chair, a man attempting to escape from the effects of his own words. 'Look, kid, don't fly off the handle. I believe you met a guy who told you a story.'

'And ended up dead. And nobody's found the body.'

'You had a few drinks, kid.'

The knowing look now, almost the nod and wink. McBride felt the chill in his body. This was the realisation that nobody would believe him, believe in all that had happened to him the night before. There was no proof, no body, no trace of Billy Sandrup.

He had to reassert himself. 'I saw and heard it all. I saw the body and the bullet wounds. And I was sober.'

Neaman sat back. He liked the Scotch kid, he could afford to indulge him. It would be a lesson in hard journalism. Show proof or you were in trouble.

'Okay, okay,' he said smiling again. 'Somebody took the guy out. And removed the body. Now, without the

43

body, we got no story. So when Harry Schuyler comes back from the Oswald thing I'll have him talk to the law. He's got good connections with the Dallas PD. They'll talk to him. Tell him if they've found anything. A personal killing or maybe a racketeer taking out your friend. Who knows?'

'And who cares?' McBride didn't conceal the bitterness in his voice. 'That's what you're saying. The old gentleman passes by, makes a pick-up and nobody cares!'

'Schuyler'll ask around. What more do you want? Blood?'

'All right. So tell him, too, if he can find out whether or not there was a Billy Sandrup . . . William Sandrup and . . . and two other characters, Buncey and Hayward in the Marine Corps in Korea.'

'Now wait a minute . . .'

'One phone call to Washington. The Marines'll have records. Charlie, I'll pay for the call myself.'

'Okay, okay, I'll tell Schuyler. But, one thing, kid. When all this is over and you find you've got no story, you go back to writing the features I want from you. That's why I give you money. Not to play Sherlock Holmes. I give it to you because you can write. But don't tell an old newshound how to run the investigative reporting bit.'

McBride sighed audibly. At least something would be done. 'Fine, Charlie and . . . thanks.'

Neaman wasn't finished. 'And take it from me, Alec, if City Hall, USA says Harvey Oswald killed John F Kennedy, then as far as this paper's concerned, he did.'

'Even if he didn't?' McBride couldn't resist the comeback.

Neaman flushed. 'In that unlikely eventuality, yeah, sure. City Hall says it, this paper says it.'

'But, for Christ's sake, if you knew he didn't . . . ?'

'This isn't the *Washington Post* or . . . or one of Mr

44

Hearst's funny papers. This is a paper owned and printed by certain people in Dallas. They'll go along with the Oswald story. Why? Because it suits them. It keeps the city clean. It says, no rich oil man took out JFK. No fascist-minded character lives in Dallas. Republicans, sure. But no killers. No right wing Texan John Birchers took the President out. It was a Commie nut called Oswald. That's what they want.'

'And you'd go along with that?'

'Who do you think I am? Lewis Stone as Judge Hardy? Lionel Barrymore running the local tell-the-truth-to-the-people rag? Get the big boys, expose corruption? Balls! The big boys own the paper. They pay me, pay you. You want crusading journalism, join Richard the fucking Lionheart. The only Pulitzer prize you'll get in this city is by telling everybody what patriotic citizens the oil men are. The holes they drill are for the USA.'

'They hated Kennedy!'

'Sure they did. And those fat cats were celebrating last night. The good ole boys are happy. But they do it privately, their celebrating. Secretly, with discretion. They wouldn't like it to be said and nobody's going to say it.'

'That's what Billy Sandrup said.'

'And look what you're telling me happened to him. If he ever existed.'

The phone on Neaman's desk rang. It was a black phone beside a red phone. It struck McBride that he'd never seen Neaman use the red phone.

Neaman lifted the black phone. 'Neaman here,' he said and listened. From the phone came fast confused sounds. 'Sure, sure, Harry we'll get the background on Jack Ruby. Mason'll get it. Sure, he owns a club, so who'd be surprised if he didn't have mob connections? Doesn't mean killing Oswald is linked with the Mafia. You want me to say the Mafia were so sorry the

45

President died, they put Oswald on the spot. Don't make me laugh. For now, we ignore the mob angle. And you, come back in. I got to have your follow-up and then I got something I want you to do.'

Neaman replaced the receiver with a knowing look at McBride, as if to say, look, I'm doing this for you, kid.

McBride said, 'What about the Mafia?'

'Ruby's got Mafia connections. Big deal. The way things are going we'll all have Mafia connections in twenty years. Doesn't mean Ruby's killing Oswald has anything to do with the Mafia. Like a truck driver kills Kennedy, doesn't mean the Teamster's Union are involved.'

'It could,' McBride replied quietly.

Charlie Neaman was exasperated. 'For God's sake, Alec, you can talk to me. I like you and I'm deaf and dumb. But don't go shooting your mouth off in the street about things like that.'

The red phone rang.

McBride stared at it. First time in McBride's office he'd heard it ring. Private line, the word was. But who had the number? Neaman put on a pair of spectacles which had been lying on the desk. McBride thought, you put on glasses to answer the phone? Strange. Why? Mark of respect to the caller? Or just Charlie Neaman being absent-minded?

Charlie looked over the rims of the spectacles. 'I may have to ask you to wait outside . . .'

McBride rose deferentially. Charlie was entitled to his private line and his private conversation. It could be a woman. McBride had seen Mrs Neaman once and he would not have blamed the editor. Mrs Neaman was loud and grating and dressed like an aging Christmas tree. Yes, Charlie was entitled.

'. . . but hold on a second,' Charlie finished and lifted the red phone.

'Neaman here.' A long pause. 'Oh, yes, Mr Dorfmann. Yes, we had two men at the police station. We're running it as big as the assassination itself.' Another pause. 'A man called Jack Ruby. Night club owner. Jewish. Not exactly the all-American hero.'

The pauses became more frequent. Whoever he was, Mr Dorfmann was important. More than that, in some kind of position of authority. Neaman was taking orders as one accustomed to taking orders. His voice was low, subdued, respectful. His tone did not vary. There was too an assumed enthusiasm about his attitude, one that McBride had never heard before.

Then Neaman's tone did vary. A higher pitch indicating surprise and genuine surprise too, came. 'Yes, as a matter of fact he's with me now.'

This pause allowed Neaman briefly to cover the speaker and address McBride. 'Sit down. This concerns you.'

McBride sat, curious. Dorfmann knew him, he did not know Dorfmann.

Neaman addressed the telephone again. 'Yes, I published his early pieces. A real honest to goodness Scotchman . . .'

McBride winced at the misnomer. He'd given up trying to explain the difference between a Scotsman and a Scotchman. It was a losing battle.

'Yes,' Neaman went on. 'I suggested if he came here from California I could use him. As a freelance of course . . . well, naturally I'm glad you liked the article . . . surely, I'll tell him. Three o'clock tomorrow. Fine. Have a nice day, Mr Dorfmann.'

Neaman replaced the red receiver and looked across the desk at McBride. 'He knows you,' the editor said, the surprise still there. 'Dorfmann knows your work and likes it.'

'Who's Dorfmann?'

'Oil. Cattle. Money. That's Dorfmann. Oh, and news-

47

papers. Dabbles in buying 'em and selling 'em. That's a lot of dabbling. You want to work, kid?'

'Of course, but . . .'

'He wants to see you. Three o'clock tomorrow at his place. The Dorfmann ranch. Twenty miles out heading for Austin. Most of the oil rigs on the way, they're Dorfmann's.'

'He's into this paper?'

Neaman smiled crookedly. 'Controlling interest in this and twenty others coast to coast. You don't think I grovel to just anybody. For some reason he liked your piece on the Britisher's eye-view of Dallas. You be there at three tomorrow.'

'Maybe. If I can . . .'

'Be there. Dorfmann wants, Dorfmann gets. That permanent job you say you don't want but you really do, he could get it for you.'

Alec McBride had always insisted he'd rather be a freelance, rather be waiting for the big movie job that never seemed to come, the novel he'd probably never write. But underneath the protestations was the uneasiness at never being sure where the next cheque was coming from, where the eating money was to be earned. And this was the USA, land of plenty, with little social security especially if you were an alien. Here, you could starve. Neaman had assessed McBride's ambivalent feelings only too well. Now Dorfmann might provide another opportunity.

'Stanley Dorfmann is President of Trans-Texican oil as well as everything else. You see him or just pack and go back to Scotland.' Neaman was underlining every sentence.

McBride left the newspaper offices and went into the street. It was now well into the afternoon but between the shadows of the great skyscrapers the sun was glaring, an over-exposed film, white light between the shade. Skyscrapers were still going up, new monoliths in the process of construction. Presidents could die but America went on building to the sky and outwards onto the prairies and deserts. There was no limit, no frontier to the spread of the concrete dream.

Walking for two blocks, McBride went into a MacDonalds and drank two cups of coffee. Walking, he'd had the uncomfortable feeling that he was being followed. He'd glanced behind him several times but amidst the shoppers, jaywalkers, business types, no face recurred. Something in his conscience, a fear based on Sandrup, his story and his end, was inducing a kind of paranoia. The coffee calmed him. He strolled for another block and went into a movie house. Large signs informed him it was cooler inside. The feature was *Midnight Lace* and Doris Day was being pursued around London by a mysterious figure trying to kill her. Her husband, Rex Harrison, seemed supportive and loving until it turned out that he was the would-be killer. Not exactly a promising theme for a man in McBride's state of mind.

Later he returned to his apartment, determined to do some work. There was a title in his head, 'Kennedy: The Death of the American Dream.' He had to try and get back to work.

In the narrow hall of the apartment building he came face to face with Genine Marks. She was nineteen years of age, with the pretty, plastic doll face of so many young American women. She lived in the apartment below McBride and he had taken her out three times, twice to dinner, once to a movie. Each time he had ended up in bed with her. All this over a period of two months which he told himself hardly constituted a steady affair. She was physically attractive and experienced in bed. Also she was lonely, a country girl who had run away from home to the big city. Unfortunately, she was rather stupid which limited conversation and, for McBride, the entire relationship. But not for Genine

49

Marks. She worked as a B-girl in some downtown club which meant she worked most nights and this limited their relationship. Yet after three dates she considered McBride her 'fella'.

'Hi, honey!' she greeted him. 'Working early tonight. Boss is trying to make up for no business yesterday. I rang your bell last night but you was out.'

She seemed to be informing him of his own absence as if it was vital he should realise he had been out.

'I was drinking with a guy,' he said.

Her mouth turned down at the corners threatening to crack her excessive makeup. 'Sure it was a guy?'

'I'm sure.'

She shrugged and smiled. 'I'll be late tonight. How about tomorrow? I just might get the evenin' off.'

'Sure, maybe tomorrow. If I'm around.'

She accepted this with surprising grace. In her life she was accustomed to being used by men and accepted it as a fact of existence.

'Gee, wasn't it terrible about the President?' she went on. 'I mean, the President. They don't get bumped like other people.'

'Lincoln did. And Harding and Garfield.'

She frowned. She'd heard of Lincoln.

'Well, gotta go. See you Alec.'

She went. Alec went up to his apartment, searched around an ancient refrigerator and found one solitary can of cold beer. He settled in front of the television set, nursing the beer can. Yesterday there had been interminable replays of the assassination. Today it was the wild shaking shots taken in the Dallas police station of the murder of Oswald. McBride thought, finish the beer, then get out the typewriter and work. Not to think just now about Sandrup or about being followed. He was in his own place and despite the vulnerability of the apartment he found it gave him a sense of security.

Alec McBride fell asleep.

He woke three hours later to the buzzing of the apartment bell. Groggily he rose and staggered to the door. Without thinking he opened it, had a flash of fear as he remembered Sandrup's prophecy that he too would be a target, and found himself face to face with Harry Schuyler. The fear vanished.

'Don't I get invited in?' said Schuyler, the yellow, sun-wrinkled features squeezed into a grin. 'After all I've been working for you today.'

'Come, come in, Harry. I'm . . . I'm sorry. I was about to do some work but I fell asleep.'

'Only freelance bums can afford that.' Schuyler came in, looked around the meagre room, the threadbare carpet, the table with the shrouded typewriter and the two ancient chairs. 'So this is the ivory tower. Guess you shed a bit of the ivory.'

He sat down, switched off the television set and looked up at his host. 'I got a thirst.'

McBride flushed. 'That was the last can of beer. I'm sorry, Harry. I can run down to the liquor store . . .'

'Forget it. A little talk and then I'll take you for a drink at the nearest bar. It's my good deed for the day. So, sit down.'

McBride perched on the other chair.

Schuyler went on, 'I hear you're going to see one of the great stone faces of Texas tomorrow.'

'Dorfmann, yes. I'd never heard of him.'

'One of the anonymous Gods. The twentieth century plainsman. Only he owns the plains. You're privileged. He who is called by the Gods . . . Sure, if you got two hundred million bucks you can be famous or you can be unknown. Dorfmann prefers to be unknown. Anyway he knows you. Don't it feel good to be known by two hundred million dollars?'

'It's ridiculous,' McBride replied. 'Who needs that kind of money?'

'Looking at this place you need some of it. What does

51

Charlie Neaman pay you in? Buttons? Don't answer. If Dorfmann likes you, you're on your way. But what did I come here for?'

'Would you like a coffee, Harry?'

Schuyler made a face. 'You want to ruin my alcoholic taste buds. I know why I came. Your little fantasy about . . . what was the name? Sandrup, that's it.'

'No fantasy, Harry.'

'No record of him being killed, Alec. Nothing. No police record on any William Sandrup . . .'

'But . . .'

'Don't interrupt. Anyway I phoned Washington about your three mystery men. Sandrup, Buncey and Hayward.'

McBride leaned forward. 'Did you . . ?'

'Find them? Of course I did. Or I found their record . . . Marine records. Master Sergeant William Sandrup, next of kin, Sonia Sandrup, 24, West Fork Avenue, Dallas. Not in the phone book.'

'That'll be him.'

'Discharged from the Marines in 1958. Honourable discharge. Previously seen service in Korea.'

'That is him! That's the man I met. The man that was killed . . .'

'At the same time, from the same unit were discharged two other sergeants. Orrin Buncey and Booker Hayward. Right.'

'That's it. Now Neaman's got to pay attention,' McBride was excited now, a young man who'd been proved right. 'And the police. I think we should take this story to the police . . .'

'Sandrup, Buncey and Hayward,' Schuyler said. 'You got the names right. But for all the rest of your story, McBride . . . no way.'

'What do you mean? Sandrup told all about . . .'

'Sandrup told you nothing. Three weeks after their discharge from the Marines, your three stoogies were driving a car out of the District of Columbia into the state of Virginia. Their car ran into a gasoline tanker. Blew up. Exploded. All three ex-marine buddies were killed instantly. Unless you were talking to a ghost there's no way you could have been talking to an ex-marine called William Sandrup. His sister even identified the body . . .'

3

Alec McBride insisted, 'It can't be the same man!'

Schuyler said, 'Come and have a drink.'

Later in a bar across the road McBride argued further but to no avail. Schuyler was adamant.

'Only one William Sandrup in the Marine Corps. Five years dead with his two buddies.'

'He only died last night in that hotel room!'

'Goddam it, Alec, the police have no record of any death like that. No body, no report of a disappearance. I told you the body was identified by the sister five years ago.'

After a time they stopped arguing and drank in silence. After five rye whiskies, Schuyler, showing no signs of alcoholic intake, rose.

'Go home and sleep it off, Alec. You got the big career day tomorrow. The meeting with Mr Make-or-Break Dorfmann. Break a leg, kid.'

McBride returned to his apartment and went to bed. He didn't sleep but lay, staring at the street lights flickering on the ceiling, going over again and again all that had happened to him in the last twenty-four hours. Sandrup had been only too real and still all he had said made a kind of sense. He would die, disappear and no one would know. Yet he had already died five years before according to official records. Why not? You train men to be hired assassins, it becomes convenient for them to lose their old identities. To appear to be dead.

But how to prove it without Sandrup's body from the hotel?

The sister. Sonia Sandrup had identified her brother's body five years before. Could she have been certain? Three burnt corpses, could anybody be certain? Or had she deliberately and knowingly pretended to identify her brother?

Some time later he heard Genine Marks coming home, heard her open and shut the door of the apartment below. He was grateful that she did not climb one floor more and knock on his door. She had tried it twice in the past. He went back to thinking about Sonia Sandrup. Schuyler had mentioned an address . . . what the hell was it? West Fork Avenue. Twenty-four, that was it. He would visit her if she still lived there. He would do that tomorrow.

Finally he slept.

He woke to another sun-lit, over-exposed morning. There was plenty of time before he had to set off for the Dorfmann ranch. He would spend the morning looking for Sonia Sandrup.

An hour later he was in a cab driving up West Fork Avenue. Used car lots lined the approaches, row upon row of shining metal bodies summing-up the consumer society which bred them and discarded them. After the used cars came rows of small wooden houses, bungalows back home, but here decaying into shacks, paint on the wood starting to fade and peel. Number twenty-four was no exception. A television aerial perched at an odd angle on the roof. A patch of grass in front of the house was overgrown. The windows were none too clean. McBride paid off the cab-driver and rang the doorbell.

Sonia Sandrup was faded, like the paintwork of her house. Blonde hair straggled around a face that bore a vague resemblance to the ex-marine he had met in the bar. She was tall for a woman, five-ten at least, big boned, somewhere in her forties, McBride reckoned. The make-up was hastily applied but could not hide the crevices in the skin or the deep lines around the neck.

'Yeah?' she said, stading in the doorway staring at him with an obvious lack of interest.

'Miss Sandrup?'

'I don't want to buy nothin'!'

'I'm not selling anything. I was a friend of your brother.'

Did the eyes open fractionally wider? Was there a tensing of the facial muscles? McBride couldn't be sure if he imagined it or not.

'You say you're a friend of Billy's?'

'Yes. My name's Alec McBride. Could I speak to you for a few minutes?'

'You were in the marines? No, you ain't an American.'

'I met Billy after he left the Marines.'

The face was a tight mask now. 'Afterwards? You couldn't have known him very long. I don't believe you, mister. So beat it or I'll call a cop.'

'If I can speak to you inside for a few minutes, there'd be some money in it.'

'How much?'

McBride thought, how much can I afford? In movies, money is no object. With him it was life's blood and in short supply.

'Twenty dollars,' he said. That much blood he reckoned he could do without.

She stared at him for a moment, then said grudgingly, 'Okay, you can come in. But one fresh move and I holler my head off. These places got thin walls.'

The parlour was small, untidy and overfilled with furniture. A sofa vied for position with two battered armchairs, both of which bulged ominously, threatening to shed stuffing. A television set, the only new item in the room, faced the armchairs, its twenty-six inch screen, a giant eye. The set was on, sound down but picture flickering brightly. The morning soap opera enacted its agonies in dumb show. A half empty mug of coffee stood on top of the machine. On a side table stood a bottle of gin, almost empty. Beside it a cracked flower bowl held a clump of dying prairie flowers. McBride thought, this is your life, Sonia Sandrup.

The woman motioned him to sit on one of the armchairs. He did so carefully.

'I gave up a lot for Billy,' she said inconsequentially.

'Why do you say that?'

'It's the truth. Little brother, big weight. Huh, I suppose it's expected of you to bring up your kid brother when your folks die early. They shouldn't have died. They should have had more care. Instead, what do they do but get drunk and crash a car. You know, I could have married. In '56 I could have married. But the guy wanted me to go to New York and I wouldn't. Stayed here to keep the house going for Billy. That's a laugh.'

'I think it's very commendable,' McBride said with elaborate politeness.

She seemed amused by this. 'Yeah, sure. Commendable. That's a good word. But what was the point. You know . . .'

'Tell me.'

She took a deep breath, as if having to force herself to speak. 'He . . . he got killed.'

McBride had been looking around. Behind the expiring prairie flowers, a photograph in a cheap frame. He rose and went over to stare down at the young unlined Billy Sandrup's face.

'That's him.'

'Sure. Heh, you said you knew him.'

'I knew him.' Not then, not the boy in the photograph but the man with the tired eyes, the veins under the

58

skin that came from too much alcohol. The man before he died for the second time.

'You couldn't have known him long if you met him after he came out of the marines.' Her face screwed up. Puzzlement or something else. Fear?

McBride turned from the photograph to face her. 'I drank with him in a bar downtown the night before last.'

The reaction was slow in coming. A silence first, then the face set hard.

'Get the hell out of here!' she said from behind clenched teeth.

'I saw him later too. At a hotel . . .'

'Get out, you fucking bastard! Get, before I call the cops!'

'No. Wait, I have to tell you . . .'

She didn't intend to be told. She shouted now. 'You never knew my brother!'

'I've told you . . .'

'My brother's been dead for five years!'

'No,' he insisted.

'Don't tell me. I identified the body. Dead. Five years. You're sick, mister, real sick. I don't know what you're trying to pull but you just get the hell out of here . . .'

He wasn't used to this. He wasn't used to screaming, angry women. One of the reasons he'd not been a good reporter. So many things embarrassed him. But she had to know. He pointed to the photograph behind the flowers.

'I drank with that man the night before last. And later I saw him. He was dead. He'd been shot . . .'

Her face drained of colour. White drawn skin suddenly trembling slightly.

'No!' she screamed, an agonising, keening scream.

'I'm sorry but it's true.'

She was making an effort now, fighting for control. 'You're sick. As sick as he was.'

The question was automatic. 'Why do you say your brother was sick?'

'I don't have to talk to you.' She'd regained her control now. 'For Christ's sake, get out of here! Billy's dead. Okay. One way or another, he's been dead for a long time.'

He clutched at the words, last straws in the wind. He knew she was determined to get rid of him out of something more than anger. That fear he'd sensed, perhaps.

'He was shot the other night, Miss Sandrup. I'm sorry, but its true.'

'Shot? No, he was burned, years ago. But if he had been shot I wouldn't have been surprised. Guns. Guns, all the time. Guns and killing people. That's why he joined the fucking marines. To kill people. So it's over.' Then, with emphasis. 'Five years over. Five years. Not the night before last. Five years. So whoever you are, leave me alone. I done my mourning and buried him. He can't die twice . . .'

She said nothing more. McBride walked away from the house, cold, her fear infecting him. He walked along the dusty avenue, sure she'd been lying. Sure but not certain. Was there a difference? The man in the photograph had been a younger Billy Sandrup, of that he was certain. The rest was fear and questioning.

Later a Greyhound bus took him towards Austin and dropped him on a dusty road with a sign pointing along a track. The sign, metallic and permanent said 'DORFMANN'. One word that was obviously considered enough. McBride started to walk along the track. He'd been on a road like that recently, not with grass and scrubland around but with wheat. High corn growing to the horizon. A movie, that was it. Hitchcock's *North by North-West*. The crop dusting scene. This was the same, but different. No wheat, no crop dusting. And oil derricks on the horizon, all around on the

60

horizon. And a quarter of a mile up the road, there were oil pumps, like steel alligator jaws moving up and down, pumping into pipes that joined with bigger pipelines and stretched to infinity.

The entrance to the ranch was over a rise a mile from the road. There was a fence broken by a gate and over the fence again the word, 'DORFMANN'. The gate, twelve feet high, was secured in some fashion McBride could not see. At the side of the gate was a telephone. He lifted it from its attachment to the side of the gate. After a moment a hoarse voice said one word.

'Yes?'

'Alec McBride. To see Mr Dorfmann.'

Silence. Then a click and the gates swung open. McBride walked through.

He was ten yards in when a puff of dust appeared on the horizon ahead of him. As it came closer it took on the shape of a jeep. The jeep pulled up only feet from McBride.

'Mr Dorfmann didn't realise you hadn't a car,' The speaker was a long thin impersonation of Gary Cooper. 'Else he would have sent one to pick you up in town. Climb aboard.'

Ten minutes towards the horizon and the ranch house loomed ahead, a low single storey building which seemed to spead in several directions. McBride was deposited at an open door where he was greeted by a small Japanese houseman who said nothing but indicated that he was to be followed.

McBride thought, it didn't matter, someone once said, whether you were rich or poor as long as you were happy. And then added, but rich is better. The ranch house proved it. It was casually comfortable in a way that only the rich could afford. Deep rugs covered polished floors. Large antique chairs stood in corners waiting to be used. The room McBride was ushered into was enormous with one wall of glass staring out onto the vastness of the prairie. Although it had seemed that oil wells dotted the countryside on all sides of the house, somehow there were none to be seen from this window. Another wall was lined with books and beside it a large table was stacked with more books, bookmarks protruding from many, reference points for the reader. The reader himself rose from a deep armchair in front of an enormous fireplace. Other armchairs invited occupation. A side table displayed an array of bottles containing every kind of liquor imaginable. Newspapers were open on the floor around the reader's chair. Untidy elegance of wealth in vision.

Dorfmann. Of medium height, he was thin, gnarled and brown like an old tree; in his sixties with a fringe of white hair and a wide smile to match the outstretched hand.

'Welcome, Mr McBride.'

Their hands met. The grip was strong, almost too strong as if Dorfmann had to prove he was glad to see his guest. Above the smile there was one thing out of true. The eyes were grey and cold.

'Damn it, man, if I'd known you hadn't a car I'd have sent someone into town to meet you.'

McBride allowed himself a degree of curiosity. 'How did you know I didn't have? I could have driven to the gates yet you sent a jeep?'

'Closed circuit television. I can see anyone who approaches my property. One of my toys.'

And what are your other toys, McBride asked himself. The wall behind him he could now see was lined with rifles in cases, rows of weapons, a small armoury.

'Sit, Mr McBride. Relax. Take off your jacket. As you can see I live casually and I dress casually.'

In an open necked silk shirt and tailored blue jeans, Dorfmann was certainly expensively casual.

'You'll have something to drink? Or would you prefer coffee?'

'I'd . . . I'd like a cup of tea, if that's possible?'

'Surely.'

The Japanese was summoned again. The tea arrived, Earl Grey in a large pot. Two cups were poured.

'I like your British tea habit. The only drink for a hot afternoon.' Dorfmann said. He was being expansive, pleasant and patronising.

'You'll have been told about me, I'm sure,' Dorfmann went on. 'Filthy rich, like many Texans. Oil does it. Can't get enough, the world, so people who're lucky like me become rich. Dorfmann's oil may not make me the Lord's anointed but it sure makes me the Stock Exchange's anointed. All over the world. I'm grateful though. But it brings its own responsibilities.'

'I can imagine,' McBride replied politely and untruthfully. He could not imagine.

Dorfmann sank back into his own chair. 'Well now, did Charlie Neaman tell you I'm an admirer of yours?' He didn't wait for a reply. 'Sure, I am. That piece on the Britisher looking at Texas . . . that was perceptive. But then you come from a perceptive race, Mr McBride. May I call you Alec?'

McBride assented. The only millionaire he'd ever met wanted to call him by his first name, who was he to object? And he noted nothing was said about his reciprocating. Anyway he couldn't imagine himself addressing his host as Sidney.

'Yeah, you Scots are perceptive, Alec.'

'The article was not entirely complimentary to Texas,' McBride said.

'Hell, son, anybody can lick ass. But the truth, that's something else. Takes a man. I like the truth, Alec. You can rely on a man who writes the truth.'

'I've always believed that,' McBride replied suddenly aware that he sounded quite naive.

'Sure you do,' Dorfmann went on. 'I know you Scots. Like the country. Played golf at St Andrews. Like your Presbyterian honesty too. Straight forward. Like me. German Lutheran stock. Oh, way back. A hundred and fifty years back. Family got to Texas early. Staked our claim, put down our roots.'

'They obviously stuck.'

'Sure. Family laid the ground work, my daddy and me made the money. I'm a rich man, Alec. But then you know that.'

'I was told.'

'I don't flaunt it like some. You take Mr Hunt over there now . . .' His hand gesticulated vaguely in the direction of the window. 'He lets it be known he's rich. Me, oh, it's known, but I'm silent about it. You know how I did it?'

'Oil, I thought.'

'Oil laid the foundations. With cattle and land. But then it's how you use it. Some guys play the market, some go into commodities. Some of them try to corner the market in this or that commodity . . . in shares, in futures. Me, I just decided early on to try and act like I was cornering the market in money. Of course you never actually make it but you make a hell of a lot of money trying.'

The economic philosophy was beginning to bore McBride. Was this why he had been ordered out here? To listen to the story of Sidney Dorfmann? Or was that part of the reason?

'You want me to write about you, Mr Dorfmann?' he asked.

'Hell, no! Maybe I sound as if I do, but no, no way. I talk a lot but that doesn't mean I want the words spread around. Words pick up dirt when they're spread around. I don't want no dirt. But I like your work, your . . . style . . . that's it . . . of writing. I like to help people whose work I like. You got a work permit?'

'Yes.'

'See, among a few things I picked up along the way was an interest in newspapers. A financial interest. Oh, I'm no Hearst . . . though I knew him . . . spent time at San Simeon when I was younger. Anyway I own part of a newspaper in Chicago. Could use a good feature writer like you. You interested?'

'Can't afford not to be.'

'Good. Pay to start with around fifteen grand a year. But it'll go up quickly. Few years you could be on forty thousand. Still interested?'

'I'm not actually a reporter.'

The older man grimaced. 'Reporters! A dime a dozen. Good feature writers . . . with a bit of investigative flair, that's what the paper needs. Things only you can see and write about. Other eyes seeing America. That's good. Could be another Alistair Cooke . . .'

The right thing to say was important now. 'I'd rather be the first Alec McBride.'

'I like that. You work mostly on your own ideas . . . well, the editor throws in some. You like it?'

'I like it. But . . .'

McBride paused. It was still there, nervously gnawing at his awareness. Bill Sandrup. All that he knew. And underlying it, a hint of fear. Chicago would take him away from that. Maybe. And should he try to run with it all still unresolved? Was there a resolution?

Dorfmann said, 'You're hesitating. Why?'

McBride drank another cup of tea and told him. He told Dorfmann it all from start to finish. After all Dorfmann had money and money spelt protection. Or so it seemed.

Dorfmann listened. Then asked questions. Like, you saw Sandrup dead . . . like, but Sandrup died five years ago. The sister confirmed it.

McBride replied, but did she? Why was she so frightened? Why did she want to get rid of him so quickly?

Then Dorfmann said, 'Sandrup was supposed to have been burned up in this car smash. But if the body was badly burned it could have been anybody.'

McBride said he had already thought of that.

'So you want to know what I think?' Dorfmann went on. 'Now I was no JFK lover. Most big money in Texas wasn't. But he was the President and he should never have been killed. That's straight, my feelings, okay?'

McBride nodded his agreement.

'Now I've been thinking the Oswald business was all too neat and tidy. Especially this man Ruby killing him. Trouble is whether or not people believe it was Oswald, they'll say nothing, do nothing. It's cosier that way. Neat and tidy. If they start believing it was someone other than Oswald, then it could be anybody. Your daddy or your uncle, or the guy next door. That's uncomfortable. Nobody's going to want that.'

'Yes, I know, but if I do know something, do I keep quiet?'

'Never said that. But it's how it'll be, I'm telling you. Now, me, I said I was no Jack Kennedy lover. I knew him. Knew his old man too. Liked the boy better than old Joe. But not the boy's politics. But he could have shaped up to be a good President. Better a rich boy in the job. Nobody can corrupt a man who's got everything.'

It was Dorfmann's turn to pause. He did so, rising, walking to the enormous window, a man in thought. After a time he turned to face McBride.

'Tell you what I'm going to do. Before you take on the Chicago job you go and see a man I know, FBI. A friend. You tell him everything you've told me.'

'Will he believe me?'

'You come from me, you come strongly recommended. The other attribute of money. Power. They listen to money. To me and my friends. Sure, you could go to the police. They listen . . . and laugh. They want

66

it to be Oswald. And your Sandrup character is, in their books, a long time dead. This friend of mine in the FBI, he'll listen. And he'll dig. You want to do that?'

'Yes, of course.' McBride felt the tension ease out of him. Dorfmann had taken over. Had provided a solution.

'Afterwards you go to Chicago, you start work, and you leave all this Sandrup business to Bill Sullivan. He's one of the deputy directors of the Bureau. Got the ear of J Edgar. You understand, you leave it to Sullivan. Otherwise you go on about it, you become some kind of crank. I don't want cranks working on my newspapers. You leave it to the FBI.'

'I . . . I could write about it . . .'

'Only if the FBI says so. Understand that?'

'Yes, sir.' The sir came automatically. Later he wasn't sure he liked himself for using it.

'I may not agree with Jack Kennedy but I agree a lot less with him being killed in Dallas. My town. My people. Dirties them all. Town that killed the President. Don't like that. Tomorrow you fly to Washington . . . I'll pay for it . . . and give you an advance of salary . . . no, hell, a bonus. Then you come back and pack for Chicago. My people will fix it all. Tickets and cash will be delivered to your apartment tonight. I'll say goodbye now, Alec, and you must not hesitate to call on me if you have any problems.'

The dismissal was abrupt but, on the way to Dallas, McBride realised that there was nothing more to be said. Everything had been covered, agreed, tied up in neat little packages. He was being driven back to Dallas then, in a large Cadillac, chauffeur driven, in deep luxury. His first connection with wealth. It soothed, took away problems, eradicated fear.

That evening at his apartment a messenger appeared and presented him with a large envelope. Inside it was a return airline ticket to Washington for the next morning, an open ticket to Chicago, single, and five thousand dollars in cash. A neat typewritten note explained that the money was for expenses and bonus. He would be expected to join the newspaper in Chicago within three weeks. The note was signed 'in the absence of Mr Dorfmann by his secretary'.

Five thousand dollars. More cash than McBride had ever had at one time; he thought, you had to admire the efficiency of the rich and powerful.

His plane was at nine in the morning. He went to bed early. He dreamt he was sleeping under the wing of the American eagle.

Washington, District of Columbia, in the first days of the administration of Lyndon B Johnson. It was grey and damp except for the buildings which retained a quality of whiteness, a facade of purity. Not that McBride saw much of the capital city. A glimpse of the Jefferson Monument from a taxi, the Capitol Building at the end of that long avenue; and signs of preparation for the funeral of the century. His first time in Washington and that was all he could say he had seen. That, and the FBI Building, new, clean and efficient.

He was shown into a pleasant room with deep chairs, a coffee table on which were copies of *National Geographic* and *Reader's Digest*. 'I was a Teenage Sex Fiend for the FBI and found God.' An old joke about the *Readers' Digest* McBride remembered as he waited. Finally a young man with close-cropped hair and a grey flannel suit that spelt Brooks Brothers came in and thrust forward a well-manicured hand.

'Dempsey,' he said. 'Mr Sullivan's assistant. He's heard your story from Mr Dorfmann on the telephone, Mr McBride. I'm to take a detailed statement.'

McBride gave him a detailed statement. The telling of it took over an hour. Dempsey brought in a

68

stenographer. Together Dempsey and the stenographer looked like Mr and Mrs Clean-Cut America.

When McBride had finished, Dempsey asked him a number of pertinent questions: 'You saw no one following you and Sandrup? No one saw you leave the hotel? You'd never met Sandrup before? You're sure he was dead in the hotel room? He gave you no reason for his employment as one of the President's assassins? You feel, ever since, that you may be being followed?'

McBride answered as truthfully as he could in memory.

Dempsey said, 'Thank you, Mr Sullivan will be most interested.'

'But will he do anything?'

'The most strenuous investigations will be pursued. And your statement will be read by Mr Hoover himself.'

Like God proof-reading the Bible, Mr Hoover would actually concern himself with Mr McBride's statement. There's glory for you, Dempsey seemed to be saying. McBride tried, within himself, to be suitably impressed but he couldn't quite manage it. But then he was, to them, a foreigner.

'Mr Sullivan regrets he cannot personally see you but he asks me to assure you, as he has already assured Mr Dorfmann, that everything will be done. And Mr Sullivan or myself will contact you the minute we have anything to tell you, any corroboration of your statement.'

McBride could only say 'Thank you.'

'Also, of course, we wish to be assured of your personal safety, Mr McBride. The FBI will be available to you if you feel in need of protection. You only need to contact any of our field offices. You don't, I gather, feel any immediate danger?'

'No, no, not now. Now I feel reassured.'

'That is our purpose both with our own citizens and guests in our country like yourself. Oh, one thing more,

Mr Sullivan asked me to tell you that it is certain there will be an official enquiry into the assassination of the President. Should your evidence be required you would of course be willing to appear before any such enquiry?'

'Of course.' Foreigner or not, there was the Atlantic alliance, Lease Lend, hands across the ocean and all that. McBride would not let his country's ally down.

'It will naturally be more than just an enquiry,' the FBI man said. 'A Commission and the word is it'll be headed by Chief Justice Warren himself. The truth will come out, Mr Hoover has assured us all of that.'

McBride thought, if Mr Hoover did the assuring, it must be so.

Dempsey shook hands again. 'We'll keep in touch. I gather you're going to Chicago shortly.'

'In about three weeks. Just have to clear up in Dallas. I can let you have my address in Chicago when I get one.'

Dempsey, he thought, almost winked, but it would not have been in character, not within the requirements of the role he was playing.

'No need. We'll know your address all right.'

A taxi was waiting outside the building to take him to the airport. The Bureau took care of everything. McBride could sleep now, unafraid. Everything was in the hands of Mr Dempsey, Mr Sullivan and, most important of all, J Edgar Hoover himself. Nothing could touch McBride now.

Except Billy Sandrup's words. 'Now I've told you, you're a dead man too.'

McBride's plane flew through the night back to Dallas.

He prepared to leave Dallas. He gave notice to his landlord. He drank with Charlie Neaman and Schuyler and other newspaper men he had come to know. He noticed, too, that there came, with the knowledge that

70

he had been selected by Dorfmann, a change in their attitudes towards him. Previously he had been treated with a patronising condescension. Now he was accepted as a colleague. Hence the farewell drinking bouts.

Seven days before he was due to leave he met Genine Marks on the stairway to her apartment. She knew he was leaving and her attitude at first was cold. However when he invited her to dinner that night, his own personal farewell to her, she warmed.

'Where we going?' she asked, assuring him she could get the night off from her job. 'Nowhere too fancy. I get sick of too fancy. I just want to relax, have it quiet. Maybe you can romance me a little with the old soft lights and sweet music.'

He assured her he would do his best. Her desires, he knew were coloured by a million movie stories where Gable or Taylor took Lombard or Margaret Sullivan to a small restaurant with gypsy music somewhere in the background provided by the full MGM orchestra. She was a simple girl, expert only at conning drinks from travelling salesmen and, for payment, going further. But this was a professional and not personal expertise.

They went to a small Italian restaurant two blocks away. The tables had candles in bottles with layers of wax around the necks of the bottles. Genine adored this. It epitomised all her romantic ideas.

When they got back to the apartment building he realised she wanted to sleep with him. And he found that the feeling was reciprocated. He wanted her. No romance but a purely physical desire. Why not? She expected it as a farewell gesture. He needed it as a biological urge. They climbed the stairs to his landing.

The door of his apartment was not locked. He should have been warned. As it was he simply thought he'd forgotten to lock it. He pushed the door open and stood aside to let her enter. The room was in darkness.

Then . . . two bright flashes.

And the sound afterwards. Two loud, earsplitting roars.

Later the police told him the bullets were from a Magnum 44, the most powerful hand gun . . . something like that. It didn't matter then. Texans were used to guns. Scotsmen weren't.

Genine took the two shots in the center of her chest. She was lifted inches from the ground and thrown backwards across the landing. She was already dead when she hit the floor.

Thought of what he might do never entered into it. McBride, struck by the girl's shoulders as she went past him, flattened automatically against the wall. Astonishment came before fear. And self-preservation next. He waited, pressed against the wall. He could run down the stairs but he could also see himself being shot in the back as he ran. So he hesitated momentarily.

The man came out of the room. Short, squat with wide shoulders he came out quickly, eyes fixed on his recent target, face frowning. As if, McBride said later, he'd hit the wrong target. As he had. Then fear took over McBride, adrenalin coming into the bloodstream. The man would turn, see him, and fire. Inevitable. Unless . . .

The right arm holding the gun was nearest to McBride. He flailed forward wildly but concentrating on the gun arm. His fists came down on it. The Magnum fell. Its owner half turned. McBride punched him on the face as hard as he could punch.

The result was not quite as he had hoped for. The gunman's head went back a foot and he grimaced.

The two men came together on the top of the stairway, overbalanced and fell downwards, both rolling over. McBride felt little pain but only an awareness of his fall, as if he was outside himself watching himself roll and thump down stairs, arms and legs

72

entangled in the gunman's limbs, feeling the wooden stairs moving and hitting his back.

At the half landing they came to a fractional stop. Then the man kicked out at McBride and missed. The heavy shoe flew past the Scotsman's eyes and hit the wall.

McBride pulled himself to his feet. The gunman did so just behind him. And they faced each other.

The man's face in close-up. Yellow skin, pockmarked. His breath hot, edged with garlic. Shaven but unable to conceal a thick stubble. Dressed in black. The man hit out, punching McBride in the stomach.

Pain exploded in his midrift. He jackknifed, his head coming forward. And the memory of an old Glasgow fighting trick. One with the head. Despite the pain he struck forward with his head. The hairline connected on the bridge of the gunman's nose. Bone cracked and blood gushed from the man's nostrils.

The gunman staggered back onto the bannister, twisted around and slid downwards, eyes dazed.

Sound came back to McBride, an awareness of noise. The gunshots had not gone unheard. People appeared on the landing above. And below. Shouting. A woman screamed. Roman holiday. Bread, blood and circuses. But McBride thought of that later.

'Phone the police!' someone shouted.

McBride felt angry. This man, this intruder had hurt, shot the girl he was with. How badly he had no means of knowing but he knew he should feel angry. And now he had disarmed the man he should do more. He should do it before the police came and he stood accused of not defending his lady. That was a matter of some kind of honor. Even if she was his lady only for the night. The anger surmounted the fear.

Launching himself after the man he was so full of rage that he was unprepared. At once he was kicked in the groin.

Pain again, but greater than before. His body jack-knifed onto the steps. Above him the ceiling spun around, blurred. Below him only pain. Sliding now down the stairs, the edges of wood biting into his back, phlegm and nausea in the throat, he was dimly aware of footsteps, fast, running, moving away. The gunman was escaping.

McBride tried to cry out but he couldn't find a voice, couldn't summon air from his lungs to his throat. To do with the pain. He could hear more distant sounds, shouts and screams.

And then a purple darkness embraced him.

In the end it was Dorfmann who sorted it all out. Not personally but through his lawyer. McBride had come to consciousness to find himself suspected of conniving at the murder of Genine Marks – an initial reaction by the Dallas Police Department that fortunately was soon dispelled.

But before McBride could make an official statement, Dorfmann's lawyer was at his side, and then closeted in his apartment while the police waited outside. McBride was never sure how Dorfmann's lawyer got there or who called him. He suspected Charlie Neaman whom he had contacted in his double capacity of victim and newspaperman. Neaman had surely informed Dorfmann of his protégé's trouble.

The lawyer was a tall neat man. Everything about him was neat; his face, his grey eyes, the crease in his trousers. And his tone of voice.

'Mr Dorfmann has informed me of a certain matter regarding which you recently saw operatives of the Federal Bureau of Investigation. He has asked me to point out that his contacts in the Bureau would consider it unwise to link this affair with that matter.'

McBride stared at the lawyer, open mouthed. 'But if it had anything to do with that . . ?'

74

'There is no evidence to indicate such is the case.'

'But . . . but . . . that man was there to kill me.'

'No evidence, as I said. Furthermore, Mr Dorfmann's contacts feel even if it were so, no useful purpose would be served by informing the Dallas Police.'

'But the girl . . . Genine Marks, she's dead.'

The face was utterly bland. 'That is so, and regrettable. But now the police are assured you yourself were not connected with the affair, they are inclined to think that an attempt was made to burglarize your apartment. The burglar was disturbed, panicked and shot his way out. The police I assure you, Mr McBride, are pursuing their investigation in order to apprehend this man. Your statement should not incline them to believe anything else.'

He talked more like an English barrister than a Texas lawyer. There was, too, something else familiar in his tones. The Harvard accent. The man sounded like John F Kennedy.

'But what the hell would anybody burgle my place for? There's nothing of value.'

'The burglar would hardly anticipate that.'

Eventually and inevitably Alec McBride agreed to announce to the police that he believed they had surprised a house breaker with tragic results to Miss Marks. The police accepted this so quickly as to seem almost grateful there were no other complications.

Four days later McBride attended the funeral of Genine Marks. And two days after that he flew to Chicago. The police, he was informed before he left, were diligently following up several leads. He heard no more. No one was ever found who could be accused of the murder of Genine Marks.

McBride was sure her death had never been intended. He knew that he had been the target. Billy Sandrup's words were true. His life was endangered by his knowledge.

Again he was afraid.

He could only hope his removal to Chicago might put him out of sight and out of mind. Whoever's mind it was. But in the end he didn't believe that, not for a moment.

4

1964

Untidy, plump and perspiring, Clyde Anson crossed the newsroom to his desk. An aged sixty-three and bald on top, hair grey, haloing the skin of the skull, he sat heavily on the chair he used to claim Mencken had sat upon, eons before. He'd given up the claim of recent years as young journalists, unimpressed, asked who the hell Mencken was.

Outside it was snowing. The Loop was a snake of infinitely slow-moving cars, each embraced by an icicle wind from the Lake. Buildings, scraping the cloud, blazed with light, illuminating the falling snow. Chicago, Anson thought, my home town. God damn the writers of popular songs. It was too fucking cold to be proud. There had been a time. He'd told young McBride often of that time.

When Chicago had been the cradle of the profession of journalism in these United States.

He'd told McBride of the city still haunted by Mencken and Hearst and Colonel McCormack. When newspapermen all aped Ben Hecht, wore hats on the backs of their heads and looked towards Hollywood for the call to riches. And to hell with that call if it never came. This was the city of *The Front Page*, of *Five Star Final*, of Al Capone and Dion O'Banion. And all the others: Greasy Thumb Guzik, Machine Gun Jack McGurn; and don't forget Mayor Big Bill Thompson who had threatened to punch King George V on the snoot if he ever came to Chicago.

And it was still the city of the Mob. Give it an Italian name now, it was just the same. Cosa Nostra, Mafia, call it what you wanted. To Chicago and to Clyde Anson it was part of a romantic history. And Clyde, despite much to deter him in life was still a romantic. He could tell McBride about seeing Capone – benefactor, not gangster in this appearance – handing out Christmas turkeys to the poor. He could remember Capone, politician now, with a touch of the gangster, kicking the then mayor of the city down the steps of city hall. Wouldn't be done today to the present Irish-American incumbent. He'd do the kicking himself.

Anson could talk too of Capone the gangster, braining two of his dinner guests with a baseball bat. Not that he'd been there to see it but he'd seen the corpses later. And he'd remember Colonel McCormack and that damn renegade priest, what the hell was his name, expound on the fact that National Socialism wasn't too bad a philosophy. Indeed the good old US of A could benefit by a touch of it. A touch of anything to get that bastard FDR out of the White House.

And there'd been the time too, young Alec McBride, when he, Clyde Anson, had shaken the hand of William Randolph Hearst – with Marion Davies a discreet two paces behind. Those were the days, Clyde Anson's days. Trouble is there was always an end in sight.

Trouble would be that he was getting too bloody old. He knew it. No future but one day the notice. Time to go. Time to retire and vegetate. With damn all behind him to keep him going. Having to rely on his daughter. Or other sources. There were the other sources of income.

He stared at the desk. One piece of copy. The Cook County Pedigree Dog Show. Jesus! Was that how it was to end? Friend of senators, gangsters, hucksters, now reduced to reporting dog shows. And looking after greenhorns.

Three months ago he'd been on his old beat. Crime in the city. Told to keep an eye on the new boy, McBride, who was to do features, he'd introduced himself in the old way.

'Clyde Anson. Hollywood would call me the ace crime reporter. In this city that's the big time.'

Not that it ever had been the 'big time'. But he wasn't going to tell that to McBride. New feature writer. Anybody with sense could write features. Anybody literate with their eyes open. But crime needed knowledge, the awareness of the way around the scene, the ear of the big men, the trust of the informers. Hell, Mayor Daley himself tipped Clyde Anson off on one or two stories, mostly grafting by the opposition. Never Daley's own people who were on the take. Anson knew when to keep quiet on that. Some stories you buried deep.

'Man with the most secure job in Chicago,' Anson had told McBride. 'On the crime beat in this city. An occupation for life.'

Unless you were Jake Lingle, he might have added. He'd known Lingle when the word was he fell out with Big Al. McGurn gunned him down on a station platform, as a favor to Al. You avoided that kind of thing, you were set for life.

Until you were sixty-three and the booze was having its effect and they gave you dog shows to write up.

It was later when he met McBride in a bar off the Loop. By that time he'd cheered himself up, was warm with three shots of bourbon. He'd let McBride buy. Why not? He'd shown the kid around, fixed him up with a decent apartment off South Water Street. So the Scotch kid was a comer, best to be decent to him. For a hell of a lot of reasons. After all the word was he was Sidney Dorfmann's boy. And Dorfmann, when he visited with the paper was way up on top of the building, executive level, nearer my God to thee.

He leaned across the booth they sat in. 'They say Mencken used to sleep here. This very bar. You know who Mencken was?'

'I know who Mencken was,' McBride replied. 'I read a lot of his pieces. I read him on the Scopes Monkey trial.'

The kid was better than most, Anson thought. He knows things he should know. 'Did I ever tell you I once met Clarence Darrow? More than once. Covered the Leopold and Loeb trial.'

Two sickly kids who should have burned were saved by Darrow. They should have burned, especially Leopold. White-faced rich kid who was as vicious as they come.

'You told me about that,' McBride replied again. 'Told me three months ago when I first came to Chicago.'

'You're right. So I did. I'm getting old. I keep repeating myself. How about another drink, Alec?'

McBride ordered another drink for him. But not for himself. Anson didn't notice he was still nursing his second drink.

'So you've been here three months. Glad to get out of Dallas, you were. I remember how glad you were.'

'I was glad,' McBride admitted. Strange, he thought to himself, I like Clyde Anson and yet he can be such a bore. Still he'd been decent, helped McBride settle in, found his apartment, showed him the city, talked the city; talked it like it was the history of Scotland or England. Maybe it was to Anson. The Americans had so little history, what they had, they treasured. Good and bad, like Capone and the mob, they nurtured the memories.

'I was in Dallas once,' Anson went on. 'Oil and cows. And money. All new. Trying to make the cowboys into history.' It was as if he was echoing McBride's thoughts.

'Didn't like it. Like it less now. President killer, that city.'

'Can't blame all of Dallas.'

'Yeah, you can. The climate of that city killed JFK. So Dallas bows down in shame, says it wasn't all of us. Just a kid called Oswald. Not me. Hell, Oswald did what they all wanted to do, those fat oil cats.'

'If Oswald did it,' McBride said. It was something he hadn't talked about since he'd left Texas, something he'd been told by the FBI not to talk about. And since coming to Chicago the fear had ebbed away. He'd been too busy to remember to look over his shoulder. James Ellon McKinlay, his editor had seen to that. McKinlay, too, had put him in the hands of Clyde Anson.

'You have doubts Oswald did it?' Anson said. He seemed to sober up slightly, curiosity clearing his mind perhaps.

'I have the thought.'

'Not good enough. You need to know something. Otherwise forget it. Forget it anyway, even if it's true.'

'Why do you say that?' It wasn't like Anson. He'd told McBride he could blow up a whiff of a story into a front page spread. Even if it wasn't true. Who remembered the next day? Who read the denial? That was Chicago journalism, certainly in the old days.

Anson sighed. 'It's like an old vaudeville routine. If he didn't, who did? What? No, who? Who did it? That's what I'm saying. Who's on first base. Anyway you don't want to know. Because they . . . the big boys don't want to know. Bury it with Oswald and sing another tune.'

Finishing his drink Anson stared bleakly at his watch. 'Time we went home. I gotta houseguest.'

McBride was surprised. Anson boasted of being a loner. No real friends. Except in the press room. And among the seats of the mighty.

'My daughter. Don't look so goddam surprised. I was

81

capable once. And stupid enough to get married. Thank God it didn't take.'

A girl passing the booth. 'Hi, Clyde!'

Anson grinned vaguely in the girl's direction. 'You look great, sweetie.'

McBride thought, a little too much make-up but a nice figure and large eyes under a mane of blonde hair. It had been a long time; no one since Genine Marks in Dallas – and the end of that he didn't want to think about.

'She looks nice,' he said.

Anson scowled. 'So does poison ivy. Keep clear of that one.'

'A bar girl?'

'Boy friend's in the rackets. The Mob. You say, hello sweetie, you smile nicely and you stay away.'

'They are still around? Gangsters?'

'What do I tell you? Big Al was good but the boys today are better. They cover up better. Strictly legit. On the surface. Underneath . . . slime, maggots, corruption. I tell you about Giancana. Little guy, big man. Walks with kings, sleeps with their ladies.'

'What does that mean?'

'Shared a lady with John F Kennedy. See, you come to Clyde Anson for all the stories in the world.' Another look at his watch. 'This time I have to go.'

It became a daily ritual, Anson and McBride drinking in the same booth, in the same bar after work. It was interrupted only when Anson was on a story – more dog shows, as he put it – or McBride was doing research. His first articles had appeared on the paper and had actually been approved of by the Managing Editor.

'One of the demi-Gods has looked down and blessed your efforts with his fucking condescending praise. You are in, kid.' Anson had commented, with an encouraging grin.

Then it was another night a few weeks later, in the booth. Anson was restless.

'So my daughter's come to stay. For Christ's sake I'm not a family man but what can I do? Throw her out into the snow? She has one marriage that goes wrong, so suddenly I'm a daddy again.'

McBride commiserated politely. He could afford to do so with other people's problems. His seemed to be receding into the past, fading from memory. Nothing to fear now. Except . . . except that he had expected to hear from the FBI and so far had heard nothing. The Warren Commission were setting up to investigate the assassination of a President and he felt he should have heard something.

'Should introduce you to my kid, Alec,' Anson went on. 'Maybe you could be taking her off my hands.'

McBride jerked his mind away from Washington, the FBI and the Warren Commission. Anson's daughter? He'd never met Anson's daughter. So far it had been all talk, no description. He wasn't sure he wanted to meet Anson's daughter. And yet he should meet her, it might just be a good idea. He knew so few people in Chicago outside of the office. Oh, the people he came into contact with seemed pleasant enough, better than those in California. At least here people smiled without knowing how much you had in the bank. But so far, the smile was all. Life was work, the television set in his apartment, the odd movie and drinking with Clyde Anson. Oh, and there was the car. He'd bought himself a year old Mustang and he spent Sundays and other days off exploring the Illinois countryside. Alone. He'd hoped the car might attract company, female company, but he'd soon realised it was too commonplace to provide attraction. Maybe Anson's daughter wasn't a bad idea. If he only knew what she looked like.

But the man had changed the subject. He was on to his favorite theme again, old Chicago.

83

'Ever hear about the Everleigh sisters? Ran the best goddam bordello in the country. Maybe the world. Those were the days. Michigan Avenue had more vice dens than a dog's got fleas. Had my first woman in one of them. Just regret I never visited the Everleigh Club. They say it had cut-glass chandeliers like your Buckingham Palace. And silk drapes and a kind of elegance you never see now. The anti-vice boys killed all that. Until Capone came along and made it a business. Looked at Cicero when he couldn't operate in the center of Chi' and said . . . this is virgin territory for whore houses. Trouble is there was no elegance any more. Just bath-tub gin, pick a lady, get it up and out and go home. I reckon they put sex on a conveyor belt. No elegance, like I said.'

Time to go, McBride told himself. There was only so much he could take from Anson, even though he was fond of the older man. And tonight Anson seemed edgy, nervous, strained.

'Sure, I am,' Anson admitted, when McBride mentioned it. 'Used to living alone. Maybe now and then entertaining a lady. But now Dorrie's there, so I have to behave. You want to go home, Alec, you go. In fact I'll walk with you. Put off the dreaded hour I have to get in.'

'Come up for a drink.' McBride felt bound to extend the invitation. 'You helped me find the apartment but you've never been there.'

They walked. McBride rarely brought his car to the office and then only if he thought he was going to need it for work. Anyway taxis were on the expense account. The Mustang nestled in the subterranean car park beneath his apartment building. Anson, he knew, possessed an aged Chevvy but like McBride preferred to leave it outside the small house in Cicero he called home. He actually liked to travel in by the El, Chicago's rattling, shuddering, elevated railway system.

84

They walked through snow falling thickly now. Anson grumbled, didn't seem keen on visiting McBride's apartment despite the prospect of a drink. As if he was nervous of the weather, anxious to get back to Cicero and his daughter. Yet he came as if obligated, unable to resist the invitation, perhaps to approve of the place he'd found for the younger man.

The snow was coming in flurries now, borne by freezing gusts of wind from the lake and beyond the icy wastes of Canada. Surely, McBride told himself, the snow must ease; they'd endured it for weeks. It must die away with the coming of spring.

In the foyer of the apartment block steam seemed to rise from their coats, Anson's spectacles misted up momentarily. The central heating was like a heavy blanket of warm air suddenly cast over them. They took the elevator to the fifth floor, McBride's floor. The corridor was flooded with yellow light, the heat climbed with them, increasing as it rose.

McBride unlocked his apartment door with a sudden feeling of *déjà-vu*, a memory of opening a door in Dallas and the death of Genine Marks. This time however, there was no instant, deadly welcome. They stepped into the narrow hallway and McBride switched on the light. Everything seemed to be as it should.

'Take off your coat,' he said to Anson. 'We'll soon dry off.'

Anson had his coat half off when he hesitated, eyes focussing across the hall. 'What the hell's that?'

McBride followed his gaze. A paper bag lying against the door of the living room, wires exposed, linked to some kind of minute terminal; the rest hidden in the depths of the bag.

'Bloody untidy,' he laughed. 'I don't know what that is. Unless it's something the cleaning woman left . . .'

For a slow, ponderous man, Anson could move with remarkable speed when necessary. He reached out and pulled McBride back to the front door. His hands were surprisingly strong.

'Out!' he shouted. 'Move!'

McBride was about to resist, astonished at the outburst. But before he could do so he found himself again out in the corridor. Anson didn't relax his grip but, tightening it, threw McBride away from the door down on to the floor and followed him. McBride tried to struggle up only to see the door of his apartment burst outwards followed by an enormous swelling bubble of flame.

Then came the roar of the explosion, and dust and cement flew into the corridor.

Later, much later, Sergeant Clayton of the Chicago police department handed over cigarettes to the two dusty figures sitting in the janitor's office of the building. The older man, Anson had a long scratch across his forehead surrounded by an amount of matted blood. Beyond that the two men were unharmed.

'Clever little bomb somebody put there,' Clayton said. 'Minute you opened the door you triggered it. Timed to go off a minute later.'

'How the hell do you know that?' Anson asked, right hand tentatively feeling the scratch on his head.

'I been with the bomb squad for twenty-three years,' Clayton drawled. 'That's why I'm here. I seen this kind of thing before.'

A smaller, better dressed man, Inspector O'Hara, joined them.

'Reckon Mr Anson saved your life, son,' he addressed McBride who barely concealed wincing at the mode of address. He thought, I'm not your son, Inspector whatever-your-name-is, and I'm fed up being adopted instantly by anyone who could claim age superiority.

'I know he did,' McBride responded, feeling now genuine gratitude towards Clyde Anson.

O'Hara looked at Clayton. 'Home made explosive device, sergeant?'

'Sure. But made by a pro, you can bet on it. Anson hadn't been there, McBride would have had no face no chest and no balls, that's what I reckon.'

Then followed the interrogation, conducted solely by O'Hara.

'You got enemies?'

McBride determined to say nothing about Dallas, Kennedy or Billy Sandrup. He denied knowledge of enemies. He was still following the FBI line. Say nothing except to us. He would have a lot to say to the FBI.

'So you got no enemies. Any friends who don't like you? You got woman trouble? Ex-wife trying to collect blood for alimony?'

McBride assured him he had no ex-wife.

'Doll, then? Girl-friend, mistress, whore?'

McBride denied all this.

'Jealous husband, jealous boyfriend, you forgot to tip some head waiter?' Deadpan, a further firm denial.

'You write for the papers? Had any crank letters? Anybody who don't like your grammar?'

A final rebuttal of all suggestions.

'OK,' O'Hara went on. 'You live an unblemished life of virtue. But somebody did just try to blow you up.'

'I know it, too. I just hope the hell you'll catch him, whoever he is!'

'We'll keep looking,' O'Hara replied. 'That's our job. As to finding, I can't give you any guarantees. You got someplace you can sleep for the night? What's left of your apartment looks like it's been badly barbecued.'

Anson said, 'I can put him up for now. And longer if he wants.'

McBride demurring politely, picture of a young man saying all the things he should say. Also knowing he didn't mean them. He needed a place and he'd hoped Anson would volunteer. He didn't want to go back to the apartment, not only not now, but he doubted ever. Sandrup's warning might just be coming true.

He went to Cicero on the El.

In the living room of Anson's house, he drank a large whisky as if it was water. He was also introduced to Anson's daughter.

'Dorrie,' she said, shaking hands. 'For Dorothy Macklin, nee Anson.' She was tall, long legs, the right shape, and black hair falling over an intelligently pretty face. She was the best thing he'd seen in years in America.

'She's too tall,' said her father. 'But she is, somehow, the fruit of my loins.'

The fruit of his loins disappeared with a grin to make up the spare bedroom. Anson proceeded to pour them another drink.

'Damn clever girl, Dorrie,' he went on. 'Even though I say so myself. Only done one stupid thing in her life and that was to marry that whey-faced advertising man, Albert Macklin. Good old Al, everybody's pal, except that he likes to beat up on his wives. Dorrie was number two. Only thing was, she belted him back. Made me feel proud. The divorce'll take her a couple of weeks in Reno and she'll be rid of him.'

He took a long gulp of whisky then and stared up at McBride.

'But tonight I want to hear your story, Alec. Somebody tried to erase you from the page. There's got to be a reason. If you can't tell O'Hara who and why, maybe you can tell me. Or is it all innocence and light and a terrible mistake. Come on, kid, talk. Did you do something back in England . . . or Scotland?'

McBride suddenly felt he had to tell someone. To hell with the FBI, Anson made a good someone. The old man had saved his life, risked his own. He deserved to be told. Yet if Sandrup had been right back in Dallas, he wouldn't be doing Clyde Anson a favour.

'If I did tell you . . .' he said hesitantly, 'You'd . . . maybe . . . you'd be taking a risk.'

'Take a risk every time you cross the street. Take a risk every time you go to the john. Do you know more heart attacks happen on the john than anywhere in the world?'

McBride told him. Started at the beginning and brought it right up to date. Anson listened without comment, occasionally sipping at his whisky. When McBride came to the end of the story Anson, despite the amount he had been drinking, was stone cold sober.

'So you think whoever killed Sandrup, whoever was behind killing Kennedy, put that mechanical device in your apartment?' he asked.

McBride nodded.

'Okay,' said Anson. 'Now Clayton said that bomb or booby trap was made by a pro. Now I know who made the thing and so does Sergeant Clayton. But he'll never be able to prove it. He knows that, so he won't even try.'

'You actually know?'

'A pro . . . professional bomb-maker. What is it they say in England? By appointment . . . to the rackets, to anybody who'll pay him.'

'But if you know who made the bomb, you'll know who's behind it all.' McBride could barely conceal his excitement.

'I said it. The guy makes them for whoever pays him. I recognised the package which is why we're both here just now. If I hadn't we'd be on the mortuary slab. But you have to understand, this bombmaker, he doesn't talk about who pays him. If he talks he's out of the game.'

McBride's excitement died. 'But we could try and make him talk?'

89

Anson laughed. 'You fancy yourself as a hood, a mobster. No way, Alec.'

'Who is he?'

'That little firecracker he left in your place, he might have left his signature too. It's Caretti. Aldo "Jellyroll" Caretti. The jelly comes from gelignite. Little Aldo, employed by the famous to blow safes, cars, people. Mafiosi. Old Sicilian family.'

Anson frowned before continuing. 'You sure this Sandrup story is the only reason somebody might want to kill you? You haven't been screwing around with a nice Italian girl. Or a mobster's lady? Or maybe they think you just don't like ice cream?'

'I like ice cream, Clyde. Honest.'

'Okay so I'm gullible. You've gulled me. I believe you. Tell me it again. Go on, tell about the rabbits, George. One more time.'

McBride told him again.

'Right. Right, right, I believe what happened to you, happened. As to whether your late friend Sandrup killed Kennedy, I don't know. Sure enough, though there have been some strange little legends coming out of Dallas.'

'What legends?'

'That the Oswald version stinks,' Anson rose and paced restlessly. 'Aw, hell, there's the Warren Commission anyhow. They should bring everything into the open. They should . . .'

'Only if people testify. Only if people are allowed to tell the truth.' McBride sounded petulant. But then he had cause, he told himself.

'Sure. Right enough. It only comes out if there's no cover-up.' Anson nodded vigorously.

'So what do I do now?' The petulance was giving way to a plaintive plea for help.

Anson stared at him again. 'That's easy. For now you stay here.'

'That's good of you but I can't . . .'

'Can and will. No argument. Anyway your apartment's uninhabitable. We've got a spare room. I can use the company and I think Dorrie'll welcome it. And we can use the money. I'm not putting up a working bum for no rent.'

McBride found himself now actually smiling. There was reassurance in Anson's manner.

'Rent in cash, by the way. Not declarable for tax purposes. And the other thing you have to do is phone the FBI. This Sullivan or his side-kick. They've taken enough time to leave you alone. Meanwhile I ask around about little Aldo Caretti.'

So it was done. Two decisions, however small. McBride could relax a little, sit back and feel the warmth of the whisky, knowing that some kind of action was underway.

The next morning he phoned the FBI in Washington.

'I'd like to speak to Mr Sullivan.'

'Which Mr Sullivan are you calling?' The voice was female and, as usual, nasal. Or did all American telephones distort the female voice?

'William Sullivan . . . Deputy Director.'

'Who is calling, please?'

'My name's McBride. Alec McBride.'

'Will you hold the line, please?'

Some static followed, then nothing. For two minutes. McBride was beginning to get restless when a voice came on. This time it was male.

'Mr McBride. You are the Mr McBride that saw Mr Sullivan some months ago. Late November that would be or early December?'

'Late November. But I didn't exactly see Mr Sullivan. I saw a Mr Dempsey. Are you Dempsey?'

'No, I'm not. Unfortunately the Deputy Director isn't available to speak to you at this time.'

Did he even exist, William Sullivan? McBride wondered.

'I'd like to speak to Mr Dempsey then.'

'Mr Dempsey is no longer on station in Washington. I believe he's in Nebraska . . . or is it Omaha? I'd have to check. Is there any message I can pass on to Mr Sullivan?'

McBride thought, what do I say? Someone tried to blow me up. They're still trying to kill me. The man at the other end of the line had almost certainly heard nothing of his story, probably knew nothing of it. Forget it just now, that was the best idea; try again later.

'I'll try again later.'

'You do that, sir. I'm sure Mr Sullivan will be free later. Have a nice day.'

If he lived through the day, it could be considered nice. A matter of simple survival. Or would they take their time, wait another three months before trying to kill him again? Open season on Alec McBride every three months of the year.

He spent the day in the library of the paper doing research on Englishmen and Scots who had emigrated to Chicago. Pinkerton the detective, he found had been born in Glasgow and had fled the city under suspicion of being a dangerous radical. Ironic when you think he ended up running a detective agency that, among other things, specialised in smashing trade unions in the old days. Was that what the United States did to all the bright, idealistic young radicals? Turned them into the running dogs of big business, the lackeys of capitalism. For God's sake don't use the phrase, lackey. How corny could you get. In fact maybe it wasn't worth going into Pinkerton at all. Unless he employed the agency to find out who was trying to kill him. There was a thought. Only he doubted if he could afford the Pinkertons.

That evening he tried the FBI in Washington again.

Again Mr Sullivan was not available. Who was the

agent he had spoken to that morning? A short delay. Then the reply, that would have been Agent Beauclair. Could he then speak to Agent Beauclair again? I'm sorry but unfortunately Agent Beauclair was not on duty. Can anyone else help? No? Certainly do try again, sir. Have a nice evening.

Two days passed. McBride worked in the office on his feature. After work he took the El to Cicero where Dorrie Macklin, nee Anson, made him a meal before dashing out to what she called her 'classes'. She dashed out with a genuinely apologetic smile leaving him to watch television. He suggested they eat out one night and was pleasantly surprised when Dorrie agreed with enthusiasm as soon as she'd finished her 'classes'. What were her classes, he asked? Advertising, she said. She was determined to be successful at her job. Later Anson himself would come in, mutter 'no news' and sink into a chair, making alcoholic pronouncements on the inadequacy of the television news. He would also ask about Washington. McBride would reply, 'No news.'

They would retire silently to their bedrooms. Anson seemed always to be out on some reporting job so they did not meet in the office.

On the third day McBride tried Washington again.

'I'm trying to get through to Mr Sullivan, the Deputy Director. I phoned a couple of days ago and spoke to a Mr Beauclair. Are you Beauclair?'

A well modulated masculine voice. 'Clark is my name, Mr McBride. Jim Clark. Unfortunately Mr Sullivan is not available.'

'Like two days ago?'

No change in tone. Still pleasant, obliging. 'Exactly like two days ago, Mr McBride. Mr Sullivan left Washington to go into the field about a week ago.'

Exasperation welled up. They were as bad as British civil servants. Worse. They were so damned polite in Washington.

'Couldn't anybody have told me that two days ago?'

'Indeed, Mr McBride, they could have and should have.'

'All right, so where can I get hold of him?'

'I'm not at liberty to tell you that, sir. However I can pass a message. Alternatively, can I be of help?'

Exasperation dominant now. 'Look, I was told the FBI would help me. Protect me. So what's happened? An attempt been made to blow me into small pieces and I get the runaround when I call you people . . .'

A pause followed by a deep breath. At least they're still breathing in Washington. Then Clark spoke again. 'Perhaps if you could give me some details. You do realise of course that murder is not necessarily a Federal offence. The local police would be the right people to handle . . .'

McBride slammed the telephone down. Why bother? They were taking him round in circles. And it was as if it was deliberate. As if they didn't want to know. In the end it came down to the fact that he had to look after himself. Keep an eye open for bombs or bullets; for the watcher in the night. Or perhaps get out, go home to Scotland. At least there he'd only be threatened by muggers, street gangsters and burglary. No conspiracies, no political assassination. Except for the IRA, but he'd never been involved with the IRA.

He was sitting at his desk in the corner of the newsroom. The bustle and hustle of the room did not affect him. He was working on features. Sedentary, thoughtful, that was what was expected of him. He was thoughtful all right. Not about the job in hand though. Too concerned about keeping alive.

Anson came up to the desk. 'Sorry I haven't seen much of you, Alec.'

'That's okay. You've been drunk every night. And absent all day.' It was said with unconcealed bitterness.

Anson flushed, offended but trying not to show it.

'Yes, I have. Sorry. But among other things I've been trying to get hold of Caretti. The guy who made up the bomb, remember?'

'Yes, sure. The one the police won't bother about because they know he's guilty. Of course, I suppose you got to him.'

Anson blinked. 'You could say that. But somebody got to him first. You see, when that bomb went off in your apartment and didn't kill you, Caretti was in trouble. He became one of the great American majority. A loser.'

'Clyde, skip the vernacular . . .'

'Can't. It's second nature,' Anson said, settling on the edge of McBride's desk. 'Alec, in the USA the losers don't inherit the earth. They may just get along but nobody cares.'

'What a bloody country!'

'Except the Mafia. The Mafia doesn't like losers. Don't care to see them around. And the Mafia are the ultimate in efficient capitalists.'

'What are you talking about?'

Anson shrugged. 'Aldo "Jellyroll" Caretti. He won't tell us anything. He was found a few hours ago down by the lake. Stuffed into a trash can. Garrotted. Very efficiently. Quite dead. You see, Alec, now the Chicago police will never find out who paid Caretti to make the bomb for your apartment. More, they'll never find out who killed Caretti.'

5

1964

The next day it stopped snowing and the thaw set in. The purity of the white mantle which had covered the city disappeared, leaving in its place a dirty greyness, a corruption of snow into mud and slush. Rubbish, discarded in the snow, appeared on the streets.

McBride was frightened again. He had slept little the night before, tossing and turning between the sheets, half dreaming of Bill Sandrup, large face grinning, flanked by his two companions. They were without faces, two figures, Buncey and Hayward, heard about but not seen. Almost certainly never to be seen. Almost certainly both were dead.

At noon, McBride phoned Sidney Dorfmann at his ranch outside Dallas. It was something to do, a straw to be grasped that just might turn into a lifebelt. After all, Dorfmann was powerful, perhaps he could get the FBI off their butts, perhaps he could find the elusive Sullivan; find anyone in official Washington who would listen and help.

The pleasantries were brief. 'So how are you, kid? We like the stuff you're turning out. You've got an eye for the scene, you know, a sense of what's going on. Time we forgot the Britisher tag and just let you do your own thing, featurewise. The editor agrees . . .'

Cutting in, incisively now, McBride said, 'Mr Dorfmann . . .'

A pause. A mild irritation at being interrupted in full flow. Then, 'Okay, son, what can I do for you now?'

McBride told him about the bomb.

A deep breath, possibly a sigh at the other end of the line. 'Yes, I was informed about your place being wrecked. I was hoping I could believe it was some kind of accident.'

'No kind of accident, Mr Dorfmann.'

'I take your word for it. What have you done about it?'

'I . . . I've been trying to get hold of Mr Sullivan.'

'Sullivan!' Dorfmann responded as if he'd never heard of the name before. 'Oh, yes, sure. Sullivan. I talked to him after he saw you in Washington . . .'

'He didn't see me in Washington. One of his assistants did.'

'Well, he got the report. Said he was very interested. Said he was instituting enquiries.'

'All I got from Washington was a runaround.'

'These people have their methods, son. You don't rush them.'

It was McBride's turn to sigh. 'I just wanted to tell him what had happened! Nobody seemed very interested.'

The old man gave a throaty chuckle at the end of the line. 'Deceptive, aren't they? These people hear horror stories every day. You don't expect any kind of . . . of outward reaction. Anyway I told him about your apartment being bombed minute I heard.'

Came a thought, an uneasy one. 'How did you hear?'

'I have my sources, Alec. In this case your editor told me. Anyway Sullivan's people, the FBI, they're already looking into it all, believe me. Meanwhile I hear you're staying with old Clyde Anson.'

'Yes. He's been very decent . . .'

'He's a regular human being is old Clyde. Getting a little past it, maybe, too far down the hill. But we look after our own. So Clyde'll be all right. Be looked after.

So will you, son. I've already informed the editor an eye's to be kept on Alec McBride. Oh, nothing heavy. Just a little quiet observation. Don't like my feature writers being blown up. You'll have some protection although you may not notice it.'

I want to notice it, McBride felt like shouting, I want to see myself being looked after, guarded like the Crown Jewels. I am my own Crown Jewels, for Christ's sake.

'Anyway, I have to go now, Alec,' Dorfmann went on. 'It's not just enough to pump oil from the ground, you have to sell it too. Just relax, don't worry, and stay in there pitching with those articles.'

Before McBride could say anything else the receiver at the other end of the line was replaced. He sat back. So that was it. The advice. Relax, forget it, someone is watching over you. Reassuring, but it was becoming less easy to be reassured. It was becoming habit-forming to look over the shoulder, to tread with care. It was a time to look under stones for scorpions. And where there were no scorpions, there was only darkness.

Yet he had to relax, force himself away from the threat at the back of his mind, do something else when you weren't working, cultivate another garden; and pray they would not try again. But what was there to cultivate on one's own? Alone, the mind turned back to the deaths of kings. Solitary, he dwelt on his fears.

The next night he took Dorrie Macklin, nee Anson to dinner.

It was a Chinese restaurant on the North Side. The walls were decorated with paper lanterns and paper dragons. Fortune cookies, McBride told himself, were to be resisted. They might tell the truth of the future. Dorrie, opposite him, was bright-eyed, talkative and attractive. She could just be attractive enough to make him forget.

'Albert Macklin,' she said over the bird's nest soup.

99

'Very bright. On the outside. Sharp. Needle point, ideal for advertising. A good accounts executive. Handled Amalgamated Canning Corporation.'

'Canning?' McBride questioned abstractly.

'Of beef. Very big account in this city. From the stockyard to your own backyard. American beef. He'd no time for anything else. Just the big account. No time for a wife. I felt he might have been more interested if he could have put me in a can.'

'Isn't there a rumor he tried?'

She stared at him, a cool appraising eye. 'You've been talking to Dad. Oh, sure, Albert could get heavy when he'd been drinking with the boys. But I could get heavier. Could get him canned.'

'Tinned Macklin. Sounds fishy or is that just a lousy pun?'

'Yes, it is,' she grinned.

A young waiter removed the soup bowls. He looked like Charlie Chan's number two son. Not number one, that was Keye Luke, who looked an intelligent actor. They were re-running the old movies on television just then. McBride thought, these days he could use Charlie Chan.

The rice and Peking Duck arrived.

'Tell me about yourself, Alec McBride,' Dorrie said. 'All I know about you is that somebody blew up your apartment and the rest, which Dad told me, is equally lurid.'

'Your Dad only knows the dull parts of my life. The really exciting bit was being born in Scotland . . . Paisley, to be exact. A town which they named a shawl after. On a hectic Saturday night you can easily get drunk in Paisley. There's nothing else to do. So, in the end it was a case of choosing between cirrhosis of the liver or coming to America. Until tonight I'm not sure if I made the right choice.'

She pursed her lips. 'With a girl like me flattery can

100

get you anything you want. After my life with Albert I've become a predatory female.'

He couldn't make up his mind whether she was joking or inviting. A bit of both. Either way he was beginning to think he'd found a way of taking his mind off the prospect of being blown up. And that, after all, had been the intention.

He'd left the Mustang outside the house in Cicero, so after the meal they walked a little way to a cab rank. They walked carefully through the dissolving slush. Underneath, the sidewalks were becoming recognizable.

'I'll be moving out of your father's house shortly,' McBride said.

'But why? We like having you . . .'

'Time I found a place of my own again.'

'I'll miss you. So will Dad. Apart from the rent he likes having someone to sound off to. But, look, if you're serious, I'd love to help you look for a place. Men have so little idea of what can make a comfortable home.'

He let the easy presumption pass. Of course she may be simply interested. Or was she stretching out feelers? Not that he minded. They arrived at the cab rank and, after McBride gave the driver the address they settled into the back seat.

'Of course what you really want,' she went on. 'Is early Hugh Hefner. Soft lights, press a button and the TV appears, or the drinks, or a hot dinner or two Bunny girls. Be bad for you. That's why you need me.'

'No Bunny girls. I'm allergic to fur. And to bombs.'

She was nestling close to him. 'I'm good on bombless premises. So it's settled. I help you find your new apartment.'

He put his arms around her. It felt comfortable. Dorrie was both attractive and intelligent. He moved to kiss her.

101

As he did so, out of the corner of his eye he saw, through the rear window, a car moving out from the opposite curb and slowly taking its place behind them. The car looked familiar. It, or a similar model had been parked opposite the Chinese restaurant. The headlights were dipped, the eyes of some medieval dragon on the scent of its prey. He was sure at once it was following them. There was no reason for his certainty; the car had simply moved off at the same time as their taxi moved. It could be late night diners on their way home. What else? Nothing sinister there. And yet he was at once convinced the car was following them. He couldn't see behind the headlights, couldn't make out driver or companion. But the certainty was with him. Two men had driven after them from the restaurant, waited for them to enter a cab.

Now a mist, blurring the tops of the skyscrapers, was moving down into the streets. Lights from the neon signs and office windows were misted to a watery yellow. As they drove the lake appeared on their right, a lighter darkness, a grey haze stretching to infinity and eventually Canada. McBride was barely aware of anything other than the darkness and the lights of the car behind them.

'What is it?' Dorrie asked, sensing his alertness. She would have sworn she was about to be kissed, expected to be and then the moment had gone . . .

The cab turned onto the North Branch moving slowly now through the mist rolling in from Lake Michigan. McBride was now twisted away from Dorrie, eyes fixed on the rear window and the headlights beyond. The car following was large, shiny, black, probably a Chevrolet. He could still make out little beyond the bonnet and the lights. He told himself his imagination was working overtime. The car was merely going in the same direction as their cab. But still the certainty that they were being followed was with him.

102

'What is it, Alec?' Dorrie repeated, insistent now.

'It's . . . it's still going on. We're being followed.'

She twisted around, straining to follow his gaze. The Chevrolet seemed momentarily to drop back. The fog embraced it, partially shrouding its headlights. Then it increased speed until it was back behind them, not more than ten yards separating the two cars.

'Sure, we're being followed,' Dorrie said quietly. 'It's misty so they're dogging our rear lights. They're going in the same direction. But it doesn't mean they're following Alec McBride.'

'They are. I'm sure of it.'

She stared at him in the dim light. There was something obsessional about him, she decided. He'd made up his mind and would have it no other way. Her father had told her to watch him. After the bombing and all that had happened in Dallas he would be obsessional. And it was a dangerous trait.

McBride turned, and leaning over, tapped the glass and mesh that separated them from the driver. The driver leaned back, took his left hand from the wheel and eased the glass partition back a couple of inches.

'Yeah?'

'The first turn off, take the first turn off!'

'Thought you wanted to go to Cicero, buddy?'

'I do. But just now take the first turn off. Slow down when I tell you.'

The driver half turned in his seat and glared at McBride before turning back. 'What is this? I ain't no sucker for a mugging, mister.'

'Nobody's going to mug you. An extra ten in it if you do what I tell you.'

'For twenty I run over my old lady.'

'Okay. Twenty then.'

The cab driver grinned, peering ahead at the road signs. 'My old lady I would have run over for nothing. But okay, I'll take twenty.'

103

A quarter of a mile on they came off the North Branch into narrower city streets. The outlines of tenements were on either side, the mist still twisting, now at kerb level. The headlights of the black car still followed.

'Alec, it's nothing. They're still just dogging our rear lights. Following, sure but just so as they know they're going somewhere.'

'No.' His voice was flat, toneless. 'Too much of a coincidence. They shouldn't have turned off unless they were following us.'

'They could live in this neighborhood.' She peered out the side window, almost afraid to admit to herself that he could be right.

The apartment blocks gave way to open spaces, derelict ground, then used car lots, drenched in fading light from spotlights fighting a losing battle against the fog, their light diffuse, yellow, dying with distance. More narrow streets running off the road.

'Now . . . hard right!' McBride shouted to the driver. He turned the wheel obediently. A car passed, moving fast in the opposite direction. It's headlights lit up for a second the interior of the cab. Dorrie saw McBride's face, shining with perspiration, pale white against a background of darkness.

The black Chevrolet followed them into the narrower street. Another bomb, this time thrown at the cab? Or the old gangster trick he'd seen in a hundred movies. A machine gun poking from the car window, a line of bullets puncturing the metal of the taxi, cutting through both driver and passengers. Or was that really just in the movies? Perhaps one shot would be enough, aimed at his head.

The method didn't matter but the threat did. Dorrie was in the car beside him. It was nothing to do with her yet she could so easily be killed with him. He couldn't rid his mind of the dead face of Genine Marks.

Traffic signals were coming up ahead, turning from

green to red. The cab driver gently applied his brakes. Behind them the Chevrolet slowed down.

Glancing out, McBride saw they were coming to a busy intersection. Kids stood outside a drugstore, leaning on the windows, ignoring the mist, oblivious to the cold. A policeman in a long shining black raincoat sauntered by, eyes on the loiterers. Now McBride saw his chance. Would they dare to try anything here?

Perhaps he was role playing. Certainly he had an image of offering himself in sacrifice, taking the area of danger away from Dorrie Macklin. But later he could think more honestly and realise that the tension within him was too great to be borne. By facing the adversary he was easing that tension, ensuring the point of danger would come at once.

'Pull in at the curb!' he shouted to the taxi driver and, as the cab veered to the right, he twisted the cab door open. Dorrie made an ineffectual effort to stop him but the moment he was out he shut the door leaving her pressed against the side window.

He walked towards the Chevrolet.

It was still directly behind the cab and forced to draw to a halt. As he approached the headlights a feeling of nausea came over him. Sweat broke out on his face, the dew of fear. What was he doing, thousands of miles from his birthplace, walking perhaps towards his death?

An age passed with every step.

Beyond the headlights now he could make out something of the two faces in the front seat of the Chevrolet. Or rather he could make out two patches of whiteness behind the windscreen. And for a moment it seemed as if the faces were featureless, anonymous ovoids, blank pallid discs.

Then he was at the passenger window and the faces came into definition as he bent towards the glass. Two men, the driver slightly in shadow, stared up at him, faces expressionless.

105

The passenger was a thick-set individual, full, fat lips and a prize fighter's nose, long broken and spread to the cheeks. The driver had a long thin face, eyes bright despite the shadow, lips, in the light, a thin gash. They were both in their thirties.

As McBride reached them the passenger lowered his window.

'Yeah?' Somehow the man made it a gutteral sound.

'Why are you following me?' A flash of pride at eliminating the tremor from his voice.

'What's the guy saying?' asked the driver.

'Wants to know why we're following him.'

'Who's following him? Who's following anybody?' The driver's voice was more highly pitched, almost girlish.

As if aware of this trait and anxious to avoid it the driver went on. 'Who does he think we are? A couple of faggots looking for a pick-up?'

The gutteral man gave a wheezing laugh. 'Maybe he's hoping.'

'You've been following me all the way from the North Side,' McBride insisted, but with less certainty now. He felt gauche, young, awkward. But he persisted. 'What do you want?'

The driver replied, 'On a bitch of a night like this all I want to do is get home. Though what the hell it's got to do with you I don't know.'

'The guy's nuts,' said the passenger.

'Then tell him to fuck off and get that cab out of the way. I want to get on.'

McBride took a deep breath. 'Who's paying you to follow me? Who's behind you?'

The two men looked at each other. The driver shrugged.

'Go back to your cab, mister, and go home. The fog's got into your brain.'

He revved up the engine and eased the car forward,

turning the wheel sharply so that the Chevrolet could veer out from behind the cab into the centre of the road. The passenger gave McBride a sneering gesture of farewell. McBride stepped back. Had he been mistaken? Were they merely two men coasting through a bad fog on their way home? There had been no sign of weapons, no aggression beyond a cynically truculent quality. The Chevrolet edged away from him.

The passenger said, 'Have a nice day, Mr McBride.' The car disappeared into the fog.

An hour later, after a slow journey through the fog, McBride and Dorrie sat in the living room of the house in Cicero.

'Am I paranoiac?' McBride asked her.

'Probably. But with cause. I'd like to have seen their faces in that car, though.'

'But, Dorrie, they knew my name . . .'

'You think you heard your name. You could have been wrong.'

'I could have been wrong about a lot of things. Maybe Oswald did kill Kennedy. I don't see Lyndon Johnson . . . or for that matter Bobby Kennedy saying he doesn't believe it. God, Bobby Kennedy would shout surely if they'd got the wrong man.'

'He might have to.'

Alec McBride frowned. 'What does that mean?'

'The public face of the American politician. Stone face. How you get carved on Mount Rushmore. Don't make waves. Don't rock any boats. The system must go on.'

McBride nodded. 'It's a point. I wonder where your father is?'

Dorrie smiled. 'At the local hostelry. Creating his own fog. And maybe being a tactful father. Giving us time to ourselves.'

107

'And I wasted time talking about insanities. But what can I do?'

'Why don't you go and see Bobby Kennedy?'

He stared at her. 'I suppose it can be done. But . . . he's Attorney General . . .'

'The word is, not for long. President Johnson doesn't like dynasties.'

'Kennedy would think I'm a crank.'

'Maybe you are. But a nice one.'

'That doesn't help if I imagined it all. A nice schizophrenic. Huh! Billy Sandrup. Maybe the character I met was some comic singer pretending to be Billy Sandrup. After all Sandrup was killed five years before. It's documented, it's there. They were all killed. Sandrup, Buncey and Hayward. Three discharged marines, drunk and celebrating in a car.'

Dorrie's forehead creased. 'Whoever the man was, you saw him dead in that Dallas hotel. And you recognised the photo in his sister's house, didn't you? Dad told me it all. And there was the bombing of your apartment. And that girl friend of yours killed in Dallas.'

'It's not healthy to be a girl friend of mine, Dorrie.'

'Life's full of risks.' She rose and crossing to a cupboard brought out a bottle of Scotch and two glasses. 'We need this.'

He nodded. 'But don't you see, only I can link it all to Sandrup and the assassination. The killing of Sandrup . . . nobody's found a body. Genine's killing . . . a burglar trying to get out of my place. Like tonight. I thought these two men were following us. They say they weren't and then one of them knows my name. But only I heard it. Even you ask me if I misheard.'

She poured the whisky and passed the glass to him.

'What about the bombing here?'

'God knows! There's nothing to connect it with the death of the President. Nobody really believes me.'

She took a sip from her own glass. 'Didn't Dorfmann believe you?'

McBride took his time replying. He thought about it.

'I don't know. He seemed to. But there were lots of stories going around Dallas in those few days after . . . after the assassination. Nightmares became reality to a lot of people. Anyway Dorfmann listened.' He paused, frowning. 'And then after he listened, he offered me a job away from Dallas. Here. And paid me a lot of money.'

'He liked your articles, your work.'

He smiled across at her. 'You're letting me hold on to my vanity. And it's true. I'm good. I'm a good writer.'

She returned the smile. 'Okay, you're good. And somebody did try to bomb your apartment. You've the best and worst of witnesses. My father.'

But it was Clyde Anson who, arriving home later that night as McBride and his daughter were about to go to their respective beds, presented them with yet another theory about the bombing of the apartment. Surprisingly Anson was comparatively sober.

'I saw that copper today, Alec. Clayton. He's come up with a new theory about your bomb. Very neat, very plausible. Almost lets them off the hook.'

'Tell me, Clyde.'

'The guy who had the apartment before you . . . one, Jake Coraldo, disappeared a few weeks before I found the apartment . . .'

He paused for effect. McBride felt irritated. Much as he liked Clyde he was in no mood for the playing of games.

'Go on. What about Jake whatsisname?'

'A nasty little man. In the rackets. Button man for the Mob. Nice little police record. Charged over the years with assault, robbery, procuring and two counts of murder. Convicted only once, of robbery. But apparently he made a few enemies in the Mob. Ran a little

109

gambling operation and was under suspicion of skimming off the top. Which is probably why he disappeared.'

'What's this to do with the bombing?' Dorrie asked.

'The police, and Clayton in particular, reckon Coraldo got out before the boys went after him. Ergo, they didn't know he'd gone. The bomb was not for you, Alec. It was for Coraldo.'

McBride looked across at Dorrie.

'See? What I was saying. Another explanation for everything. No connection with me, with Sandrup, with JFK.'

Anson looked from one to the other questioningly. Then his eye became attached to the whisky bottle now standing on a side table. He moved towards it, a man with a mission.

McBride went on. 'I'm the only person who believes my own story. Funny, isn't it? Everyone wants to believe something else.'

6

1965

A year passing. Like a newsreel, events occur. Lyndon Johnson announces the beginnings of the Great Society. And he fails to announce the escalation of a local conflict in Vietnam. The Warren Committee investigates the assassination of John F Kennedy and concludes that it was committed by one Lee Harvey Oswald. Through all this Alec McBride works in Chicago.

There had been no further attempts on his life. That was, he told himself, if the original attempts were meant to be on *his* life. With the passing of time, the tension within Alec eased until after some months he was able to go out and walk the streets of the city without looking over his shoulder. It was a small triumph.

With the help of Dorrie Macklin, he found a new apartment high in a new block overlooking the lake front. Together they celebrated his moving in by going to bed together for the first time. It was a funny, passionate bedding and they both enjoyed the experience. So much so it became a regular affair three or four times a week.

In work McBride progressed. His articles began to be syndicated all over the United States. He was asked to appear on breakfast television programmes, first being interviewed, later commenting on current issues. There was talk of a new Alistair Cooke arising in the Windy City. It was gratifying.

He began to be known in Chicago. He achieved a

nodding acquaintance with local politicians, was even introduced to the Mayor. Daley's pudgy face creased into what passed for a smile as they shook hands. The hands McBride grasped were slightly damp.

'Howl your head off, kid,' Daley told him. 'But not against Chicago Democrats. Otherwise you'll be looking for a job in another city.'

This was the voice of power in the City of Chicago, in the heart of the great democracy. Free speech, provided you only said what was wanted. Other characters he met were, he was surprised to learn later, of dubious morality. Most of them, he noted again with surprise, looked like respectable if rather tired business men. But, as Clyde Anson pointed out, that's exactly what they were, in their own *metier*.

Alec McBride began to enjoy his life. For the time being. The time being ended late in February, 1965.

McBride was at his desk in a corner of the newsroom. He was typing a story revealing the signs of unrest among young men threatened with being drafted into the army and on to Vietnam. The phone on his desk rang.

'Commissionaire here, Mr McBride. There's a dame here wants to see you. A Mrs Kathy Raymond.'

'Never heard of her.' Genuinely, the name meant nothing.

'You want I should get rid of her?'

'No. Find out what she wants.'

A distant obscure series of sounds came from the other end of the telephone receiver.

Then, 'She says she's from Dallas. Was referred to you by a Miss Sonia Sandrup.'

His hand trembled slightly as a measure of tension returned.

'Send her up. Right away.' Whatever it was, better to face it, get it over.

She was small, neat and tidy. In her forties, McBride reckoned. Once pretty, still attractive but slightly faded. Cobwebs of tiny lines on the skin under the eyes.

'Do sit down,' he indicated a seat facing him. She did so. Around them the noise of the newsroom.

She leaned forward, her voice dropping, to reply. 'Thank you, I didn't know whether or not you would see me.'

'What can I do for you?'

'I'm . . . I'm not sure.' The voice was low, pleasant, surprising for a Texan, albeit a female.

'I'm from Dallas, Dallas, Texas. But you know Dallas. You lived there.'

Dallas, he thought. God, please, no more of Dallas.

'My mother lives in Chicago, you see. She hasn't been well which . . . which is why I'm here. But, some time ago I was friendly with a lady in Dallas and . . . and, well I told her something that happened to me. And she . . . she said I should contact that newspaper writer . . . that's you.'

'Who was this friend?'

'Sonia Sandrup.'

McBride sighed. It was all over, he felt like telling this woman, he had nothing more to do with it.

'Sonia told me you'd come to see her once. Guess she said it was before you were writing for those big newspapers. She said she'd . . . she'd refused to speak to you. That right?'

'Something like that.'

'She told me I should come and see you. Tell you what I'd seen. You'd be interested, that's what she said.'

'I'm surprised,' McBride said sincerely. 'I got the impression, over a year ago, that Miss Sandrup hardly wanted to talk to me.'

The woman nodded knowingly. 'Sure. That was then. But later it was different.'

'Why should it be so different?'

'Because . . . because Sonia was on her deathbed.'

McBride was suddenly aware that all the sounds in the newsroom seemed to have been reduced to nothing. People yelling had become people whispering, even if at the top of their voices.

'She's dead?' he said.

'Last month. But she remembered you.'

'I hardly knew her. One brief meeting . . . I think she thought I was crazy. Trying to convince her her brother was still alive in 1963.'

'But he was,' Kathy Raymond said.

'What did you say?'

'I saw him. I was in Dealey Plaza the day the President was killed. I saw Billy Sandrup just afterwards.'

McBride was aware of some kind of shock within him, a surprised jolt. He had to confirm what he'd heard. 'You saw Billy Sandrup in Dealey Plaza?'

'My husband saw him too. You see we thought we saw the shots that killed the President. Yes, then we thought we saw them.'

McBride frowned. 'From the book depository?'

The woman shook her head. 'No. From behind the stockade wall.'

'You mean, you saw other shots?'

'We told the police at the time. Made statements. But we never heard any more about it. And of course we saw the three men. But . . . but we didn't mention that to the police.'

'Why not?'

'They were coming from behind the stockade wall. But that didn't mean it was them that fired the shots. And especially since I knew two of them.'

McBride looked around the newsroom. Everyone was working as usual. Sounds came back to him – the clatter of a typewriter, a telephone ringing, Horsley, the sports reporter, declaiming loudly to a copy boy. McBride

114

turned back to the woman. She was about to prove the nightmare he had endured for over a year was fact.

'You knew two of them? One was Billy Sandrup?'

She nodded. 'I was sure it was him. Of course until I visited Sonia in hospital I didn't know Billy was supposed to be dead. See, we'd been neighbors for a time in the fifties. Then we moved to the other side of town. Then when I heard she was in hospital . . . you see I've got a job in the hospital . . . secretarial work . . . so I went up to visit with Sonia. And . . . and I mentioned I saw her brother that day in Dealey Plaza. She kinda went white . . . God knows, she was white enough, her being ill and all . . . and at first she was mixed up. Then she told me to get in touch with you. You being a big newspaper writer and all.'

'You said you recognized two men. Who was the other? Buncey? Orrin Buncey?'

'No, no, that wasn't his name. It was a boy came on leave in the early fifties . . . just after Korea . . . big lad, clean cut, in the marines with Billy. Hayward, that was his name. Bunker Hayward.'

McBride lit a cigarette, hand trembling slightly. Then he remembered his manners and offered Kathy Raymond one.

'Never touch 'em,' she said. 'Bad for asthma. I get asthma pretty often. Say, is all this helping you, what I'm telling you?'

McBride inhaled. 'It's helping. These three men came from behind the stockade, you're sure of that?'

'Sure I'm sure. Don't mean they were the ones fired the shots though.'

There was no point in saying anything else now. He had someone who backed up his story about Billy Sandrup. That was enough.

'I'm glad you came to see me, Mrs Raymond.'

'Well, I was only doing what Sonia said I should do

115

on her death bed. You got to respect folk's wishes on their death beds, I always think.'

She rose to her feet, a small, sad, faded figure, nondescript in her ordinariness. 'Anyway I'm flying back to Dallas tonight. You see my mother's much better, much improved, that's what the doctor said.'

'Would you do something for me?' McBride asked. He had to hang on to her, keep contact with his only witness.

'Depends what you're askin', Mr McBride.'

'Leave me your address. I'll come to Dallas as soon as I can . . . within the next few days . . . and I want to contact you, ask you to tell what you've just told me to a . . . a friend of mine.'

Her forehead knitted together. 'I wouldn't want to get nobody into trouble. Not Billy, if it was Billy. Nor his friend.'

'You won't get them into trouble. I think they're both beyond trouble now. Please, will you do what I ask?'

The frown remained. 'Don't know. Have to ask my husband. Anyway what do you mean, they're both beyond trouble, Billy and Bunker?'

'They're both dead, Mrs Raymond.'

'That's not so!' With emphasis, certainty.

'I can assure you, Billy Sandrup is dead. Oh, not back in '58. After the President was killed.' He took a deep breath. 'I saw Billy's body.'

'Not Billy. You may be right about Billy. But, Bunker Hayward . . . I saw Bunker Hayward in Dallas two weeks ago.'

A slow motion effect. McBride watched himself stub out his cigarette in the ashtray on his desk, hand moving with slow deliberation. This was something else. Something unforeseen.

'You saw Hayward?'

'Outside the Hilton Hotel. Know him anywhere. He was a good-looking man and . . . and in 1958, I won't

116

say I wasn't attracted to him. I won't say more, except that my husband and I . . . then we was having problems and a young woman don't exactly ignore a good-looking soldier who goes out of his way to be polite to her. No, I saw Bunker Hayward, clear as I see you now. Bit older, bit greyer but it was him. And still a good-looking man.'

It was even more important that she should agree to talk. Dorfmann would be the one to talk to, the one to be convinced, once and for all. And then Sullivan and the FBI. Maybe now even right up to Bobby Kennedy.

'Will you do as I ask?'

'You come and see me in Dallas. That's my address.' She scribbled it on a scrap of paper, leaning heavily on the edge of his desk. 'I'll talk to my husband. Work out what's best to do. Now I got to go. Got to be at the airport . . .'

He ordered a cab for her and ushered her to the foyer and into the cab. Inside him there was a growing, seething excitement.

After work that evening he buttonholed Clyde Anson and took him to the customary bar, to their usual booth. After the drinks arrived, Anson stared across the table at him. 'Okay, okay, so where's the fire? Who really sank the Titanic? Who really killed the Lindbergh baby? Tell your future father-in-law all about it.'

McBride ignored the comment on his future marital status. 'I've seen a woman this afternoon who knew Billy Sandrup. And saw him in Dealey Plaza just after Kennedy was shot.'

Anson blinked. His eyes were red rimmed, veined minutely with blood. He took a sip of whisky.

'So what are you going to do about it?' He sounded sober now.

'The woman comes from Dallas. I want her to tell her story to Dorfmann.'

'Good old Sidney. *Deus ex machina*. He's not all-powerful, you know, Alec. He's just a man . . .'

'He's a man the FBI will listen to. They always listen to a few million dollars in this country.'

Anson stared into his whisky. 'And what's this woman's name?'

'Raymond. Kathy Raymond. She was a neighbour of Sandrup's at one time. She knew Billy.'

'Don't you think she'd just be another voice making noises? Uncorroborated evidence.'

'But it's not uncorroborated. Her husband was with her, saw Sandrup too. And not only Sandrup. Bunker Hayward. They knew him too. And he's still alive.'

'How the hell do they know that?'

'Kathy Raymond saw him in Dallas two weeks ago.'

It seemed there was nothing more Anson could say. He finished his drink, silent, thoughtful. Then he said, 'Come home for dinner. Tell Dorrie. See what she thinks.'

Dorrie Anson listened over the dinner table in silence. When McBride finished, Anson added the rider. 'He's determined to go to Dallas. Get this woman and Dorfmann together.'

'Don't go!' Dorrie said. 'Tell him not to go, dad.'

Anson gave a silent shrug.

'For God's sake, Dorrie, this is my chance to prove I'm not a liar or a fantasist,' McBride insisted.

'Alec's made up his mind,' Anson said.

'Tell him what you found out!' Dorrie went on.

McBride looked from one to the other. 'There's something I should know?'

Anson sighed heavily. 'I've been doing a lot of research into the assassination.' He paused and then, as if to justify himself, 'Well, I've had damn-all decent journalism to do. I . . . I'm a newspaperman . . . even if they think I'm . . . I'm too old . . . past it . . . So I looked into it all.'

'You could have told me,' McBride said.

'I . . . I didn't expect to come up with anything. I thought I'd prove you wrong or . . . or even right and . . . if you were right . . . we might get together on it. Even do a book.'

'So what did you find out?'

'The shots from the stockade wall . . . if there were shots . . . that's not new. Quite a few people reported it. And, like your Mrs Raymond, nothing was done. Don't ask me why. Maybe the police were just happy to have arrested Oswald. I don't know why.'

'Go on!'

'There were also a lot of questions about the autopsy on the President. It seems to have been botched. Seems, I say. Nobody knows for sure. But whether there were two bullets or three, that's a question mark. And the angle of entry of each bullet, that's another.'

'He could have been shot from behind the stockade wall then?'

Anson shifted in his seat irritably. 'I don't know. It's an outside possibility. There are other things though. About the witnesses. People who had information about the shots coming from the stockade. People who knew something about Oswald or . . . or Jack Ruby. There were quite a few of them.'

'What about them?'

'You should look it up for yourself.'

'Save me the time just now. Tell me.'

'They keep dying.'

'What do you mean?'

'A high death rate. Higher than normal for any group of people. All of them die in violent accidents . . . or they're suicides. At least that's what it looks like. Either way they keep dying.'

Dorrie leaned towards McBride. 'Alec, there's something wrong.'

McBride shook his head. 'Coincidence?'

119

'It's statistically crazy that all these people should die in such a short time.'

Turning to Anson, McBride said, 'Where did you get this from?'

The old man gave a wan smile. 'You're not the only one who didn't like the Lee Harvey Oswald story. A few good newspapermen have been doing their own digging. Doing it quietly, Alec. Not shouting about it.'

'You mean like I've been shouting? Okay, but were attempts made to kill these good newspapermen?'

'I don't know.'

'All right!' McBride leant forward over the table. 'This is all the more reason why I should follow this through. See Dorfmann, get him and the Raymond woman together.'

'Dorrie's afraid you'll become one of those statistics.'

'If what you've told me is true I could become one anyway. And what about Mrs Raymond? She's a witness. And she's still around.'

'I don't know,' Anson replied, shaking his head wearily. 'If there is some lunatic going around arranging accidents for these people she may have got missed out. He may not know about her. I think you should leave it alone, Alec, I really do. You've had a peaceful year. Forget about the whole business and maybe it'll never touch you again.'

McBride stood up. He felt more confident now, knowing there were other witnesses who could back up all he had said in the past. There was a time to go on with this and it was now.

'I'm going to phone Dorfmann. Tell him I'm coming.'

The line was bad, crackling with static. Somewhere across middle America lightning storms were building up.

'Okay,' said Dorfmann. 'I'll see this woman . . .' a burst of static rose and fell, 'Do more than that, son. If what you tell me's true I'll get hold of Bill Sullivan in

120

Washington. Maybe even go to J Edgar himself . . .'
More static. 'Between you and me, Alec. I'm not exactly
happy about the way the FBI's handled this business.'

'I'm glad you said that, Mr Dorfmann.'

Between the crackling McBride heard Dorfmann
laugh, a throaty laugh. 'So am I. What does Earl Warren
and his commission know anyway. Months of talk and
all they'll come up with is Oswald killed the President,
Ruby killed Oswald. Finish. Nice and easy. Ruby paints
himself as a phoney patriot. That's a laugh. Yeah, you
come and see me soon as you like. Between us and this
Raymond woman we'll shake up this town.'

'I thought I'd fly down on Friday.'

But Dorfmann, despite the static, was in full spate.
'Too many people too darned pleased to blame it all on
Oswald. And that includes Warren. It's up to us to
show them the truth. When did you say you were
coming?'

'Friday.'

'Good, good, see you then.'

With a final explosion of static, the line went dead.
McBride went back into the small dining room. 'Friday,'
he informed them.

Anson turned away to stare bleakly out of the
window as if he had developed a sick fascination for
the side wall of the building opposite.

Dorrie rose to her feet.

'I'm going to bed,' she announced, scowling.

Next Thursday in Dallas a boy called George Hampton
Kleberg, on the way to making his first million, was
doing a newspaper round early in the morning. That
is, he started off early but it was nearly eight-thirty by
the time he came to the small house on a quiet side
street. The method of delivery was simple. One bicycle
and a strong throwing arm were the only necessities.
George prided himself on the expertise with which he

managed to ride, steering with his left hand, deftly removing papers from the large open saddlebag and throwing them to within a foot of the front doors of the many small houses on his route.

This bright Thursday morning, as he came up to the Raymond house, he saw Mrs Raymond in a large towelling dressing gown, obviously borrowed from her husband, standing at the front door.

'You ring the doorbell, George?' she called out as he passed.

'No, ma'm,' George replied, slowing his machine to a halt. 'Just got here. Your paper's coming over.'

He threw the thick lump of newsprint over the small hedge, slightly to the right for this one occasion with Mrs Raymond on her own doorstep. Wouldn't do to knock one of your customers down with the newspaper.

'Could have sworn I heard someone at this door just a minute ago,' Kathy Raymond said, reaching down to retrieve the newspaper.

Pretty woman, thought George, near as pretty a woman as you'd find in his whole newspaper round. Except for Gloria Stover and everybody knew what she was. Seen her in town on her 'professional business', that Gloria Stover. But Mrs Raymond, now she was different. Just the right amount of make-up on, when she had make-up on; and, anyway, she didn't need it. And with those boobs, she was quite a looker. Of course he reckoned he always preferred older women and he'd sure prefer a piece of that one. Be better than groping Lizzie Calderwood at the back of the Bijou on South Street every Saturday.

He started to move off again, warmed by the smile she'd thrown him as she lifted her paper. There was a roar of traffic from the main highway ahead, he remembered that afterwards, because it seemed just then the

122

roar stopped, evaporated and there was a silence marred only by a rustle of warm air.

George half turned on the seat of his bicycle to look back at Mrs Raymond again. But he could no longer see her. A billowing, rising cloud of smoke and orange flame reached out towards him, obscuring the house and the woman.

And then he was thrown from his bicycle, found himself being propelled over the dust and gravel of the road, hands scraping the surface, back hot, almost burning. He wasn't aware of anything else until some hours later when he woke up in the hospital.

Alec McBride never went to Dallas on that occasion, much to Dorrie Macklin's relief. There was no point. His witnesses were dead.

Dorfmann phoned him.

'An explosion. Accidental. They still used gas in that house. The police reckon it was a gas leak.'

McBride said, 'No accident. Another statistic.'

'Either way you lost your evidence, son. Nothing to be done.'

'It might be a comfort if I thought the Dallas police were looking for whoever blew up the Raymonds.'

'I told you. An accident,' Dorfmann insisted.

'All right. But what about your FBI friend, Sullivan? What's he supposed to be doing?'

'Investigating. As far as he can. As far as Hoover will let him. Trouble is, nobody wants to know any more. It's all buried with Oswald. Even if people don't believe he did it, they don't want to know the truth. Might be too painful. And nobody wants to disturb the smooth running of the Republic. That's it.'

'What about Bobby Kennedy?'

'Bobby wants to be President. He knows stirring up that kind of thing will do him no good. You want my advice, Alec. Stay in Chicago, get on with your job and your life. Forget that day in Dallas.'

Everybody wants me to do that, McBride thought. Forget. Obliterate. Maybe that way stay alive.

'Yes, yes, I'll do that. You're right. No point,' he lied.

'Good,' Dorfmann replied. 'If Sullivan came up with something that might be different. Otherwise, as I say, forget. And I can tell you that we in the executive boardroom of the paper like what you're giving us. Keep on.'

McBride assured him he would do so. But, as he hung up he knew he would not forget. And he knew too that Kathy Raymond had provided him with one piece of information that would stay with him.

Bunker Hayward was alive. The third man in Sandrup's assassination team had survived.

Interlude
In Another Place

7

1969

It seemed to Turvey that the square in Saigon was filled with white light. A combination of the sun and a kind of dust, he supposed. And his coming from a dimly lit hotel room. Perhaps too, the weeks spent in a green, not yet defoliated jungle, were affecting his eyes.

He strolled across the square, a tall figure, green beret on the side of his head, clean if crumpled uniform, slightly ill-fitting. Of course he'd lost weight. About twenty pounds he reckoned. Better for it, if not the method of losing it. He was walking now past the corner of the square with the scars and indentations on the stone of the building where the bomb had gone off last year. In a bicycle pump, they'd hidden the damn thing, surrounded by nails, so the word was. The Cong were clever little bastards. The hell with them, he had a week of R and R before going back. And he was walking easily now, John Wayne in uniform leading his men with that slightly puzzled frown and the simple condescension to the peasants who were on his side.

Role playing, that's what the quack at the hospital had called it. Living an image, unreal but necessary. It was healthier than other ways of keeping intact. He hadn't yet followed the way of the private soldier, smoking grass, and more than grass; a lot of men were mainlining heroin, God help them. Didn't they know they'd never shake it off, not without going through all kinds of hell? But they were going through that anyway.

And maybe role playing was just as addictive. He'd seen men acting tough and unconcerned, until they'd cracked up, lost any kind of identity, didn't know who the hell they were any more. He'd have to watch that.

The bar was crowded. A few Vietnamese and a lot of soldiers. The Viets looked all the same to him, like when he'd first arrived. Thin Chinese, that what they looked like. Only out of the city, in action could he begin to differentiate between one and another.

The newspaper guy was sitting in a booth near the bar. They were in adjacent rooms in the hotel and had arranged to meet and have a drink. Turvey made his way through the crowd. A small Viet girl, about fifteen, he estimated, stopped him momentarily, hand on his arm, and the usual muttered invitation.

He brushed her aside. One thing he'd avoid in this goddam country, getting involved with the women. Sapped a man's strength, took too much from him. If he was going to survive this whole crappy war he needed himself intact.

The newspaper man saw him and waved. The drinks were set up. Canadian Club and the local equivalent of branchwater only it tasted more like piss. Turvey thought, what was the guy's name, he'd thrown it across the table in the hotel at dinner last night. He was in the drab greens of a soldier but with accredited correspondent's badges, and, although he came from America, Chicago to be exact, he wasn't an American. Some kind of Limey. Still he'd provided the bottle last night and was paying for another today.

Alec McBride motioned the major to sit. The man was a formidable figure and, according to all he'd said, he'd just come from fighting the Cong up north. Turvey sat heavily.

'How are you today?' Turvey said, the tones of the South unmistakable.

'Fine. I've set up your dram.'

128

That's it, the guy was a Scotsman. Better maybe than some Yankee.

They drank and talked.

'You never been up north?' Turvey said.

'Flew up briefly. But it's not my bag.'

'What exactly is your "bag", sir? Thought you were a war correspondent. You report the war, you got to see that war.'

McBride gave a tired smile. 'I'm not exactly a war correspondent. In fact it's tough for me to get permission to go where the fighting is. You see, I'm a British subject. Your people aren't too happy about us running around the battlefields.'

'Fuck them, the whole goddam country's a battlefield. Or soon will be. So what the heck are you here for?'

'Sent out by my paper in Chicago. Three to six months' tour. To write about how the boys doing the fighting feel about it all.'

'The fucking boys don't feel anything except fucking terror. That's what it's all about. Living through sheer terror. But don't you quote me on that. Not by name anyway. But I don't get what the heck you're after.'

McBride shrugged. 'A year ago my paper got a new editor. A man called Marinker. This Marinker got me reporting on the draft card burners, the young men who went up to Canada to avoid being sent here. The whole damn anti-war movement in the States.'

After a moment Turvey replied with a harsh, humorless laugh.

'Bastards!'

'Yes, well; then Marinker decided to send me out here to find out what the boys here felt about the whole anti-war business. So I'm here. Interviewing anybody that'll talk. Anybody that's allowed to talk.'

'I can tell you how they feel,' Turvey said. 'They wish they'd burnt their draft cards, wish they were nice and neat and cosy in Canada. Me, I just want to be back in Georgia in one neat piece.'

McBride waved the barman over. The small yellow face smiled down at them, a grinning mask. 'Sa?'

'Bring the bottle of Canadian Club and leave it with us.'

The man nodded and on spindle legs, tottered back to the bar, produced the requested bottle and brought it back. McBride paid him.

'Tell you, Mister . . . mister . . . what did you say your name was?' Turvey asked.

McBride told him.

'Mr McBride, I'll tell you, the whole fuckin' war here is being run by amateurs. Amateurs. Oh, some of them are West Point amateurs but they're still amateurs. Ever since Kennedy was killed, the amateurs have taken over. Me, I'm a Southern Democrat and so is Mr President LBJ. But they don't know back there whether they're dealing with asses or elbows. They're all "good ole boys" sitting back and saying we got to knock out the Cong. And they don't know who the Cong are. Commies sure, but which gook is which? And what's it to do with us anyway? Now if Kennedy had lived, he would have known. I'm a Kennedy man myself, see.'

'But didn't Kennedy start the whole Vietnam thing?'

'Sure, he did, but not in such a big way. And if John F had lived, he would have seen what was going on and pulled us all out. Kennedy would have known. Hell, he was a combat man himself in the big war. If that bastard, Oswald hadn't shot him . . .'

McBride was silent for a moment. Silent, remembering.

Then he said, 'Perhaps Oswald didn't kill him.'

Turvey gulped his drink, slopping it down the corners of his mouth.

'Sure, I heard that said. But if it wasn't Oswald, who the hell was it?'

A B-girl slid by, eyed them with an inviting look and then, receiving no reaction, shrugged and moved on to a party of infantrymen. McBride looked around. The place was dim, hazy with cigarette smoke, a low wooden ceiling broken only by occasional bare electric light bulbs. The motley collection of customers were engrossed in their own conversations – punctuated occasionally by loud, hoarse laughter. Nobody was concerned with Turvey or himself.

'I'll tell you a story,' McBride said to Turvey.

He hadn't told it for some years now. After the news of the deaths of Kathy Raymond and her husband, he had kept his own counsel regarding Billy Sandrup. But it had always been with him: the story, the events just afterwards; and the knowledge that Bunker Hayward might still be alive. But now, in the noise and heat of a Saigon bar he felt like talking to a stranger. He couldn't have explained his reasons to himself. Perhaps every now and then it was necessary to pass the story on, make sure it didn't fade or die.

He told the story to Turvey.

The Major sat over his drink in silence for some moments after McBride had finished. Then, ordering yet another round of drinks, he finally spoke.

'That's a helluva story.'

'It happened. It happened to me.'

'And you're still alive. Nobody tried to kill you again since?'

'No.'

'Wonder why?'

'Perhaps they felt I'd been silenced. Perhaps they just haven't got round to it.'

The Major ran his hand across his damp brow. 'I was in Korea, you know. Got my commission in Korea. Fought with marine units too.'

Like a tiny, stabbing electric shock, the statement got to McBride. 'I don't suppose you ever came across a Sergeant Billy Sandrup, or Buncey, or Hayward?'

'That's like asking me if I know a John Doe lives in New York City. There was a lot of guys in Korea. But I'll tell you this. I knew a couple of guys called Hayward.'

The small anticipatory shock was wearing off. And Hayward was a common enough name. 'But not a Sergeant Bunker Hayward, eh?'

'Not a Sergeant Bunker Hayward . . . not then. But I do know a guy called Bunker Hayward. And he was an ex-gyrene.'

McBride trembled, a shiver in the heat, a small reaction. 'Tell me about Hayward.'

Turvey stared at the table. 'Been in and out of this country since the Tet offensive in '64. Maybe longer. He said something about being here for a while when Diem was killed in '63.'

'He was in the army?'

'He wore a uniform. Captain in intelligence. That's what he said. Look, I only met the guy last year. Talked a lot for an intelligence man. And he was never in the fighting, not that I heard. Just coming and going, minding his own business, whatever that was. Fair hair. Good-looking guy.'

'So you didn't know him well?'

'Can't say as how I did. Knew him like I know you. To drink with. Oh, a few times. Last year was the last time. See, I haven't seen him recently. But then that doesn't mean anything. He was always coming and going from the States, so he said. Lucky bastard. Rest and Recreation for most of us means getting pissed here in Saigon. Unless you're lucky and you get to Japan.'

McBride was oblivious to the noise around him now. He leant forward straining to hear Turvey. 'Anything else you can tell me about him?'

'What more's to tell. Told you all there is.'

'You haven't any idea what he was actually doing?'

'Look, McBride, intelligence people don't exactly shout from the rooftops.' The next round of bottles arrived. 'Stay close,' Turvey said to the barman. 'I'm drinking quickly to make up for a big thirst.'

He turned back to McBride. 'What you're really saying, McBride, is this Bunker Hayward may just have had something to do with the assassination of the President. Well, after two tours in this shit hole of the world, nothing should surprise me. But I don't believe you. Just don't believe an officer wearing the uniform would get into something like that. So I just don't think I should hear any more crack-pot ideas. You want to drink, we'll drink. You want to pick up an almond eyed hooker, I might do the same. But that's it.'

They spent the rest of the day together. They drank in various bars and eventually Turvey, a tiny slant-eyed girl on his arm, bade McBride a drunken good night. McBride went on drinking for a while.

In the years since Dallas and the night of his meeting with Billy Sandrup, McBride had matured. The twenty-four-year-old expatriate Scot had become a thin, wiry, thirty-year-old American newspaperman. He had acquired a degree of experience and a degree of cynicism. He had learned from Clyde Anson and others the tricks of his chosen profession. He had almost learned to ignore the feelings of the bereaved and the bereft. Almost, but not quite. He had held on to a degree of humanity. At the same time he had sat in bars with characters who might have crawled out of the primeval jungles which existed in the cities of the USA. He had listened, too, in elegant hotel suites to men who would tell him how they would run the world; men who indeed had the potential and the power to run it the way they wanted.

He'd written of all this with, he believed, some kind of objectivity. He'd looked on the callousness of power

133

and the ruthlessness of those trying to attain that power.

Then Marinker had appeared. He was a smooth man, Alan Marinker, reputed to be another Dorfmann protégé recruited from the New York *Herald Tribune*. He was tall, slim with an overemphasized elegance. He was quietly spoken and deadly. Anson called him a plastic man, compared him to a razor blade honed to sharpness. But then, in Marinker's eyes, Anson was negligible, an old man on the way out.

As to McBride himself, Marinker was different. He stated that he liked McBride's work but felt it lacked the cruelty of the great columnists. He insisted that it was his task to inculcate McBride with that cruelty. And to emphasise this Marinker suggested McBride go to Vietnam.

'I want to hear the voices of those poor bastards out there fighting the gooks and wondering whether or not they're being betrayed at home. What they think of the draft dodgers, the peace movement. What they think about fighting for a country that not only assassinates its President but also his brother . . . and Martin Luther King.'

McBride thought of Bobby Kennedy's death, following five years after his brother's. Could he, McBride, have done anything? Would it have made any difference if he had gone to Bobby Kennedy with Billy Sandrup's story?

Marinker had gone on with his diatribe. 'I want to hear the GIs moaning about being stabbed in the back by the folks at home . . . I want it to be read by Mr and Mrs America and all the ships at sea. I want it to shake them.'

McBride ignored the plagiarism from Walter Winchell. 'Supposing they agree with the peace movement? Supposing they wish they'd burnt their draft cards?'

Marinker gave a slight smile. 'Then we may even print it.'

'Look, I'm not a war correspondent . . .'

'You're what I make you, Alec. Oh, you're good but with me as editor you'll be better. Go out there and write about it. I'll bring you back when I'm ready and you'll be a big name.'

McBride's first impulse was to refuse and to resign. He didn't want Vietnam and that kind of nightmare. He could admit he didn't want to risk death in a war zone. At the same time Marinker seemed genuinely to be interested in promoting him as a columnist. And McBride went to discuss it with Dorrie Macklin.

In respect of Dorrie, they had avoided matrimonial entanglements but enjoyed a good healthy relationship, both physical and mental. They liked the same things, they laughed at the same jokes. And they made love together well and without monotony.

Marinker's parting remarks he reported to Dorrie. 'Go to Nam, Alec. Come back and you'll be able to ask for a lot of money. Play it my way and with luck you'll win a Pulitzer Prize.'

That night, lying in bed with Dorrie he was surprised when she urged him to go. 'The mortality rate on correspondents isn't high,' she insisted. 'And despite Marinker you can go out there and tell it like it is.'

'All you Americans want that horrendous fallacy, to be told how it is,' McBride replied. 'There's no such thing. It's different for everybody. Each dog soldier, each correspondent sees it differently. Syphons experience through his own psyche and produces the different picture. Some people will hate it, some . . . the sicker ones . . . may even enjoy it. It's the same in every godawful war.'

He could ask himself how he knew that. But he was not in a self-questioning mood.

'Okay!' Dorrie said. 'Say that. Say this is how you see it. Maybe even try and say how others might see it.'

It was an interesting approach. It could almost convince him it might be worth going. But for one thing.

'How about us?' he asked.

A small pause.

'I'll be here when you get back. I'll be with you when you accept your Pulitzer. So now that's settled, make love to me. Hard.'

There was no Pulitzer.

There was, had been up until now, heat and dust and hollow-eyed private soldiers, college boys who'd become old men overnight, young negroes, embittered at fighting what they believed was the wrong battle in the wrong country. There were the atrocity stories, whispers and nudges and bland blank looks. Lieutenant Calley was in some guardhouse but the dead of May Lai were no less dead for his incarceration awaiting trial.

McBride soon realized his stories were being edited before appearing in the paper in Chicago. Marinker, he reckoned, was personally editing them. Oh, sure, they were good slick journalistic comments but somehow, in the editing, the rough edges, the truer scenes were not appearing quite as clearly as McBride intended. The change was subtle but definitive. But then, he should have known. The paper had consistently supported Richard Nixon.

And then, in the middle of his tour of Nam, he met Major Turvey and he heard the name of Bunker Hayward again.

No sign of Turvey at breakfast the morning after. Well, McBride thought, can't blame a man after a tour up country. Only second day of R and R. Come lunch and still no sign. McBride propped himself up in the bar, a mildly lascivious picture in his mind of the major and the girl passing the entire day in bed. By dinner Turvey had still not appeared.

Why did McBride want to speak to him again? Perhaps to catch the major sober, dig into his memory, learn more about Hayward. What, for example, did the man look like? That would be a start. Finally that evening McBride enquired about the major at the reception desk of their hotel.

'No here,' said the Vietnamese receptionist, a boy in his late teens who had been discharged from the Vietnamese army for obvious reasons. He had lost an arm and an eye. 'Go back to unit early this morning.'

Turvey had returned to his private jungle, recalled for God knows what reason. At least he had left McBride with the knowledge that Bunker Hayward had been in Vietnam.

During the following weeks, McBride did his best work in Saigon. Interviews at the military hospital with young Americans, some of them horrendously wounded, others with light scars of combat. McBride talked, cajoled, even joked with them. The jokes were in a vein of blackness. They were young men who had lived through personal nightmares and the only relief was to joke. It was either that, or as some did, to retire from the conscious world. Those ones would sit at the edge of their beds clutching blankets, staring at walls, seeing nothing.

It was a big story, the wounded of Vietnam, too big to try to encapsulate in weekly newspaper articles. McBride did his best and, for his readers, his best was good. To himself it was nothing, a scratching of the surface.

And there were other questions in his mind. He made enquiries at Saigon HQ, US Army in the Field, for an officer called Bunker Hayward. He described himself as a friend looking for a friend. He became accustomed to blank looks, shrugs, apologies, excuses. Didn't he know they were fighting a war? He suspected some of them would like to have admitted it was a losing fight.

He asked if someone could consult army records, find out whether or not his old friend Bunker Hayward was still in the country. He was told army records were strictly confidential, not for the eyes of correspondents; not even to be seen by old friends.

In September President Nixon announced that 35,000 troops would be withdrawn from Vietnam.

A day later an Army doctor from one of the MASH units, on R and R in Saigon, a man who had treated McBride for a comparatively mild bout of dysentry when he had first arrived, contacted the journalist.

'You still looking for a guy called Hayward?'

'I'm still looking.'

'Came across him a month ago.'

McBride sat quietly facing the doctor, saying nothing. He'd learned enthusiasm was counter-productive. Get excited, show keenness to hear about Hayward and for some reason people went silent. Waiting produced a response more easily. And regarding Bunker Hayward, McBride was used to waiting. Six years was a long wait.

'Up in Da Lat. Went over with a medical team. Some of our boys had been shot up pretty badly. There was this captain there . . . seemed he'd just flown in from the States. Some kind of intelligence mission. A couple of local Nam politicos had been shot the day before. Supposed to have gone over to the Cong and somebody had taken them out. Found with a bullet each in the head.'

'That had something to do with Hayward?'

'He said he'd arrived to conduct an investigation. Not that he seemed to be doing much investigating. Hanging around, drinking with a marine colonel, then he disappeared. Back to wherever these characters disappear to.'

'That was all?'

'Not exactly. One thing funny struck me. He'd come to investigate the deaths of these two guys, but he'd actually arrived the day before they were killed.'

Play it calmly now. No excitement. Just another quiet question. 'How does that strike you, doc?'

The doctor was non-committal. It was a trait among middle-ranking officers in this country. Never commit yourself in any way. Then you stayed out of trouble.

'He might have come up to Da Lat to parley with these guys. Government business. Or investigating to see if they turned.'

'And then they were dead.'

'That's it. Look, this Hayward guy, he may be a friend of yours but he's a cold fish.'

'Did I say he was a friend?'

'Yeah. Weeks ago when we first met. You were looking for this friend and the army wasn't being helpful.'

He'd said it all right, he knew. He'd said it to not only HQ but to individuals. A damn sight simpler than saying he was looking for a professional assassin.

'Yes, I did say that. More of an acquaintance, really.'

McBride was a good liar. In the last six years he'd found he had to be, to make a living as a newspaperman.

The doctor frowned. 'I guess I just didn't take to him. Cold city boy, that's how I read him. Said he came from Dallas but he was street wise, more like a New Yorker.'

Another picture of Bunker Hayward. There'd been Turvey and now the doctor. And then there was a GI in hospital who'd lost half his right leg treading on one of the army's own mines. He said he'd served with a Captain Hayward for a few weeks.

'Intelligence job up near Da Lat. Never did know

139

what we were doin' up there. They helicoptered the captain out and left us to walk. Didn't tell us we'd be walking through the edge of a mine field.'

'What was Captain Hayward like?'

'You mean, to look at? Okay. Big, clean, Buck Rogers type. But I'll tell you this, underneath he was one ice-cold bastard. Except when we was shooting at anybody. He seemed to warm up then. Enjoyed shooting at people. Still I'm grateful to him. See, losing this leg gets me home for good. Reckon it's better losin' a part than losin' all of yourself in this dirty country.'

The GI would say no more.

Then McBride received the telegram from Chicago:

DOING GREAT JOB STOP KEEP IN THERE STOP HARRISON OUR FRONT LINE MAN DOWN WITH FEVER STOP TAKE HIS PLACE FOR TWO WEEKS STOP HELP US STOP MARINKER

And he'd told the bastard he wasn't a war correspondent. Well, he was now. He went to Army HQ Saigon to receive his accreditation. It came through three days later with a note informing him that he was to report to Captain Albert Manzetti, Information Officer, Room 31, GHQ, Saigon.

Manzetti looked like an ex-Mafiosi. He was dark, Italianate but with a surprising Boston accent. A Harvard man.

'Your first time in the field I understand, Mr McBride. You've been mostly in Saigon until now, isn't that so?'

'I wasn't sent out as a war correspondent.'

'Lucky for you. Until now, eh? Well, a couple of newspapermen, one of them English, by the way, good man too, are going up possibly as far as Da Nang. Thought it would be a good idea if you went with them. They'd show you the ropes, so to speak.'

'I have to go where I'm sent by you people?'

'Of course. Can't have you gentlemen of the press running wild in the country. Wouldn't want you to end up in a cage in Hanoi.'

'Or being fried by your own napalm.'

The captain's mouth twitched. 'Hardly likely. Our people indulge only in precision bombing.'

'Defoliation doesn't call for a great deal of precision.'

Another twitch. Indicative of irritation. 'You will, of course, have to clear your dispatches with this office.'

'Since when? Haven't you heard of the freedom of the press, captain? Or the right of the people to know?'

The irritation was now causing a reddening of the captain's skin. 'We check for accuracy. You people can often get things wrong.'

'Or perhaps right, as the case may be.'

The interview ended with Manzetti giving McBride instructions as to where he should rendezvous with his fellow correspondents. These were issued in a distinctly chilly manner.

The next day found him in a jeep driving up a long dusty road.

Amersham, the English correspondent for the Manchester *Guardian* was a tall man, seemingly relaxed. Chivers, the American, was small and square, with short hair fringing a round head. Both were young-old men, with humor bereft of illusion.

'Sooner we're out of this country like the French the better,' Chivers said with lazy conviction. 'Preferably all the way to Paris.'

The jeep bucked and jumped over the rutted road, framework protesting against the terrain. Amersham tried to light a cigarette with difficulty.

'Vietnam is one of the few places they should issue a government health warning against,' he said finally managing to sustain his lighter flame long enough to fire the cigarette.

McBride tried to smile. But he didn't feel like smiling, he felt like being sick. Chivers stared at his pale face.

'You get used to anything eventually, Mac. That's

141

why Hell wouldn't work. The inhabitants would get used to it.'

'Anyway, they look after us pretty well,' Amersham added. 'They don't like foreign correspondents being killed. Bad for the image. And if you look at the casualty lists the Americans who get killed are predominantly negro. Funny none of you American journalists mention that in your reports.'

Chivers, who worked in Washington but had been born in Kansas nodded. 'It's true. But who'll let us say it? And I'll bet you something else. No senator, no member of the House of Representatives will have a kid killed here in Vietnam. Just won't happen. Same for the kids from wealthy families. Makes you think . . .'

McBride thought. Mostly about not being sick. And about the countryside which was new to him. Not that it was of any great interest. Paddy fields on either side of the road, deserted, lines of water and what might be rice or weed stretched as far as the eye could see. Occasionally, on the road or the verges, were the signs of war; shell craters, acned earth pitting the country-side. There was a haze over the fields, damp, humid and hot. There were low rumblings in the distance which McBride did not wish to identify.

'Of course you do get the occasional ambush,' Amersham said, laconically. 'But I shouldn't worry. They mostly go for columns rather than solitary vehicles.'

The driver, an army corporal from Arkansas, snorted loudly. 'The fuck they do! The gooks go for anything that moves. And we're moving, ain't we?'

'Corporal Anderson is a cheerful man,' said Chivers. 'His mission in life is to keep us all happy.'

'My mission,' Anderson replied without taking his eyes off the ribbon of dusty road in front of him, 'Is to get you guys where they tell me to take you. Preferably in one piece. My intention is to get myself there in one piece. And anyway what about the goddam mines? We're just as liable to hit a mine and blow up.'

The man makes it a wide-awake nightmare in bright lights, McBride thought. If there was darkness he would expect the fear, be able to cope with it somehow. But in daylight fear became greater because it was out of place, away from the dark corners.

They drove on.

An hour passed and the countryside remained monotonously the same. Eventually they came to a command post, manned by dishevelled marines. They were under the command of a very young lieutenant who looked as if he might be kept busy if he shaved once a week. He was from the South, probably Georgia. He gave them mugs of coffee and asked how the war was going.

'You see, suh,' he said to Amersham who, because of his height, was assumed to be the leader. 'We don't know what's goin' on in the war. Sometimes they even forgets we're here and they don't bring up the rations for a whole day. And, since I got promoted to officer in the field they been tellin' me to use ma initiative. If I used ma initiative we'd withdraw all the way to Saigon and take the first boat out.'

Amersham muttered suitable words of sympathetic understanding. The lieutenant ignored them.

'Which way you goin' now?' he asked without much interest. Corporal Anderson showed him on the map.

'There's a crossroads up ahead, and I reckon, if you go the way they told you, you'd be taking the wrong road,' the lieutenant said. 'Leastways it wasn't exactly recommended last week. Mebbe they done cleared it now.'

'Of what?' Chivers inquired.

'They don't tell us, suh. They jest warn us.'

They moved on, driving past the crossroads on the designated route. Corporal Anderson did what he was told.

Fifteen minutes later they hit a mine.

PART TWO

Bunker Hayward

8

1970

For a time there were only faces. They flitted through his consciousness, coming in and out of auras of light; or looming out of blackness, round moons fully risen. Gradually they came into definition. Features became clear, eyes, ears, noses. The eyes filled with a kind of dispassionate concern.

Then he came to complete consciousness. He was in hospital in Saigon. He was wounded. The mine had exploded under the jeep, killing Corporal Anderson and injuring the three correspondents. Amersham was in another hospital and would soon be recovered enough to fly back to London. Chivers had escaped with cuts and bruises and was already back at work somewhere in the battlezone. But he, McBride, had suffered multiple fractures in his right leg, had several broken ribs and a hairline fracture of the skull.

He had been semi-conscious for over a month.

Now, he was told, he was fully conscious and the prognosis was good. The surgeon wanted to fly him to Tokyo where he could rest, recuperate and undergo some final work on his right leg. Arrangements were made for him to be flown to Tokyo. But before he left, an officer from Intelligence would like to speak to him if he was willing and felt able.

Major Danvers was small, fair and intense. He was only concerned about one issue. Why the hell the jeep was on the mined road. That road had been off-limits to all military personnel. It was reckoned to be a route used by the Viet Cong guerillas and had been extensively mined for that very reason.

McBride told the Major he understood it had been the route issued by the information people.

'That's what Chivers and Amersham said,' Danvers nodded. 'But the routing was given to the corporal driver and he's dead. We'd like to know who issued the orders to take that route.'

Despite his injuries, McBride's memory was unaffected. 'I was briefed by a Captain Manzetti, information officer. That's what he called himself.'

Danvers swore loudly and graphically. 'Typical fucking SNAFU! Information people say they have no record of issuing such a route. And your bright Captain Manzetti has been sent back to the States. Not available for questioning.'

From the white pillows McBride stared up at the Intelligence man. 'You're saying that . . . that we were deliberately sent along a mined road?'

Danvers smiled. 'Am I saying that? Why should you be deliberately sent along that route? Do tell me.'

McBride was silent. There was a time to talk and he didn't feel it was now. He knew nothing of Danvers.

The major went on, 'Actually, all I'm saying is that a mistake was made. I'd like to make sure no further mistakes of that nature occur. Especially concerning newspapermen.'

'Wouldn't look good in print, is that it?'

'Dead right, McBride. I've no idea how it happened. Perhaps that stupid bastard Manzetti ignored official memoranda. Or perhaps he misread them. If he was still here I'd probably break both his fucking arms. But at least he's been removed to where he can do no more damage.'

Danvers turned away and went to the door of the

148

hospital room. 'Anyway I just had to check I wasn't missing anything. You comfortable here, McBride?'

'Yes, I think so.'

'You ought to be. This kind of room's usually reserved for the top brass. Nothing I can get you? Cigarettes, anything?'

'No. They're flying me to Tokyo for a few weeks. And then back to Chicago.'

Danvers opened the door. 'Well, have a good trip. Count your blessings you're out of this ashtray of the world.'

McBride took a deep breath. One thing to be asked. 'There is something, Major Danvers.'

'Yeah?'

'Do you know a man called Bunker Hayward?'

Danvers stopped, a still frame in a movie, for a fraction of time. Then he deliberately shut the door again.

'Why do you want to know that?'

There was no use, McBride thought, in telling Danvers that Hayward was an old friend. He could get away with that with some people but not Danvers, he knew that instinctively.

'He's a man I want to meet.'

'You know him?'

'Not personally.'

'Then why do you want to meet him?'

A pause. You could tell the truth, McBride said to himself, but it would be a long story and his wounds were acting up. That seemed as good a reason as any for not telling long stories.

'It's a personal matter.'

'Okay, so I know a man called Bunker Hayward.'

Another pause. This time from Danvers.

McBride broke the pause. 'What's he like?'

Danvers was staring across the room, eyes on the man in the bed. 'You mean physically?' he asked. 'Physically he's a big guy. Good looking. Sometime

149

Captain in the Intelligence Corps. Sometime, other things.'

'What does that mean?'

'It means I've seen him around,' Danvers said irritably. 'I've seen him sometimes in uniform, sometimes not.'

'Apart from physically, what's he like?'

'Very bright. You don't usually find that kind under a stone. But that's where you should find him.'

'Why do you say that?'

Danvers bridled. 'I'm the goddamned interrogator around here. Not you. Anyway I shouldn't be talking about other officers. Especially in the intelligence game.'

McBride told himself he was being fenced with. And he had an advantage. His questions were somehow embarrassing Danvers. He pressed on, ignoring a deep ache from his ribs.

'Go on. Tell me more. After all you don't like the man.'

'I don't know the man! And I don't want to. He enjoys his work. And I've just heard his kind of work nobody should enjoy.'

'What kind of work is that, Major Danvers?'

Danvers put his hand again on the handle of the door. 'The kind of work we don't talk about. The kind of work we may have to do but we don't have to like.'

'Tell me more.'

Danvers had his head averted from McBride's gaze. 'The dirty jobs. Cleaning up. Like a scavenger. That's all I know about Hayward. He does dirty jobs for the big people. I shouldn't even be saying that to you. And if you print it, I'll deny it and sue you, you bastard.'

'You don't have to show your affection for me, major. And I'm not going to print this. I just want to know about Hayward.'

'I don't know any more than I've told you. I don't even know that for sure. I just hear stories. The sooner you get to Tokyo, the better, McBride. Otherwise you might just find another bloody great mine under your bed. You got involved with Bunker Hayward, I'm not surprised your driver took the jeep up the wrong road. If you've got something on Hayward, don't tell me. You have to go higher up on that one. Maybe all the way to the top. And maybe at the top they don't want to know.'

Danvers went out, shutting the door firmly behind him.

McBride stared at the door. People heard stories about Hayward, people told stories about Hayward. But people didn't like to know about Hayward. They didn't think the man should be discussed. Didn't think he should be mentioned. When he was, it was in whispers. You could hear the voice drop. Bunker Hayward, who might be the executioner of Presidents, was not to be acknowledged.

And McBride wondered where Manzetti had received the routing for these three journalists. Who had given him the routing?

He fell asleep remembering for the first time a thought which had flashed through his mind as the jeep had exploded beneath him. What was a man from Paisley, Scotland, via Chicago, doing on the edge of a paddy field in South East Asia?

Four months in Tokyo. And the most he saw were the grounds of the military hospital. Neat, tidy, army and Japanese style. A Japanese garden, courtesy of the US Army.

There was one night on the Ginza. He was about to fly back to the States pronounced a fit man again. He didn't remember much afterwards about that one night. A deal of liquor was consumed. Mostly Japanese-style Scotch whisky which wasn't in the least like Scotch whisky. One bottle of genuine Highland Malt appeared,

151

Laphroiag, which in the early hours tasted like iodine. Of the Ginza itself he only remembered more neon than he'd ever seen in one place. Neon coloured strips and loud Western music somehow synthesised through Japanese culture. It was terrible and made him laugh.

Then he was on a plane for the States.

Chicago was the same. Warmer as spring came.

Marinker greeted him with the set-piece fixed smile, outstretched hand and a deliberately generous offer of two weeks further vacation. Then back to work. McBride accepted the vacation with no show of gratitude. Somehow he'd learned. Never really thank anyone. There was always an ulterior motive. In this case to rearrange the work on the paper. Someone else had been doing his column. Not very well, he later learned. That someone had to be moved out. And was. The two weeks vacation for McBride gave Marinker time to breathe, feel out the management, assure himself they wanted McBride back in his old spot. They did.

On leaving Marinker's office he came face to face with Clyde Anson. Anson was greyer, smaller it seemed. His skin was mottled, veins redder, more prominent. Too much booze, too little enthusiasm left.

They greeted each other warmly but McBride felt a barrier. Before he'd gone to Vietnam, he felt the beginnings of the barrier, the foundations being laid. The old man was drawing back from their relationship, their friendship. He wondered whether it was because Dorrie and he had never actually married. The only one who'd ever mentioned marriage was Anson himself. Dorrie had accepted their relationship, seemed to prefer the unspoken thought that they were still free individuals if they so chose.

'She's waiting for you at your apartment, son,' Anson

informed him. 'Guess she wants a kind of quiet celebration for your homecoming. I'm not invited.' He said it cheerfully enough but the last sentence had an edge to it.

Dorrie met him at the apartment door. They fell into each other's arms without speech but with a small sob from her. They fell into bed still without speech.

McBride was nervous. He had been celibate too long. His wounds still gave him traces of pain. Yet he needn't have worried. She guided him, caressed him, moved him slowly towards excitement. And as he entered her she spoke only one word.

'God.'

Afterwards he asked her what God had to do with it. Or was she addressing him. She blushed.

As he thrust into her there was an overwhelming feeling of joy. One human being to another in love. He needed that more than the act itself; the expression of the emotion. And yet as she writhed beneath him, breasts thrust upwards, nipples hard, for a fraction of time he thought, how mechanically she was behaving. Doing everything she should do and yet there was something, a lack of spontaneity there. Then he lost the thought in the heat of his own passion.

Afterwards they ate. She had prepared the perfect dinner, even to placing the two thin candles on the table between them. He moved them to the side so they could talk.

She asked about Vietnam and he told her everything he could remember. Especially did he tell her about Bunker Hayward.

'Not that still, Alec,' she responded bleakly.

'But, don't you see, it's some kind of proof.'

'I thought you were finished with that.'

Somehow her lack of enthusiasm did not surprise him. She went on, 'I suppose you'll tell me he killed Bobby Kennedy, too.'

153

He remembered his feelings at the death of the second Kennedy brother. As if the ground had been pulled out from under him. The one man who might have listened; the man he had planned to go to when he had enough evidence. And then he too was gone.

'Sirhan, whatever his name is, killed Bobby,' he said to Dorrie. 'Okay, that was proved. But Hayward could have been behind that.'

'Or it could have been the act of one single crazy.'

He nodded. 'Sure. I would believe that. I would believe that Oswald killed JFK. If I hadn't met Billy Sandrup. If I hadn't heard of Bunker Hayward. Now I keep hearing about Bunker Hayward.'

After a time she poured the coffee in silence. Then she finally said, 'Forget it? It's past history. It doesn't matter any more. The Kennedys are dead, whatever. New things are happening. Nobody's interested any more.'

'Hayward's still operating.'

'If it's the same man. You don't know . . .'

'A lot of people died. Innocent people who happened to see something they shouldn't have seen in Dealey Plaza that day.'

'You don't know they were killed. People die . . .'

'Statistically . . .'

'What the hell does that mean? Statistics aren't an immutable law. Something my father told you and you believed him. And half the time he was drunk then. More than half now.'

'But if I can prove it, apart from anything else, it would be the news story of the century.'

'Big deal!' she said. 'Another Pulitzer prize. Of course they forgot to give you one for Vietnam.'

He was irritated now, and puzzled. Why the attack?

'Okay, so I didn't do anything to merit a Pulitzer in Nam. That was Marinker sounding-off to encourage me to go. But this is something else. This man Hayward,

154

there's something about him . . . he frightens everybody he comes near.'

She was sneering now. 'So there goes the bogey man.
And what's he supposed to be? A crackpot army man.
Maybe he's a Commie. A character who's infiltrated.
Yeah, maybe Khrushchev ordered Kennedy dead . . .'

'Why not? It's one possibility. Maybe Lyndon
Johnson ordered him dead so as he could be President.
Or maybe Nixon. Dorrie, it doesn't matter who . . . not
at this stage. It matters that there was more to it than
Lee Harvey Oswald. And it should come out.'

She stood up, placing her crumpled napkin on the
table. 'I think I'll go home, Alec. I'm pretty tired. I guess
it's the excitement of waiting for you to get home.'

'I thought you'd be staying the night . . .'

'So did I. But I'm too tired. Rather be in my own bed
tonight. Okay?'

He accepted her decision with ill-concealed
annoyance.

'Okay. But just because we're arguing . . .'

She turned angrily towards him. 'Not just because
we're arguing. It's what we're arguing about! Christ,
it's been seven years of your life and you keep coming
back to it. Just when I think it's over.'

'It's an unfinished story. I want to write the finish.'

'They tried to kill you last time. They blew up your
apartment. Now you tell me they might just have blown
up the jeep in Vietnam by sending it through a mine
field. Every time you come back to it they try to kill
you. They'll do it in the end.'

'Maybe. But that's just it, Dorrie. Who the hell are
they? I've got one name, Bunker Hayward. But there
must be others behind him. That's who I want to nail.'

She was at the door now, light coat on her shoulders.
She looked across at him.

'Why?' she asked.

There was no easy answer. He had asked himself the

155

question several times in Saigon and in Tokyo. And he had avoided answering himself. He could consider it a kind of obssession. An obssession to know the truth. He could tell himself it was a story, a newspaperman's dream. But that wasn't enough. Time had made the story old; it had moved from the pages of papers into the pages of history. Perhaps he had a desire to put history right. If he only knew what the truth was.

She could almost read his thoughts. 'Okay. Think about it,' she said. 'And call me.'

'Tomorrow?'

There was no smile. 'When you know what you're going to do, Alec.'

She went. He was alone now. In his own place for the first time in months. He was glad to be alone, grateful to her for going. He needed to be alone. He could avoid the question alone. No one to ask it but himself.

The apartment was chilly from disuse. McBride sprawled on a rug in front of a large electric fire. He never could get used to the central heating. He needed a red glow somewhere in front of him to be really assured that he was warm. Lying there he could shut off his own questions regarding Sandrup and the story that had lurked in the back of his consciousness for seven years.

He was good at shutting things off, closing down on uncomfortable concepts. He thought for a time about Dorrie. Wanting her for so long, he was angry at the outcome of the evening. Yet he refused to blame himself. Anyway there would be other evenings. Or was he expected to renounce his search for Bunker Hayward? Was that her condition for their relationship to continue?

After a time he fell asleep. He slept without dreaming.

He went back to work after a week. Marinker accepted his early return as a sign of enthusiasm and suggested he do a series on the returning Vietnam veteran. McBride was uncertain of his qualifications to talk to men who had really seen combat there but he accepted the challenge.

The series entailed travelling all over America. He found himself interviewing men who had left part of their bodies in South East Asia and others who had left part of their minds there. He interviewed outwardly undamaged men who were inwardly empty. He travelled to Montana, California, Virginia, Alabama, Nebraska, Kentucky, Kansas and most of the other states of the Union. He avoided Texas deliberately. Too many memories, too much fear.

In Washington, DC, he consulted army lists. There was no Bunker Hayward. Marine lists only brought up the name of the man who was supposed to have died in 1959.

On his occasional visits to Chicago he saw little of Dorrie. A couple of times in a cocktail bar where she was drinking with two other women. She gave him a deliberately perfunctory wave. And again he saw her dining with a man, a stranger to him. That was a painful sighting. He found wells of jealousy within him he had never before reckoned on. That night, he passed alone in his apartment, fretful, unable to sleep. Images of her in bed with the man drifted across his mental vision. He tried to shut them out. The next day he left for New York.

A veterans' hospital. After discharge from the army, the long-term disabled ended up here. Not exactly Bellevue but no picnic. Dark green walls and men huddled in corners, on beds, or sitting with faces averted from the world.

Every now and then McBride would drop in the name. An officer called Hayward. He learned nothing

157

for a long time. Then, in Nebraska, in an army hospital, when McBride dropped the name he got a reaction. The man was a sergeant who'd lost a leg. Mentally he was well-adjusted, indeed had arranged a return to his old job as a motor mechanic when he was fitted with his metal leg.

'Did you say Hayward, Mr McBride?'

'I wondered whether you'd ever come across an officer called Hayward. Bunker Hayward.'

'This guy a friend of yours?'

'Not exactly. I knew someone who knew him. In Dallas, actually I've never met him myself.'

'You say he was an army officer?'

'Or in the marines.'

McBride played it calmly, hiding a growing excitement. He'd obviously struck a chord in the one-legged sergeant.

'The guy I knew was in civilian clothes.'

'But his name was Hayward?'

'That was his name. At first we thought he was government. Yuh know, State Department or politician. Maybe even a congressman. We discovered different. See I was Top-Sergeant. Captain Ricketts, he was my boss . . . got killed in Da Nang later . . . he got his orders. Give Mr Hayward whatever he wanted.'

'What did he want?'

'Guns. Picked men. Picked them himself. Went through the unit records. Picked five of the worst bastards we had in the unit. Armed them and went off. North.'

'They came back?'

The sergeant rubbed his trousers where his lost leg terminated.

'Gets to aching now and then. As if it was still there. Sure, he came back. Alone.'

'Any idea where he'd been or what he'd been doing?'

'Not then. Later when we moved north. See, there

158

was a village and we thought one or two of the top Cong used it. Well, we got there and there was no village. Burnt out. A shell. Bodies all around. And five of them were our five men. There was a doc with us. New York Jew boy. Kinda liberal. Went around examining all the bodies. Said it was another Lieutenant Calley-type massacre. Only worse. You see, the doc reckoned that after Hayward and his five men took out that village, Hayward himself took out his own five men. No witnesses.'

'Wasn't there some kind of inquiry?'

'Hell, no! Captain Ricketts had already had his orders from Hayward and above. Ricketts was a decent man and he hated what he had to say. You could see he hated it. Almost choked him. Had to announce that our men had gone up to defend the village and obviously it was the Cong had done the massacre. Jesus, he fooled nobody. The bullets on the people, men, women, kids . . . they were from our own guns. Even the five men had been shot by one of our machine guns. And Hayward had been issued with that kind of gun.'

'So nothing was done?'

'If Hayward had been around some of us would have had him. He was a cold murdering bastard.'

Cold. Always cold. Any description of Hayward. Ice cold. Not human. What kind of creature was he looking for, McBride asked himself. And what could he do if he ever found him? More and more he doubted he would ever find the man.

Of course, he couldn't use the sergeant's story. He knew Marinker well enough to know the editor would never use it. And if he did it would provoke instant denial. It was unprovable.

McBride finally returned to Chicago to write up the last stories of his series. The city was ice-bound again, the year drawing to a close.

New Year's day came and went. Five days later he

159

received a phone call at his apartment late in the evening.

'Hold on. I have a call for you.'

And then the familiar voice, older now, more brittle in tone. And tired.

'Dorfmann here, Alec. I want to see you. I want you to fly down to Dallas. I'll arrange it with Marinker. Come tomorrow.'

'I don't know if I can . . .'

'I told you. I'll arrange it with Marinker. You have to come. I guess I haven't too much time left.'

9

There were more oil wells now; more pumps moving steadily up and down. The prairie was held together by pipelines, arteries conveying the life blood of Texas to the heartlands.

Dallas was bigger too. Giant towers of concrete and glass towering above their elder relations. In parts it was as if the old city had been gutted, thrown away and a new start made. Some of the architecture, to McBride's eye, was early 'Amazing Science Fiction'. The cars, too, seemed bigger than in other cities, certainly more garish, decorated with cow hides and buffalo horns. The city smelled of money.

Dorfmann made sure McBride would not be held up. A new station wagon was waiting at the airport, a taciturn cowboy at the wheel. He drove quickly through the city and out towards the Dorfmann ranch. Horizons were broken now by distant steel chimneys emitting flames, by storage tanks and the appurtenances of oil refineries. As if the prairie had been doubly defiled, first by the rigs and pumps, now by the steel of strangely shaped edifices.

Dorfmann too had changed. Sure, McBride expected it. Age wreaked its own small havocs. But, with Dorfmann, not small. He had withered, skin paper thin and yellowed, eyes almost glazed. Sitting out on the patio in front of the ranch-house like a dead man someone had forgotten to bury. He stood up as McBride

161

came from the station wagon, an effort sustained only by considerable willpower.

'Glad to see you, son.' The voice was thin, tremulous. 'Pleased you came.'

The handshake was a meaningless gesture. No grip, a mere brushing of flesh.

'Glad to be here,' McBride replied, the necessary lie.

'Sit, sit!' A gesture to a chair beside his own. 'My man's bringing some lemonade. Also bourbon and branchwater. Take your pick.'

Settled with bourbon and branchwater, McBride watched the old man sip lemonade. As if now he daren't touch hard liquor, a truth at once confirmed by Dorfmann.

'No liquor. Doctor's orders. I like the smell so now and then I sniff the neck of the bottle.'

A pause. The old man staring bleakly at the prairie. Unseeing.

'Why did you send for me?' McBride asked.

'Because you're on my conscience.'

He had to wait now for the full reply. Dorfmann would take his own time. However much he had.

'Told you on the phone I haven't got much time,' Dorfmann went on. 'No time at all really. If I'm in luck maybe a year. That's what's inside me. Growing inside me.'

'Cancer?'

'You British can say the word. Here it's not so easy. You know they avoid using it on television. But then it's not just the growing in the chest. More than that. In the soul as well as the body.'

McBride thought, a plea for pity. Metaphysical as well as physical. Surprise. Dorfmann believed in the soul. Never thought there was much place for the soul in Texas. The internal combustion engine, yes, but the soul was something confined to gospelling on Sunday radio and tin shack sermons for the poor.

162

'Funny,' Dorfmann went on. 'All the money in the world and all I can do is just sit here waiting. Kinda rich man's cliche, that. Can't run away from the old man in the long nightgown, eh?'

McBride felt a lack of sympathy. ' W C Fields called it that.'

'Knew a thing or two, did Fields. Still, don't be sorry, son, not on my behalf . . .'

How do you say you're not sorry? That you had no feelings for the old man, could you tell him that? Or was it too much like driving the boot in? Better to keep quiet. McBride kept quiet.

Dorfmann went on. 'Guess it's been laid on me. If there's judgement then I been judged. Been coming ever since they killed the President. Ever since I killed the President.'

In front of his eyes, McBride saw the prairie swim and buckle, an earthquake confined to the irises of his eyes, to the pictures in his brain.

'I guess I played my part,' said Dorfmann. 'Knew it would happen. Paid my dues to make it so. And then sat back and waited. It's not even Kennedy's death that troubles me. I'd resolved to live with that for a long time. It was the others. All the others. Line of shadows growing longer and longer. Need to be executed, that's what was said. But I didn't like it. Troubled something they call conscience. Like you. You troubled my conscience. Guess after they tried to get rid of you, I salved a fragment of conscience, told them I could handle you.'

'That's why I was sent for? Why I got the Chicago job?'

'Some of it, son, some of the reason. Oh, you were good at your job, that helped, made it easier. And I kinda liked you. Not that I ever believed that should have anything to do with business.'

'Even the business of murder?'

163

'Like any other business. If it has to be done, then it has to be done. But I thought I could get around the killing of Alec McBride. After all you hadn't seen Kennedy being killed. You weren't in Dealey Plaza.'

'I saw Sandrup's killing.'

'He'd been dead for years on the books. And nobody found a body. All you knew was hearsay. No proof. Trouble is you stuck with it. All these years. Like an obsession.'

'Not knowing made it an obsession. Now you really can help, Mr Dorfmann. You can tell me all about it.'

Dorfmann ran the back of his hand across his forehead. It was damp with the sweat of pain.

'Kennedy had to be killed. He was costing people money. Too much money. People around here. People in New York and Washington and California. Interests on Wall Street. Trouble with an impossibly rich President . . . it didn't matter to him that he was bleeding the rich. Trying to tame the multi-national corporations. They didn't want him in power. So they started the ball rolling. Brought in people like me. And they'd talk to the Cubans . . . the anti-Castro Cubans. Never forgave Kennedy for letting them lose at the Bay of Pigs.'

He faltered, lips dry, and sipped lemonade.

'Go on,' said McBride coldly.

'And . . . and the Mafia . . . they weren't exactly happy with the Kennedys. That was the idea. Get the enemies together. At first it was just an idea. Then the guys who knew how to make it reality they came in.'

'Mafia?'

'No. They'd help. But they were amateurs. But the others . . . the professionals . . . they made it happen.'

Dorfmann was talking a lot. But in generalities. No specifics. And the time for generalities was past, McBride told himself.

'Names? Details? I need them.'

'A lot of them. High places. Oh, you know one name.

Sidney Dorfmann. One of the middle strata. Others . . . so many. To tell you, I'd need time. And just now I'm tired. Weary right into the bone marrow. Give me tonight. Put names on paper. Then you come tomorrow and I give you them.'

'I can stay here tonight . . .'

'No. You here . . . too much of a give-away. Too many people might guess what I'm going to do.'

'But they'll know I'm here anyway, if they know anything.'

'One visit's not important. On the business of the paper. But you mustn't seem to stay too long. Tonight you can wait at the Hilton. Then in the morning you hire a car or . . . or pick up a taxi and travel around, lose any followers and then come out here. All right?'

Reluctantly McBride agreed. He had no choice. Dorfmann was white, drawn, exhausted. McBride rose to go. But as he did so, Dorfmann gripped his arm.

'You'll write, Alec? As a book for abroad. They won't let you publish here. But overseas. Somewhere, in hiding, you'll write it. It'll have to be in hiding. They have long arms and long memories. But you will write it?'

'I'll write it. But why now? Why not years ago?'

'Because now I've nothing to be afraid of any longer. It doesn't matter if they kill me now. They'd be killing a dead man.'

He relaxed his grip on McBride's arm. But his eyes, deep set, unnaturally bright still stared into the younger man's face.

'Come as soon as you can tomorrow. I'll have everything ready.'

The hotel in Dallas was comfortable, a change from 1963 and that hotel with Billy Sandrup. McBride could relax, had to relax, his brain fogged, his eyelids heavy. Yet still the sense of anticipation. Tomorrow he would know more, much more. He would know where

Sandrup had fitted in, where Bunker Hayward still fitted in. And behind them, the names. The story would have texture, meaning; the names would be big, well-known, talked-of names. And now they'd be talked of even more.

McBride ate alone in his hotel room. Outside Dallas came to life for the evening. Traffic built up, lights flashed, neon dazzled. McBride contemplated the city from his hotel window. A monument to bad taste, too much money, a statue erected to the great glory of oil, cenotaph to the power of the automobile, big rich city, USA. Christ, what a memorial to society.

McBride went from the window to the bathroom. It seemed an appropriate comment. Later he bathed and went to bed where he sat up staring at the television screen. It was a bleak vision. Eventually he slept. Tonight he had no desire to see the new Dallas.

Morning. The taxi, at his instruction, took him around the city for an hour before heading out towards the Dorfmann ranch. McBride kept an eye on the rear window watching for a following car. There was none. Or at least none he could spot. Unless they were alternating, using more than one car. But it seemed not.

On the road out to the ranch there was still no sign of a follower. Later, he realised there was no need to follow him. The matter had been attended to, without trailing McBride.

There were cars in front of the ranch, more cars than usual. Two of them from the Dallas Police Department. And an ambulance.

A ranch hand, a tall silent cliche of a Texan showed McBride into the building, ushering him into a small room to the left of the front door. There he was left alone for some minutes. Finally a large man in a stetson and a grey suit came in.

'Who are you?'

166

'McBride. Alec McBride. I work on a Chicago paper in which Mr Dorfmann has an interest.'

'Yeah, that right? I think I heard of you. Read some of your stuff. What do you want with Dorfmann?'

'I had an appointment this morning. A matter of newspaper business.' It was the safe thing to say. Already McBride was cold with anticipation. He hadn't even asked what had happened. There seemed to be no need to do so. Everything told the story.

'Guess you'll have to arrange your business with somebody else,' The large man said. 'My name's Trasker. Dan Trasker. County sheriff. This here is in my county.'

'Hello, sheriff.'

'Yeah, well, we can skip the formalities. Dorfmann's dead.'

Cold confirmation. Expected. But there were questions. 'How did he die?'

'You know he was a sick man. The big C.'

McBride nodded. 'He mentioned it yesterday.'

'You saw him yesterday?'

'Yes.'

'Why come back today?'

'Unfinished business.'

The sheriff coughed and scratched his neck. It was red, the skin of the neck. In character.

'Dorfmann took a shotgun sometime last night, put it under his chin and blew the top of his head off.'

McBride said nothing for a long moment. Somewhere a clock chimed eleven. McBride thought, this should not be a surprise to me. Like the old-time detective story. The murderer about to be revealed and then the shot from outside the french windows.

But in this case it had been the shotgun over night. Or could it have been suicide? No, not when Dorfmann had wanted to cleanse his conscience. It had been

Dorfmann's idea that he give McBride names, to open up the death of the President.

'Are you sure he killed himself?' McBride said.

The sheriff's head jerked up. 'Wha'? Wha' you saying? Who else could have done it? Hell's teeth, the old guy had incurable cancer. That's pain, Mr McBride. Real pain. I seen it in my own family. Dorfmann did what he had to do . . .'

'He had to see me this morning.'

'Think that would be important to a guy in mortal pain? For God's sake, McBride, you got no imagination?'

'Perhaps I've got too much imagination. Somebody could have put that shotgun under his chin.'

The sheriff flushed. 'You newspaper guys are all the same. You make up stories out of anything. You want to see the body? I'll show you the old corpus delicti. Maybe that'll stop you making up stories.'

McBride was taken across the hall into the other room.

It was as Trasker had said. Dorfmann sat in front of the picture window at his desk. The gun had slid sideways on firing. The shot had entered under his chin smashing the jaw, going through the mouth and upwards into the brain. The window was splashed with scarlet. The top of the head had ceased to exist.

'Now, Mr McBride, you just make sure that you've seen a suicide,' Trasker said. 'Because I don't want no stories about murders appearing in the newspapers when there ain't no murder.'

He nodded towards a small man who was closing a suitcase in the corner of the room. 'That's Doc Morrish, County Medical Examiner. Doc, tell this guy what happened here.'

The doctor didn't even look up. 'Put the shotgun under his chin and blew his brains all over the window. No question.'

Trasker looked smug. 'There. And motive, doc?'

'His own medical adviser's been telling us Mr Dorfmann had cancer of the stomach. Widespread. Inoperable. There's your motive.'

McBride took a step towards the medical examiner. 'Could someone have put the gun in his hands under his chin and fired?'

Trasker said, 'You don't give up easy, McBride.'

The medical examiner now looked up at McBride. 'Sure they could have. But they didn't, I'm pretty sure. Hell, there's cordite smelling the palms of his hands. Bet you there'd even be the signs he fired it himself.'

'Of course someone could have put the gun in his hands, forced him to fire.'

Trasker stepped forward. 'That's enough of that. Sure, pigs maybe could fly. But we ain't in that kinda business. Mr Dorfmann killed himself. Simple as that. So don't you be building sand castles with no sand, McBride. No funny stories in the newspaper. You just have to accept the official verdict.'

There was nothing to be done and McBride knew it. 'I'll look forward to reading that verdict.'

The sheriff stared at him evenly. 'In Chicago, son. Not here. You'll be returning to Chicago quickly, won't you?'

'I might stay a few days longer.'

'Stay as long as you like, McBride. But don't write lyin' stories, that's all.'

McBride was driven back into Dallas in a police car. He had to admit to himself he had no intention of staying in Dallas. But he'd wanted to see Trasker's reaction. He'd expected it all to be hushed-up. The sheriff's big act. But friendly. Stay as long as you like. The sheriff was a professional.

And McBride did want to stay a few hours longer. He did want to ask one question in one place. And then he would fly back to Chicago.

169

It was one street in Dallas that hadn't changed in all the years. The facade of the Prairie Traveller hotel was unchanged. Perhaps a little more of the stucco on the front had broken off. But it was essentially the same.

Behind the reception desk, another face, a fair-haired young man with an ingratiating smile.

'Good afternoon, sir.'

It was already early afternoon now. McBride had two hours before his plane to Chicago.

'Good afternoon,' he said, looking around the small foyer and lounge. Cheap and nasty. Not the right image for the new Dallas. Worn armchairs and a faded table.

'You'd like a room, sir?'

'No. No room. Just enquiring after a friend of mine. I thought he might just be staying here.'

The long shot. No reason why it should be so. No reason at all. Unless the man had a sense of humour. Or of irony. No, the trip to the Prairie Traveller was probably a wasted trip, a crazy thought in McBride's head.

'The name of your friend, sir?'

'Hayward. A Mr Bunker Hayward.'

The receptionist made a move towards a large red registry book, then grinned.

'No need to look, sir. I'm afraid you've just missed him. Mr Hayward checked out about an hour ago. He did say, just as he was leaving, that somebody might just come looking for him. He said I was to give the gentleman his apologies.'

So Hayward had a sense of humor. And an ability to read minds. The latter should not have surprised McBride. The man was always one jump ahead. The important thing was that Hayward had been in Dallas when Dorfmann had blown his own life away. Or had it blown away for him.

McBride took a taxi out to the airport.

To his surprise Dan Trasker was waiting for him at

170

the airport. Alone. The sheriff took him by the arm and led him into a quiet corner of the refreshment lounge.

'You got at least a half hour before your plane takes off.'

'Checking to make sure I'm on it, sheriff?'

'No. I want a word with you. Off the record. Not for publication. Not even for talking about. You wanna coffee?'

McBride nodded. Two coffees duly appeared. The sheriff leaned forward, stetson shoved to the back of his head.

'I'm an honest cop, McBride,' he said.

'Is that supposed to be a rarity?'

'Sometimes. Out there at the Dorfmann ranch I gave you the official line on the old man's death. Okay?'

'I heard you. Print anything else at my peril.'

'Heck, that was for effect. There were deputies and the coroner there. You can try and print what you like. Trouble is nobody'll put it in the paper. You ought to know that.'

'You're probably right.'

'Okay. So I have to play along too. And maybe Dorfmann did kill himself . . .'

McBride was surprised. Genuinely. 'You said . . . maybe?'

'There were scratches on his wrists. He could have been forced to hold that shotgun . . . even forced to press the trigger.'

'Then, for God's sake, why don't you do something?' McBride said, his voice rising.

Trasker leaned forward, hunched up, a tight bundle of a man. 'Because it would be no use. I'm only a small county sheriff. Means nothing. I could catch a cold tomorrow and be out of a job. Wouldn't do me any good, wouldn't help the odd guy I can help. The official word is Sidney Dorfmann killed himself. I have to go

171

along with that. Hell, the coroner had the word before he even reached the ranch and saw the body.'

'So why are you telling me this?'

'Because I've got fragments of self respect left. Because I wanted you to know.'

'If I print it you'd deny it?'

'What else? There's nothing to be done. Bigger things behind this. Things I don't know about. Maybe you do. I don't want to. Might not be able to handle them.' The sheriff took a gulp of coffee. 'Anyway, there's something else.'

'What's that?'

From his pocket the sheriff brought out a bulky manila envelope. 'This. Addressed to you. I found it in Dorfmann's desk drawer. Notebook.'

'You'll know what's in it?'

'Sure. Part of my job. Doesn't mean anything to me. Not relevant to his death, as far as I can see. So I thought you should have it.'

McBride took the envelope. He could feel the shape of the notebook inside.

'All right,' he said. 'Save me the anticipation. What's in it?'

'Lists. Of names. Means nothing to me. Just lists. Take it. Do what you can with it. But leave me out.'

'So as you can keep honest . . . and ignorant.'

'Yeah, yeah, sure, that's it.'

On the plane McBride settled back and studied the notebook. It was an ordinary notebook, imitation leather binding, white, unruled pages. A memorandum book. But no memorandum. Unless you count the lists.

The first list was of names; about seventy, with addresses. Most of them meant nothing to McBride. Most of them but not all of them. Kathy Raymond's name was there, so was her husband's. And Billy Sandrup and Orrin Buncey. The names gave him the clue. If he was right everyone on this list was dead. All

172

had in some way been witnesses to what they should not have witnessed. All of them had seen something which indicated that Lee Harvey Oswald did not kill John F Kennedy.

The second list was shorter – just names, no addresses. Only one name meant anything to him. It stared out at him from the page.

Alexander McBride. Those still to be taken care of? Unfinished business?

There followed a number of blank pages. Only at the end of the book did he come upon the third list. It was like an excerpt from the stock listings in the business section of any newspaper. Except that there were no listings. Just company names. Trans-Texican Oil. That was Dorfmann's company. International A & I; United World Communicators Inc; Betheseda International Trading Corporation. And others. Ten companies and three international conglomerates.

McBride sat back in his seat. A segment of middle America lay thirty thousand feet below. And in front of him the notebook. Business terminated, unfinished business, and the ten companies and three conglomerates. Who were they? Oh, easy enough to know. Listed in every trade directory in the country. What's good for ten companies and three conglomerates is good for the USA. A variation on an old cliche.

Were they behind the assassination of John F Kennedy? Or were they sympathizers? A part of a greater whole? The enemy? And how could one man fight such an enemy? No way. No method of combatting. Nothing to be done.

The thought angered him. There must be a way. There must be a method. Attrition. One man following a trail that would lead only to one other man. But would then perhaps lead to someone else. Another man, another group. Upwards towards the higher echelons.

No way.

Anger cooled. Nothing on which it could be vented. He sat back and closed his eyes. In a short time he would be back in Chicago. And with time to think. Leave it until then. Until there was time to think.

10

1975

On 1st January, 1975, Watergate defendants, Mitchell, Haldeman, Ehrlichman and Mardian were found guilty of conspiracy and obstruction of justice. Watergate had dominated the headlines for a long time. Of course there were other things and Alec McBride had written of them. In five years he had written himself into a commanding position as one of the country's major columnists.

In five years too, dust settles over memory. After the death of Dorfmann, McBride had contrived to bury the memories of Kennedy and Sandrup and the name of Bunker Hayward. It was of the past, he told himself, and for the future. Something to be left alone until the time was right. Not that he had done nothing on his return from Dallas after Dorfmann's death. There had been another telephone call to the FBI in Washington.

'Your people know what happened to Sidney Dorfmann?' McBride asked the anonymous agent to whom he had been connected.

'Mr Sullivan is aware that Mr Dorfmann had a terminal illness and took his own life.' The voice was flat, monotonous. An aide to Deputy Director Sullivan.

'Is Mr Sullivan aware there were indications that Mr Dorfmann did not take his own life?'

'We have the local police reports. There is no such evidence. Mr Sullivan is however reviewing the whole matter. Mr Sullivan was a personal friend of Mr Dorfmann's.'

'And what is Mr Sullivan doing about the other matter?'

A pause. Then, hesitant and uncertain. 'To what are you referring, Mr McBride?'

'The matter of the death of John F Kennedy.'

A longer pause. The agent coughed at the end of the line. There was a sound as of papers being shuffled.

Then, the reply. 'I can give you no information on ongoing investigations by the Bureau.'

'I was one of the people who provided the Bureau with information relevant to the assassination.'

'We are always grateful for every assistance given to us by the public. Indeed Mr Hoover is on record as saying that is the essence of good police work. Good public relations.'

McBride had let his emotions loose for the first time during the phone call. 'For God's sake, I'm asking about the murder of the President.'

The voice was unutterably bland now. 'Of course all this was some years ago and evidence has firmly placed guilt on the shoulders of Lee Harvey Oswald. You know, sir, that there is no real evidence of any others being involved . . .' McBride slammed down the receiver.

Dorfmann's notebook gathered dust.

The incidents at Watergate became the *cause célèbre*. And there were other stories. In Kentucky there was a mining disaster and twenty-eight miners died. After eleven years of fighting in Vietnam 53,000 Americans had died. Lyndon Johnson died and a cease-fire was signed in Vietnam. John Kennedy's old opponent was at the helm and Americans showed they would buy a used car from the from the man with the five o'clock shadow. But not for long.

When McBride had returned from Dallas, Dorrie

Macklin had come back to him. No overtures, no discussion. She had turned up at the door of his apartment and moved back into his life. He had offered no resistance nor had he wanted to. Alec McBride was aging into a creature of habit. Not that Dorrie was simply habit. He could tell himself he was in love with her and believed she was with him. It all seemed like the natural coming together of two people who cared deeply for each other. So McBride believed. They went to bed as before and there was excitement and passion. Yet, as before, McBride could not rid himself of the feeling there was still some strange, indefinable barrier between them. Physically they were ideal. But the barrier was there.

They lived together for four years. But now there was no talk of marriage. Simply an acceptance of a situation both desired.

Clyde Anson had retired from the staff of the paper after some pressure from Marinker who obviously considered the old man a passenger and wanted him out. He was still given occasional freelance work to supplement a pension which Anson persistently complained was inadequate. And, as often as he could, McBride would give the old man legwork in researching stories for his column.

Occasionally Alec McBride thought about the Kennedy assassination. It would be the book he would write when he took his long sabbatical. There was a night over dinner with Dorrie and her father that he mentioned this.

They were in a restaurant off Lakeside Drive, very new, low-ceilinged, with a cook who would move on but as yet was new enough to be concerned about food. It was becoming a rarity in America.

Over coffee, McBride told them of the book he would write.

'No. Forget it,' said Anson.

'I've forgotten about it for too long. But it's always been there. In the back of my mind. Something to be done.'

'Nobody gives a bent nickel for Kennedy now. He's with the immortals. That means he's for the historians. You say he wasn't killed by Oswald . . . nobody'll care. It'll be fiction for the reader. Anyway why should you care any more?'

McBride sipped his coffee. 'I've thought about that. Every time I've given up, put it out of mind, something's happened. Turvey in Saigon, Dorfmann before he died. Always the name of this character Hayward comes back.'

'It's an obsession, Alec,' Dorrie said.

'Yes. But . . . I can't forget that night in Dallas. Sandrup sitting there telling me. There's the notebook too.'

Anson looked up. 'What notebook?'

'Dorfmann left me a notebook. Lists of names. Everybody who died after the death of Kennedy. Because of the death of Kennedy. Others too. Lists of companies, corporations . . . the ones he believed were involved.'

Dorrie and her father exchanged glances.

'What good does it do?' asked Anson. 'Even if it were true, you couldn't touch them.'

McBride thought for a moment. There had to be an answer. He thought, injustice cannot be eternal. Cannot go on for ever.

'I could howl like a dog in the night,' he said. 'In the book, in my column.'

'You think they'd print it? Some of these people probably own the paper. That means they own us, Alec. Whether we like it or not. They want us to shut up, they cut off our sources of supply. No job, no money, in the end, no personality. Efficient economic destruction. They're good at it.' Anson lit a cigarette before going on. 'And if they don't shut you up that way, they kill you. Like they killed the people on Dorfmann's list. Oh, it was probably easier to kill them than destroy them in any other way.'

'That's why I can't leave it, Clyde. Because they kill people. As a matter of business practice.'

'Sure they do. So they need you out of the way. Maybe you stand between them and two million dollars. Or whatever. Or in the street, you stand between a mugger and two dollars. Either way you're expendable. It's business. It's free enterprise carried to the ultimate.'

McBride shrugged. 'You may be right. You're monotonously right at times, Clyde.'

The old man waved over the wine waiter and ordered brandies. 'I know it. I know I'm right. And it's a burden. That's why you prefer my daughter to me. She's wrong now and then. When are you two going to get married?'

McBride ignored the question. It shouldn't have been asked. Not of him. Perhaps Anson should have asked it of his daughter. Why not marry the man and get rid of the barrier? Whatever the barrier was. He looked at Dorrie. She said nothing. She revealed nothing. Her face was emotionless. She sipped her coffee.

McBride went back to the subject. 'There were other names in Dorfmann's book. My own. Others who are still alive. One of them was Giancana. Sam Giancana.'

Anson looked up now, startled. The waiter placed brandies in front of them. Anson waited until he had gone.

'Giancana,' he repeated the name. 'Friend of friends.'

'The one who shared a girl friend with John F Kennedy.'

'I told you that,' Anson said. 'Now everybody knows. So, Giancana. The padrone of Chicago. The Mafia Capo for this little city. I wouldn't talk too much about Sam. I wouldn't mention his name is in this notebook you have. Not that it means anything.'

179

'I'd like to meet Giancana.'

'No, you wouldn't, Alec.'

'He might want to meet me. If he knew his name was on a list in Dorfmann's book. A list of people who know something about the death of Kennedy.'

'Forget it, Alec,' Dorrie said.

He ignored her. He concentrated on her father. 'Tell him, Clyde. Tell him his name's in the book. Tell him I'm going to bring it up in my column.'

That night in his apartment, Dorrie said very little to him. He imagined she seemed sad. She slept with her back to him.

A week later he brought up the death of Kennedy in his column. Twelve years after the event.

'Who did kill President Kennedy? The question keeps coming back over the years. People are starting to write books about it. And more and more, the least likely candidate is Lee Harvey Oswald. Are we going to revive again the old question? The answer is yes. This column will be aware of all developments and will report them. This is an ongoing story. There are too many questions unanswered. More questions arise. Was there more than one gunman? The questions keep being asked. It's time they were asked in public.'

The next day Marinker called him to his office.

'I know what you're saying, Alec,' the editor said. 'And you're not the only person who is asking these questions. But I don't want the column filled with speculation over something that's for the history books. That's not why you're employed by this paper.'

McBride found himself staring over Marinker's shoulder at the large expanse of window which covered one wall of the office. Beyond the window stretched the Chicago skyline and the lake.

'I think the Kennedy story will be relevant,' McBride said. 'And become more and more relevant.'

180

'This newspaper is not interested in history. We're more concerned about another president. Whether or not Nixon will resign or be impeached. Write about that!'

'I have done. Perhaps it's the same story. Kennedy died, Johnson went and the crooks got into power.'

Marinker frowned. He was a registered Republican. 'I don't know that I like that. Nixon may have made mistakes. That doesn't mean . . .'

McBride cut in. 'Maybe it just means what different people want it to mean. A crime or a stupidity? Does it matter? But the killing of Kennedy was a crime.'

'With which, I gather, you are obsessed. Oh, I've heard, McBride, of your obsession. I don't want it brought into your column. It is of no interest. As I've said, it's history.'

'Is that official policy?'

Marinker's face flushed. 'It is my policy. Look, you were right in your column. People are asking questions about Kennedy's death. All right. But they won't find answers, take it from me. Therefore the exercise is futile. So forget it. I don't want column inches wasted. Not unless it sells papers. And an assassination twelve years ago does not sell papers.'

McBride left the editor's office. Marinker believed in brief interviews. Perhaps it was easier for him. Lay down the law and ignore all arguments. Perhaps he was right. There would be no conclusion to the story of John F Kennedy. Perhaps it was a dead end, McBride's personal obsession. Perhaps Marinker had other motives, not to be thought on.

Or perhaps it was the beginning of the nightmare.

That evening Anson phoned him. 'Giancana wants to meet you.'

It was on the north side of the city, a small Italian restaurant that looked like a set from a gangster movie. Lasagna was the speciality of the house. The owner looked like an old-time character actor called Henry Armetta.

Anson waited with McBride. They drank coffee.

Fifteen minutes after the appointed time two men entered the restaurant. Anson stood up as they approached. The small man looked ill. His face was yellow, skin tight and wrinkled like old parchment; a grey moustache crept down the side of his upper lip merging into a small, rather untidy beard.

'Mr Giancana,' Anson said and stretched his hand out to the small man. Giancana merely nodded and sat, as if exhausted, facing McBride.

'This is Alec McBride,' Anson went on. Giancana nodded again. Anson turned to the other man – a taller figure, distinguished, impeccably dressed, grey hair turning to white, and keen, alert eyes. To McBride, he looked like a distinguished political figure.

'Mr John Roselli,' Anson indicated McBride. 'Alec McBride.'

Roselli shook hands with McBride before sitting. Seated he looked at Giancana. 'Sam?'

'A little warm milk, maybe,' said Giancana.

Roselli turned to the Henry Armetta lookalike.

'Warm milk for Mr Giancana. A brandy for me.'

The orders were duly served and the four men were left alone at the table. Giancana went into a small paroxysm of coughing. Eventually it subsided.

Roselli faced McBride. 'So you got a list, Mr McBride.'

McBride nodded. He felt warm, uncomfortable.

'Tell me about this list.'

'Given to me by Sidney Dorfmann.'

A look was exchanged between the two Italians. McBride felt warmer. Too warm. It was only early summer. He shouldn't feel so warm.

'And this list, kid, what does it imply?' Roselli went on.

182

'It's a death list . . .' A wheezing sound from Giancana and McBride realised the old man was laughing.

Roselli explained. 'Mr Giancana finds it amusing he's on a death list. He's been on so many, over the years.'

Giancana leaned forward and spoke for the first time. 'I'm on another death list just now, eh? One you don't know about.'

Roselli seemed to feel the need to explain. 'Mr Giancana just arrived back in Chicago today. He's been in hospital in Houston, Texas. And the goddam police hounded him out of the city. He's not a well man, see. So you say what you gotta say and get it over, kid.'

McBride suddenly felt irritated. 'Look, you people asked to see me. Okay, I wanted to see you. But, Mr Roselli, I used to be a kid. Then, like you, I grew up. I don't like being called a kid.'

Anson visibly shuddered. Giancana coughed. And Roselli, after staring for a moment, laughed.

'You got a big lip, kid. Okay, let's start over. You say Mr Giancana's name is on what you think is a death list in this book Dorfmann gave you. Sure, Anson told us about it.'

'Your name's on the list too, Mr Roselli.'

Roselli showed his teeth. It was a smile.

Giancana said, 'I don't like my name appearing in books of lists.'

'Where is this book?' Roselli asked.

'With my lawyer,' McBride replied. 'Safe with him. In the event of my demise it gets passed to the government.'

'Huh! They do nothing,' Giancana said. 'So let's hear what this list is all about.'

'Those who have some knowledge of the assassination of John F Kennedy.'

Again the two Italians looked at each other.

Roselli said, 'We're supposed to have killed Kennedy too?'

'It's a damn lie,' Giancana muttered. 'Anybody that's dead, I killed them. That's the new story. So the Senate Committee wants me to tell them about trying to kill Castro. And he's still alive.'

'This has nothing to do with Castro . . .'

The small old man grunted. 'No? You think not. Look, years ago before the Bay of Pigs they come to me. Me and Johnny. The Central Intelligence Agency. They say they want to kill Fidel Castro. They want me to help. Me? The FBI tries to put me in jail, CIA wants me to kill Castro. Don't you think that's funny, Mr McBride?'

'I think it's interesting.'

'It's true,' said Roselli. 'Oh, we gave them ideas. Why not? We're patriotic Americans. Anyway it didn't happen. And now you say some dead Texas millionaire says we helped to kill the President . . . it's crazy.'

Giancana coughed briefly. 'I had nothing against Kennedy. I liked him. We had mutual friends,' he laughed hoarsely. 'They even write books about it. But I wouldn't get involved. Even when they came to me, I wouldn't get involved . . .'

Roselli leaned forward. 'Sam . . . dolce, dolce . . .'

Now McBride was alert. 'You say they came to you. Who came?'

But Giancana had subsided into a further fit of coughing. Roselli took over.

'What do you want from Mr Giancana? He's not a young man. He has retired. He may say things he does not mean . . .'

'Mr Roselli, he said he was approached in the matter of assassinating Castro . . .'

'That is true. Both Mr Giancana and myself are to appear on that matter . . .'

'But if you were approached about Castro, you could also be approached about Kennedy. And Mr Giancana

184

implied he had been approached. If that is so, I want to know by whom he was approached.'

Now Roselli gave a tight smile and looked for the first time at Anson.

'He's a Britisher this kid. I can tell, "By whom." I like that. That's classy. That's grammar.' Roselli turned back to McBride. 'Now I tell you. This is Mr Sam Giancana, friend of friends, friend of politicians, big businessmen, even the Mayors of Chicago, New York and Los Angeles. Friend of Frank Sinatra. And other movie stars. Now he's retired. Pestered by a Senate Committee. By the FBI. By his own business associates. All he wants is to be allowed to rest. To have a little peace.'

'Doesn't answer my question.'

'You have your answer. Mr Giancana refused any such suggestion regarding the death of Kennedy. You want to know who approached him. No. Mr Giancana does not sing for his supper. Not to the FBI, not to the Senate, not to the newspapers. So now, we'll go. Mr Giancana is tired . . .'

Roselli helped the old man to his feet in silence. Then Giancana seemed to hesitate and, turning, he stared at McBride.

'You think I deal with guns, Mr McBride. You think I'm like some buttonman for these big corporations. These government agencies. No! Not Giancana. I was never into that. Now I'm out of everything. I'm a private citizen. I know nothing. I will tell the senate committee I know nothing.'

He turned away, leaning on Roselli's arm. Roselli had the last word.

'We wasn't here tonight, McBride. We never met you. We don't talk to newspapermen. Capish?'

Roselli threw a large bill across the counter at the restaurant owner. Then Anson and McBride were alone.

185

'Gave himself away,' Anson said. 'That bit about them coming to him and him refusing to get involved . . .'

'I know.'

'Funny though. They were frightened of being seen talking to you.'

McBride drove Anson to his house in Cicero. Then he drove back to his own apartment. Dorrie was waiting for him. To his surprise she asked no questions. He was grateful for that. He didn't want to talk about the meeting, he wanted to think. Giancana had admitted he had been approached, said he'd refused the approach and McBride found the old man believable in this statement. But if somehow he could get to him again, he might learn who made the approach. McBride wondered if the name Bunker Hayward would surface. But then Hayward was the field man. The approach would have been made by someone else, someone bigger, more important. Perhaps someone linked with one of the corporations on Dorfmann's final list. And Giancana and Roselli would know who made the approach and that fact was enough to place them on the list in Dorfmann's book.

But why had they survived? Why had there been no attempt on their lives? Giancana had been a big man in the Mafia then. Leader of one of the Families. That could buy him safety. The Mafiosi did not sing. He could be left as unfinished business indefinitely.

So McBride thought on the evening of the 17th June, 1975.

Two days later Sam Giancana was in the kitchen of his apartment cooking himself a late supper. Someone came into the apartment and shot the old man seven times through his head.

186

11

'They killed a dead man,' Roselli said. 'An old, tired, dead man. He was out of the rackets. He didn't want to know any more. Yet they had to put seven slugs in his head.'

It was two nights after Giancana's death. Roselli had arranged the meeting at the same Italian restaurant. Just McBride this time. No sign of Anson. Henry Armetta served them two plates of lasagna and a bottle of chianti and left them alone.

And Roselli talked with a surprising amount of genuine sadness considering his reputation and background.

'They coulda left him alone. How long had he got? Half his insides was gone. He'd had a cholecystostomy in Houston.'

'You know who killed him?' McBride asked.

'Sure I know. Maybe Aiuppa. Maybe Joe Batters. You know why?'

'You're going to tell me.'

'He was goin' to testify before the senate committee. He wouldn't have told them anything. He knew the rules. Would have given them double talk. Maybe told them about the CIA and the Castro business. But no family business.'

'Maybe he would have talked about the assassination of Kennedy?' It was a shot in the dark for McBride.

Roselli stared at him. 'We told you about that. Sam wasn't involved. I wasn't involved.'

'But you were approached.'

'So what? It's nothing to do with anything.'

'Maybe whoever approached you was afraid Sam would talk.'

'Sure they'd be afraid. But they'd know Sam wouldn't.' Suddenly Roselli leaned over and gripped McBride's wrist. Hard.

'Did you open your mouth about the meeting the other night?'

McBride was puzzled. Nothing had been said. Or written. Or would have been. Not until he knew; not until he'd talked to Giancana again. Too late now.

'Sam's due to talk to the senate. And then they hear he's had a secret get-together with a hot-shot columnist. Big newspaper guy. What should they think? Old Sam's about to blow his top. You sure you didn't talk?'

'I'm sure I didn't talk, Roselli. I wasn't going to talk. Because I wanted to get together with Giancana again. I wanted to know who approached him. I didn't want to mess that up.'

Roselli lit a cigarette. 'If they knew I was talking to you I'd be next.' He said it coolly, unemotionally. 'But they don't know that. Not from you.'

'Not from me.'

'The little guy. Clyde Anson. He could have opened his mouth.'

McBride said nothing. Clyde Anson talking. It was Anson who had said, forget it. Say nothing. Anson. Who couldn't stop talking.

Roselli said, 'I'll take odds he ain't where he's supposed to be. I'll take odds he's moving house.' He dragged heavily on his cigarette, coughed slightly and exhaled deeply. 'Maybe we should all be moving house.'

McBride stared at the untouched plate of lasagna in

front of him. 'Look, Roselli, if Clyde Anson talked out of turn, then whoever he talked to knows Giancana talked to me. And two days later he's killed. A few people know I've been questioning the Kennedy assassination. Just maybe whoever came to Giancana all these years ago about Kennedy was afraid he might say too much to me.'

Roselli was studying the table cloth. McBride went on, 'All right, maybe they went to Aiuppa. Got him to kill Giancana . . .'

Roselli slammed his hand palm down on the table. 'Maybe, maybe, everything's maybe. We didn't want to know about a contract on Kennedy. Never wanted to know.' He looked up at McBride. 'You shouldn't want to know.'

'I want to know who approached you and Giancana.'

'I don't remember. Hell, it was years ago.'

'I want a name!'

'No names. I never knew any names. Two guys came to see us. That was all. Two guys. They knew we'd been into the Castro business. So then they wanted Kennedy. We said no.'

'What did they look like?'

'One was an operator. Nice suit, expensive. Like . . . like a corporation lawyer. A *consiglieri*. The other was younger, tall, blonde hair . . .'

'Hayward! Was his name Hayward?'

'I told you. I don't know names.' Roselli rose suddenly. 'I tell you this for your own good, McBride. Do nothing about this. Write nothing. Maybe . . . maybe, like I said, you leave town.'

'What about you?'

'I'm leaving town. Business in LA and then Florida. They don't touch me, though. They know me. I look after myself and I keep quiet. You do the same. So I say goodbye, McBride. But, one thing, watch Anson. He's a sour grape.'

189

An hour later McBride arrived at his apartment. It was empty. No Dorrie. More than that, none of Dorrie's clothes. She'd emptied the wardrobe, taken her suitcase and gone. There was no note. McBride walked around the apartment for a time. Dorrie had said nothing about going. Not for a night, or a few days. They'd had no row. She'd simply gone.

McBride lifted the telephone and dialled Clyde Anson's home number. Dorrie answered the phone.

'What's it about, Dorrie?'

A pause. Then the reply. 'My father's not well.'

'So you could have left a note.'

'I hadn't time.'

'You'd time to pack everything.'

A longer pause. 'Alec, he's worried. About Giancana being killed.'

'Yes. I should think he has cause to worry. He talked about the meeting the other night. Who did he talk to, Dorrie?'

'I don't know.'

'Then ask him!'

'He's sleeping.'

'Then wake him up.'

'I told you, he's not well.'

McBride took a deep breath. Exasperation. That was the dominant feeling. She should be helping him, not obstructing him. So should Anson. 'If he doesn't talk to me he might be even more unwell. Like Giancana.'

'That's what he's afraid of, Alec.'

Another deep breath. This time, he had to make a decision. 'The story will be in my column tomorrow. As much as I know. Giancana being approached to kill the President. That's only tomorrow's bit. To be continued. The whole story in my column over the next few days.'

'You can't, Alec!' He could hear the panic in her voice. 'You'll be committing suicide.'

190

The next thought hurt him. A pain in the mind. In the emotions. Why was she so sure? He asked her.

She stammered. She didn't usually stammer. 'They . . . they t . . . tried to kill you . . . kill you before. You write about it, they're bound to try again.'

That wasn't enough, he told himself. She had been too certain, too definite.

'More than that, Dorrie. You sound as if you know something. Something else. Do you know something else, Dorrie?'

The long silence now. He could hear her breathing. She would deny it, had to deny it. There was no way she could admit she knew more than he thought.

'I don't know anything more. I don't, Alec. What could I know?' The question underlined the lie. She went on, 'Look, meet me tomorrow. The Lake Bar. You know it.'

'One of your father's regular watering-holes.'

'Lunchtime. One o'clock. Meet me there.'

'I'll be there. If Clyde's too ill to join us, ask him that question. Ask him who he talked to.'

He heard her replace the receiver. He poured himself a long, long drink and set it down at his desk beside his typewriter. He inserted a sheet of paper and started to type. Every now and then he took a gulp from the tall glass. He was writing his column for the day after tomorrow. It was headed 'On The Death Of Kings'.

He typed five hundred words linking the deaths of the President and the old Mafiosi. When he had finished he poured himself another long drink and went to bed. He watched *The Late Show*, glass in hand. Then he went to sleep. He slept well. He'd made a decision. The story would be told.

He was being over-confident.

The next morning was hot. Chicago simmered in the heat from the early summer sun. McBride arrived at his office and filed his copy. And waited.

191

He was expecting problems with Marinker. But he was coldly confident he could overcome any objections from the editor. Since Vietnam he had insisted that none of his copy could be edited without discussion. He was prepared for that discussion.

He didn't have long to wait.

'The boss wants you.' This from Marinker's secretary, a smooth, plastic blonde, a Barbie Doll come to life.

Marinker sat in an easy chair away from his desk, at the large window, reading proof copies of tomorrow's features. He ran through them with the expert eye, tomorrow's comment today. McBride always thought it would be apt to give him a god-like arrogance. As if he knew a day in advance what the world would think tomorrow.

McBride came in, hesitated for a second and sat down. Marinker would not look up or indicate he was aware of McBride's arrival. It was his customary method of unnerving his employees. McBride would not be unnerved. He relaxed, crossed his legs and slumped back. Aware his technique would not work with McBride, Marinker placed the proofs on the thick carpet beside his chair and looked across at McBride.

'No!' he said. 'I won't run your column tomorrow. Not as it is.'

'Why?' McBride responded, easily, still determined Marinker would not intimidate him.

'I told you. The Kennedy assassination's an old, dead story.'

'Not any more. Not with the Zapruder film being shown on television.'

The film of Kennedy's moment of death had been shown on television in March. It appeared to throw into question the Oswald version.

'That was March. This is June. Nothing else has come to light,' Marinker insisted.

192

'Not so. It's all in my copy. I saw Giancana two days before he died. That's the story he told me . . .'

Marinker stood up irritably. 'There's no corroboration!'

'The man told me it. Clyde Anson heard. Even if it wasn't true, what he claimed is still a good story.'

'I do not intend that this paper should get into asking questions about the death of Kennedy. As a matter of policy. All these goddam rumours, they . . . they undermine the confidence of the nation. We've had Watergate. Now Nixon's gone, we've got to rebuild . . . something called national pride. Okay, you're not a citizen, McBride, but you must see the damage that could be done if . . . well, if someone other than Oswald killed Kennedy.'

'Everything in my copy is true. And it's news. And it's important. It has to be brought into the light.'

Marinker spun around almost violently to face McBride. 'Not in this paper! No argument, McBride. You write another column or you don't appear in tomorrow's edition.'

Calmly now. 'Then I don't appear.'

The editor suddenly seemed to relax, the tenseness leaving his body. The erect figure sagged.

'Write a book. That's the way to do it. Not now in the paper. Next year I'll give you a six months sabbatical and you can go away and write it. A . . . a paid sabbatical, of course.'

'Now is the time to do it,' McBride replied. 'And not in a book. A book can disappear in any bookshop. This should be a newspaper piece.'

'I can't print it. Either you . . . you forget or . . . or . . . you're out. Think about that, McBride. You've a good name in this business. A big name. But you can be forgotten tomorrow. With this story I can make sure you don't work for any other paper in the country.'

There'd always been the possibility, McBride told

himself, of this happening. And certainly Marinker could do him damage, at least for a time making sure he didn't go to another newspaper.

'Not even the *Christian Science Monitor* or the *Catholic Herald* would look at you!' Marinker drove the point home.

McBride did a quick calculation in his head. He'd been well paid, highly paid. He had something around $90,000–$100,000 in the bank. In American terms that was chickenfeed. To a boy from Paisley, Scotland, grown into a man it was money. He could live modestly for two, maybe even three years on that. He could write the Kennedy book, go into the country somewhere and work. At the end of three years he could probably get back into the newspaper world. Perhaps the book might even take off, something remarkable, the definitive theory.

Marinker was staring down at him, a small smug smile growing on his face. He'd used the ultimate threat. The man who earned big money in the USA, to him, this was the ultimate nightmare. The long fall down the ladder.

'All right,' McBride said. 'You've got your wish.'

Marinker smiled. 'A rewritten column. Good. I don't mind a piece on Giancana. The old *padrone* of the Chicago Mafia. Another Capone meets a sticky end . . . something like that. Just keep the Kennedy thing out.'

McBride rose slowly. Take time. Enjoy it. Even professional suicide has its charm.

'I think you've misunderstood me, Marinker. I'm quitting.'

The editor's face twitched, flinching as if he'd been struck. The man's vanity was wounded.

'You're serious? You know what you're doing?'

'Not only serious. Grim. And I know what I'm doing. If you don't mind, I'll clear my desk,' McBride smiled. 'Goodbye, Marinker.'

He was at the door before Marinker spoke again.

'I'm sorry, McBride. But they wouldn't let me print your story.'

'They? Who are they?'

'The people who own this paper.' Marinker at once drew himself to his full height. 'And . . . and they'd be quite right. In the national interest.'

'Or in their own interest.'

He closed Marinker's door firmly behind him.

He cleared his desk aware that all eyes in the newsroom were on him. He enjoyed being the centre of their silent attention. Placing everything that he could call his own from the desk into an ancient briefcase he straightened up and looked around. Most of the people in the room he'd known and liked ever since he'd come to Chicago. He would miss the noise, the jokes, the sound of men trying to report a sick city in a sick world, and keep their sanity with the semblance of a sense of humour.

His eyes met Cardwell's. Cardwell was a good sports reporter, a beetle-browed veteran in his late fifties.

'Going to write the great American novel, Alec?' Cardwell said.

'The great Scottish novel, Jos. Remember my ethnic origins.'

Cardwell shrugged. 'I forgot you were one of an ethnic minority. I've always said I'd work beside Scotsmen but I'd never let my daughter marry one.'

'Glad of that. We have to keep the race pure.'

Tansy Walker, a tall willowy brunette who wrote fashion notes for the woman's pages between feminist articles on the rising American woman, smiled at him.

'Hell, Alec, you didn't even give us time to have a whip-round and buy you a going away present.'

'My pockets wouldn't hold all those nickels and dimes, Tansy. But if you want to give me a personal

195

going away present, come to my apartment at midnight.'

'Alec, lover, you would-be great novelists need all your strength. I wouldn't want to weaken the creative impulse.'

McBride shook hands all around. Tansy and two of her colleagues kissed him with some enthusiasm. He wondered if he'd been wasting all the years with Dorrie.

The Lake Bar was quiet at lunch time. A few newspapermen drifted in and out, a few regulars sat in booths nursing beers with the reverence of hardened lunch-hour drinkers. McBride settled in a corner booth and waited. He ordered a Manhattan and sipped it without interest. He told himself his nostrils were filled with the smoke of burning bridges and there should be health warnings issued by the government about burning bridges.

McBride waited. One o'clock came and went. A half hour past. Three quarters of an hour. McBride went over to the bar.

'Any messages for me? Name's McBride.'

The barman looked at him with a jaundiced eye. 'This ain't Western Union, buddy.'

He continued the ritual of glass polishing, a thick-set man with heavy, dark eyebrows. A Polack, McBride thought, and a surly Polack. McBride stood facing him, glowering back at the glowering face. After a moment, the thick-set man looked up.

'No messages for nobody.'

'Is there a public phone here?'

The barman jerked his head to the back of the bar, a dimly lit corner. McBride made out the outline of a telephone booth.

He rang Anson's house in Cicero. There was no reply. He went back to the booth and ordered another Manhattan. He waited another half hour. Then he walked out.

196

He walked to his bank and made arrangements that would enable him to draw money throughout the United States in any branch of the bank. He put a sum of money aside to cover any bills that might arise regarding his apartment. Also, should he decide to sell the apartment, the bank would do this on his behalf. He then took a cab to the apartment.

Despite the central heating and the yellowing sun of a dying afternoon, the apartment seemed cold. McBride paced around from room to room for half an hour. Then he started to pack. Two suitcases only and his typewriter. Everything else he determined to leave. A few books went into one of the suitcases, particular books that mattered. Sandburg's *Life of Lincoln*, *Vanity Fair*, a paperback volume of the poems of Whitman, a couple of unread detective stories, the plays of Chekov, *War and Peace*. The others he would leave with regret. But at least he'd arrived in Chicago with only one suitcase and no bank account. It was something for eleven years, some kind of small achievement.

He locked up the apartment and gave the keys to the porter.

'Message for you, Mr McBride,' the porter said.

He took the envelope, his hand trembling. His name was scrawled on it in Dorrie's handwriting. At least she'd sent a message.

It was short, to the point and without sentiment.

'Alec, it's no use. This time they'll kill you. Believe me, I know. There's nothing I can do. You can only run. If you're fast enough you might just make it. Good luck, Dorrie.'

No affection, no regrets, no explanations. He'd been right about one thing. She had known more than she'd ever told him. Much more. And now there was only the impersonality of black ink, and an obviously hurried scrawl. He crumpled the note and thrust it deep into his jacket pocket. He nodded goodbye to the porter and went down into the basement car park.

The Thunderbird had long been replaced by a sleek Chevrolet, not the best car in the country but one that he found comfortable to drive. He put his luggage in the back seat and drove out of the car park.

Drove out of the city of Chicago. Heading south-west. No determined destination. Just looking for someplace that he would know would be the right place in which to stop and breathe.

12

1975–1978

Mid-America. Even if you've never been through it you've got the image in your mind. Of course McBride had passed through in the years before but never with leisure, never with time to look. He still had the images mixed up in the back of his mind. There was the Middle America of Hollywood and the Andy Hardy movies, the small towns with the trees fringing the streets, overhanging the lives of old, wise occupants and young enthusiastic Mr Americas of tomorrow. America, there was God (a very white protestant), the President (as God, but more powerful), Mom's apple pie, the girl next door, coca-cola and necking with both the coke and the girl in an open roadster. And sex was necking and nothing more.

So Andy Hardy's home town of Carvel became Peyton Place and worse. It became the America of *Easy Rider*; small towns drenched in ignorance, brutal law enforcers, thuggish Fascist townsmen in loud checked shirts. John Ford's brawling heroes could punch and leave no scars. These characters punched and kicked and wounded and killed. This was America as it saw itself. The sight, implanted in Alec McBride's mind, was the image he was about to see in reality.

He was determined to drive away from the Kennedy assassination, the search for Bunker Hayward, the idea that there were those who wished to kill him. He was driving away from it and yet still moving towards it.

199

He was determined to find time and peace to write his book. And he was searching for the place.

He drove through Springfield, home of Abe Lincoln, one of four Springfields in the USA; drove through mining country, pitheads reminding him of home and the coal mines of central Scotland. He lived in motels and small rooming houses, heading further south through St Louis. And for a time followed the Mississipi. He moved towards Cairo, Illinois, a man travelling alone, speaking to few people.

Then there was a night south of Cairo where, booked into a motel in a small town, he sat in an empty bar staring at the barman. McBride wanted to talk, to have some communication in a society that seemed to have little interest in communication outside the radio and the television screen. Communication to so many in America had become a one-way process, something to be received but not passed on. Barmen were, of course, the exception to this rule.

'There you are, buddy.' The large Scotch was placed in front of McBride. 'You want ice?'

'No ice, thanks.'

The barman shrugged. 'Thought everybody had ice.'

'Not Scotsmen.'

'That right? Gee, you from Scotland? Never met anybody from Scotland. When you're at home you wear one o' those . . . what do you call them . . . skirts?'

'Kilts. No, I don't wear one.'

A pause and a grin. American hospitality coming for the foreigner. 'First time in town?'

'This town, yes.'

'Good little town. Timber town. And grain. You staying long?'

A silent shrug. Was he staying anywhere long? The question was still to be resolved.

'You should stay around. Good prospects here.'

McBride swallowed the Scotch. It warmed him. He felt amiable towards the barman.

'Another Scotch. And something for yourself.'

'Thanks. You drink quickly.'

'I have a thirst.' McBride said, suddenly wondering if he was beginning to forget how to conduct a conversation. And he had only been away from Chicago for a matter of weeks.

The barman placed the refilled glass in front of McBride and poured himself a beer. The bar was a long thin room with a low ceiling and the inevitable strip neon.

'Where you headin'?' the barman asked.

'Uncertain. Like going along a dark tunnel.' Christ, what an answer.

The barman accepted it. 'Driftin', eh? Not many people driftin' nowadays. Now, in the thirties, everybody seemed to be driftin'. The whole population moving around. Lookin' for something. Eldorado. Yeah, that or just plain lookin' for enough to eat. What you lookin' for, mister?'

'You could call it . . . an avenue of escape. Place where I can relax, that would be more accurate.'

'We're all lookin' for that. Trouble today is everybody who's moving is doing it for different things. Stranger things. Not work, or their souls, or a woman. Blame the atom bomb for all that. Makin' folks unsettled. It was simpler in the old days. I had a cousin walked from the Atlantic to the Pacific . . . 1929, it was. Lookin' for work and an amenable woman. All the way he was carrying a pet canary in a cage. Been gassed in the first world war and he was still worried about a gas attack. Reckoned if it was happening the canary would keel over and warn him.'

'Not much fun for the canary.'

'Cousin reckoned if it was good enough to warn coal-miners of gas it would warn him. Funny thing. Damn

201

bird outlived my cousin. He got hit by a truck. The canary survived. Haven't much time for birds myself. Not feathered ones.'

They talked for an hour and the conversation, complex to the point of surrealism, warmed McBride.

The next morning he moved on, still following the Mississipi. He crossed the state line into Tennessee. In a small town overlooking the river he rented a small house for six months and made a start on his book. He would write in the mornings, directly onto his type-writer, sitting facing a small window which gave him a view of the wide brown river. Late in the afternoon he would drive into town in the Chevvy, eat at a small cafe for truckers or at a local Howard Johnson's. He passed the evenings watching the inanities of television, drinking in a local bar or occasionally going to the local drive-in movie house.

The waitress at the trucker's cafe, a tall blonde girl, somehow reminded him of Dorrie or a screen actress of his youth, June Havoc. The waitress, whose name was Gloria, had a pretty face, lived in, used by life, but she had a native wit that intrigued him. Gloria, who had been married at fourteen and widowed at nineteen, accepted his interest with a wry humour and went out with him on her occasional evening off. They went to the drive-in or to a bar and finally, after three dates, to his house.

Their sex was warm, amusing, comfortable and without ties. Gloria, who later confessed her real name was Lettice, expected nothing but the enjoyment of the moment. She was thirty-two now and had, in her own words, been around.

'I don't expect anything but three square meals a day and a little fun . . . mebbe a little love. But I don't expect it to last.'

'You must want something out of life,' McBride said as they lay together on his narrow bed.

202

'I guess some guy . . . probably a farmer or one of the lumber men'll want a little more than you do, Alec McBride. And if I kinda take to him I'll say, sure, and maybe get hitched again. But yuh cain't even rely on that. Like Tommy . . . my husband . . . any guy can up and die next minute. So . . . so I guess I got no . . . what you call it . . . . expectations. Just take it day by day.'

McBride thought, that's what I'm doing. Day by day. Except for the book. That was for the future.

Gloria knew he was a writer. But it held no interest for her. So he was writing a book. So, she was a waitress in a hash-joint. Her own words. It was the same thing. Work. To be done but not to be interested in. McBride liked her. But she didn't fill the space left by Dorrie. The more he thought about Dorrie the more he became convinced he was the one who had been in love. She had responded for reasons he couldn't fathom at this time. But it wasn't love. Sex, sure, humour, maybe, and companionship. But not love. Gloria, he told himself, was ten times more honest than Dorrie Macklin had ever been. It was something to appreciate.

In the fourth month, they caught up with him. Whoever they were, they appeared in the form of a large man running to fat, in a crumpled grey suit and a soft grey hat.

It was a night Gloria was working, for which McBride was grateful. Other people were not to be involved. He couldn't forget Genine Marks, long dead in Dallas.

At nine in the evening there was a knock at the door of the rented house. McBride, half watching television, half going over a manuscript he had completed that day, rose wearily. He thought, maybe Gloria had got off work early or maybe Jess Loper, a local barfly had dropped in for a game of chess. It was an occasional habit of Loper's to do this and it was welcomed by McBride.

203

He opened the door. The grey suit and the crumpled hat stood there. Under the hat, fleshy features, ridged between fat, scarred with long-gone adolescent acne. A stranger. A big man.

'Mr McBride?'

McBride acknowledged his identity with a nod. Then the gun appeared, a large gun, a Magnum, pressed into his stomach. He was propelled backwards into his living room.

'Who the hell are you?' McBride demanded. They had caught up with him, he knew it.

'I'm a man that's been looking for you, McBride,' came the reply. 'You're not an easy man to find.'

'What do you want?'

The fat face creased into a kind of smile. 'You must know what I want. Now jest don't you be movin' fast. This is a Magnum with a hair trigger and I wouldn't want to blow you away here. Too messy.'

'And too much noise so near town?' McBride suggested. 'How did you find me?'

'Long story. Lot of people lookin', so they tell me. Now let's jest get you a jacket and coat on and we'll move right out of here.'

'To where?'

'Where it's peaceful and quiet and we won't be disturbing anybody.'

'And if I don't come with you . . . ?'

'Then we might jest have to disturb folk.'

McBride stared at him for a moment. McBride was perspiring now. Yet the big man didn't look so frightening. Perhaps that made him even more terrifying.

'You intend to kill me?'

'Let's not get into detail, mister.'

McBride had to keep talking. If nothing else it took up time, elongated the few minutes he might have left. 'Why? Why kill me? Is it because of Dallas?'

204

The big man shook his head. 'Don't know nothin' about Dallas. Don't know nothin' about anything. I'll tell you, mister, I jest git a phone call tellin' me what I got to do and I go out and do it. That's my business, my remunerative labor, you kin call it. See I find you . . . or I'm told where to look and I go and take care of you. I don't ask questions. I don't do nothin' but what I'm paid to do . . .'

'Who pays you? Wouldn't be a man called Hayward?'

'I don't ask for no names. I'm like . . . like an actor. As if I got an agent who handles all that.'

More time needed, McBride thought. So grab at straws. He grabbed. 'How much do they pay you?'

The big man grimaced. 'Do I ask you how much you earn? No, I don't. I don't talk to strangers about money matters and they don't talk to me.'

'I could pay you more to let me go.'

'More'n five grand?'

'Ten grand.'

The man rubbed his chin.

'A thought, mister. But then you see, I wouldn't get any more work from my sources. Not if I let them down even jest once. So, much as I'm tempted I reckon I got to say, sorry, no. Now you don't bother any more but be gettin' your coat on.'

He stood easily, the big man, weapon in hand pointing at McBride's stomach. McBride reached for his jacket and felt his body tense. Something had to be done and he knew he was going to do it.

He swung around, jacket in hand, arm stretched out. The jacket hit the gun hand as much like a whip lash as he could make it. The Magnum, deflected to the right, slipped in the intruder's hand, damp fingers sliding on the blue metal. At the same time McBride put his head down and charged forward. It was something he remembered from his childhood, a Scottish streetfighter's feint, 'one wi' the heid'.

McBride's head hit the big man under the chin on the throat. The man crashed back against the wall, choking at the force of the blow to his throat. The Magnum clattered to the floor. Now at least McBride had rid him of the weapon.

But there was another disadvantage: the size of his opponent. The man pulled away from the wall, hands reaching forward, enormous and threatening. Once those hands reached him McBride knew he'd be in trouble. Without thought his right hand shot forward aimed at the one area already weakened. The edge of his palm hit the man's throat again, fractionally above the Adam's apple. The large body went back again, twisting sideways, mouth open, gasping for air.

A third time McBride hit him on the throat. This time he was balanced, with all his strength concentrated on his right hand. There was a small sound, almost a crack and the big man was gurgling, mouth moving, lips contorted. And then a gout of blood, bright scarlet burst over the moving lips. The man's hands flayed now ineffectually for a moment and McBride stood back watching with a horrid fascination.

But it wasn't over. McBride was only beginning to learn how difficult it was to disable, perhaps even to kill another human being. The flaying hands straightened out, the eyes, screwed up in pain, attempted to focus on something below.

The large body lurched forward, unidentifiable sounds still coming from throat and mouth. The man was ignoring his own agony, making his next move. He fell on his knees, hands reaching for the Magnum.

McBride uttered a sobbing sound for no reason he could fathom and, moving forward, kicked the Magnum into a corner of the room, away from the large, scrabbling hands. At the same time he kicked out, striking the large body on the left ribs. The would-be assassin rolled onto his side with a low grunt. McBride

206

kicked out again, this time hitting ribs. There was a distinct cracking sound.

Another groan. Still the large body moved in the direction of the gun. McBride moved fast around him, reached the corner of the room and picked up the weapon. The metal felt warm, damp in his hand. He swivelled round as he felt fingers clutching at his feet. Holding the gun by the barrel and resisting the temptation to use it as it should be used, McBride jumped back, staring at the bulk of moving grey flannel and flesh at his feet. He should shoot the man but any shots would be heard throughout the neighbourhood. Too many questions would be asked, too much local publicity, even if it came out as 'Man shoots intruder with intruder's gun'.

Using the gun as a club McBride hit the man on the head.

The man fell back onto his side. Blood seeped onto the short hair. A rich color. McBride hit him again on the same spot. Another sound like wood cracking. McBride thought, I've fractured his skull. I must have. He must be nearly dead.

Nearly.

But not yet. The man heaved himself with tremendous effort onto his knees in front of the Scot. More blood, flowing from mouth and nostrils now. And more choking, gurgling sounds. The man's eyes were glazed, rolling in his head but he was still moving forward, hands reaching out, searching for his opponent.

Christ, thought McBride, will he never stop?

The big man, horrible sounds in his throat as he tried to get air into his lungs, still moved.

McBride, feeling sick now, kicked him under the chin and he fell back against the wall of the room, chin streaming blood, hair matted with it. Again attempting to move, fighting himself now to live.

Got to kill him, McBride thought. Got to or he'll never

stop. *He's* the paid assassin and *I* have to kill him. Or he'll keep coming. He'll never lose consciousness, he'll keep on and on.

The Magnum would finish it but he couldn't use it. So hit him again.

McBride hit the man again and again. He was kneeling beside the body, blood on his fingers and on the gun when the door opened and Gloria came into the room.

'I got away early . . . Oh, God!' She stood, eyes wide, the whites enormous, staring down at the two figures.

'He . . . he came to kill me!' It was said with a gasp and a gesture of hopelessness. He could have done nothing less than he had. 'I can't stop him. He keeps coming at me . . .'

Gloria pushed him gently aside and looked at the big man against the wall, head and face splashed with blood. She felt the neck at the side of the throat, looking for a pulse. As she did so McBride stared at the man, wondering at the discoloration on the throat and the strange, uneven shapes under the skin.

Gloria stood up and helped McBride to his feet. 'He won't come at you any more. He's dead.'

McBride nodded. 'I had to kill him. But he wouldn't die.'

'He did. Who was he?'

'Don't know. Paid to kill me . . .'

'Why?'

'Something I learned when . . . when I was a newspaperman.'

She seemed to accept this. She was a practical woman. She stared across at the body. 'He's not from around here.'

'No. Somewhere near. Maybe St Louis. He's a . . . a professional killer.'

Gloria looked at McBride now and he imagined she almost smiled. 'How did you manage? He's so big.'

'Don't think he expected me to resist. And I was lucky . . . got him on the throat . . . lucky . . .'

The practical woman came to the surface. 'Nobody'll miss him around here. And St Louis is a big city. We have to get rid of him.'

McBride nodded. 'Yes. I suppose so. But they know I'm here now. They'll send somebody else.'

She said quietly. 'Then you'll have to move on. Is McBride your real name?'

'Yes.'

'You didn't think to change it, did you? Didn't think to cover your tracks.'

'No, I don't suppose I did.'

She smiled now, a good strong smile. 'I did it myself. Not that any guy was trying to kill me. Jest hang on to me. An' I didn't reckon to be hung on to. So I'd take off and always change my name. Okay, now on your feet.'

McBride stood and she indicated he should wash. While he did this she stared at the room and the body. She was waiting when he returned.

'The river,' she said. 'Weighed down. Oh, he'll float up eventually but it'll not be around here. Further down. And there should be no connection with you. Let's search him.'

They did so. He had a wallet containing a social security card made out to Edward Jepson, $200, some old betting slips and a piece of paper with McBride's name and address on it. The piece of paper and the social security card, they burned. The money McBride gave to Gloria. She accepted it without a qualm. In his pockets they found two sets of keys, one for a house and the other for the battered Ford which was standing outside McBride's door.

McBride drove Jepson's Ford away from the town, the body crammed into the boot. The placing of the body in the boot had somehow deprived death of any dignity and yet McBride felt no conscience about this. He suspected Jepson's life and profession lacked any kind of dignity and his manner of death and the disposal of his corpse were in keeping with that life.

Gloria, without demur, followed the Ford in McBride's own car. She waited while he abandoned the Ford in a hollow by the river. She helped him wrap the corpse in a sheet, secured the sheet with rope and weighed it down with rocks.

Edward Jepson embraced the brown waters of the Mississippi in his winding sheet. McBride never heard of his body being found nor of him even being missed. Perhaps the body never was found. It may have decayed and dissolved into the elements of the river. And whether such a man ever commanded enough concern to be missed, McBride doubted. At the same time he felt the uneasiness of conscience at having killed another man. Self-defence, certainly, as Gloria assured him. His life or Jepson's? And Jepson had been sent to kill him. Nevertheless the mechanics of killing the man horrified him and that horror would be with him for a long time.

Back at his house he sat drinking Scotch while Gloria scrubbed and cleaned away all signs of the struggle and the death. When he made a gesture towards helping her she waved him back to his seat and his drink. Only when she had finished did she join him and accept a drink for herself.

'So you've been running,' she said. 'And you didn't even try to change your name.'

'No. I suppose I didn't expect them to find me.'

'These guys who are looking for you, they're big people? With dough?'

'I suppose so.'

'So you want to disappear. You move on. You change your name. You get rid of that car, trade it in. McBride, you gotta become somebody else.'

He nodded, forcing himself to listen to her. In his mind there was still the picture of himself striking at the intruder over and over again.

'Listen to me!' she insisted. 'Goddamn it, listen! You go now. You put distance between yourself and this place. And then you do like I say. You become somebody else.'

'Come with me,' McBride said impulsively.

She smiled, leaned over and kissed him on the mouth. 'Thanks but no thanks. No way. I like you, McBride. I like you fuckin' me. But we're from two different worlds. You'd get sick of me or I'd get sick of you. Either way it would become pretty nasty. I'm happy enough here until the time comes I move on.'

'I couldn't have got rid of his body without you.'

She laughed aloud now. 'Ain't exactly the best reason for a lifelong relationship.'

'What will you do?'

'Look, what I do doesn't matter. Nobody's trying to kill me. A few characters will always be trying to lay me and . . . I should complain. If I like them I let them. I reckon, if I'm lucky, I might meet a nice guy without too much brains, we'll put what little dough we've got together and open our own hash joint. Pull-in for truck drivers. Make enough to retire to one of them small condos in Florida.'

McBride reached for his wallet. She stopped him, anger in her eyes. 'No! I went to bed with you because I liked it. I'm no whore. Anyway I got no conscience about taking money from that dead man. $200 he won't be needing. But I don't take nothing from you.'

But she took one more thing from him. They made love in his bed, in the early hours of the morning. They made love with an almost brutal passion, perhaps an affirmation of a temporary need. Afterwards she helped him pack and load his cases into his car.

'Forget what happened here, McBride. As if it didn't

211

happen,' she said, standing in the frame of the front door, dawn edging the sky over the house. 'And get rid of that car soon. Then get rid of your name. For as long as you have to. Now get the hell out of here before I start howlin'.'

He kissed her for the last time, a gentle kiss.

'You never asked me why I was running. Why they want to kill me.'

'I did. But you never answered. I'm glad of that. Hell, I don't want to know anything. If I do they might want to kill me. Life's tough enough without that. You jest take care.'

'And you.'

He drove away.

13

It was a small town on the Mississippi just north of Baton Rouge. 'Town' was really a misnomer – village would have been closer. Above the village, overlooking the river was the cabin. At least from the outside it looked like a cabin. Inside it was something else. A long low open-plan room ran from one wall of the cabin to the other, on opening the front door. Beyond the room was a small, completely fitted kitchen. Next to this, with its entrance from the living room was a large bedroom and beyond the bedroom, a well-fitted bathroom. The cabin was centrally-heated in winter, air-conditioned in summer. It stood in two acres of ground which consisted of wide lawns.

The man who rented the cabin gave his name as Max Alexander. A Scot domiciled in the USA, Alexander was to the locals, polite, even friendly but unforthcoming about his past.

Jeb Mallon, who owned the one general store in the village, viewed him initially with the morose suspicion reserved for foreigners. However when first delivering groceries to the cottage Jeb found himself invited in and offered a cold beer or something stronger. Jeb opted for something stronger and was poured a large tumbler of his favourite corn whisky. While he drank it the stranger explained that he was a writer and wanted peace and quiet to work on a book and some short stories. As the whisky warmed him Jeb thawed in his

213

attitude to the stranger. The man explained that he wanted to use whatever facilities the village would provide to supply him with the necessities of living. He seemed a quiet man, willing to fit in.

Through Jeb Mallon the word spread that Alexander presented no threat to the villagers, their daughters, or their way of life. Next Alexander made himself known to the sheriff, invited him to the cabin and again the corn whisky was dispensed. In a month Alexander was looked upon as harmless, someone to be tolerated. In six months he was accepted as an amiable visitor. In a year he was, if not one of them, at least a friend with a good supply of corn whisky.

Alexander, it was noted, did write a great deal. The typewriter could be heard at all hours. Packages of manuscript were dispatched to various publications and the only one which raised eyebrows was sent to *Playboy*. Alexander did indicate to Jeb Mallon that the manuscript was a short story, four thousand words of high adventure and nothing to do with the less salubrious side of Mr Hefner's publication. (Or more salubrious, depending on your viewpoint.) Sure enough, some eight months later the short story appeared in the magazine and those few who read *Playboy* (and would admit to it) assured the rest that the story was a cracking good yarn and Hollywood would be crazy if they didn't buy it.

There was an interesting side issue mentioned by those who read the article. Playboy was in the habit of giving in an opening editorial a short resume of the careers of their contributors. However against the name of Max Alexander was only a short note. Alexander was a new writer to *Playboy* and it was suspected that the name was a nom-de-plume for a well-known English writer.

'What's that there Nom de whatsit?' Jeb Mallon asked

214

of Carter Dewsbury who ran a local newspaper from the village.

'Pen name. Jest fur his writin'.'

'That's the name he goes by, ain't it?'

'Mebbe. Mebbe not. Some writers like usin' other names. Anyway I asked Alexander about it. Popped in this morning . . . I was passin' and I was kinda thirsty. He obliged me with a glass of liquid.'

Jeb laughed throatily. 'Bet it wasn't water you got.'

'Anyway I was askin' him 'bout this nom-de-plume. Jest laughed. Said there was a wife somewheres, looking for alimony. And *Playboy* had got it wrong. He ain't English, he's Scotch. Or Scots or something.'

'Guess a wife lookin' fur alimony's a good reason for a guy to change his name. Anyway Alexander's likker and his money's good enough fur me. He's a right hospitable man and he keeps himself to himself. Cain't ask fur anything more.'

Alone in his cabin the man known as Max Alexander studied the copy of *Playboy* which contained his short story and wondered whether or not he had made a mistake in offering it for publication. He was rather proud of the story and had taken a chance, sending it through a New York agent who had greeted it with the enthusiasm of a man who believed he had discovered a new William Faulkner. Alexander had insisted on complete confidentiality regarding any material he might submit. A phone conversation routed through Baton Rouge had underlined this. And *Playboy*, if they accepted the story, were to be given no information other than that Max Alexander might be a nom-de-plume for a British writer in other fields of literary endeavor. By the end of the phone call the agent had abandoned the vision of a new Faulkner and was soon talking to his staff about having a worthy successor to B Traven.

But to the man who called himself Max Alexander

215

the most important fact about the short story was that in its composition there was no sign of the journalistic style of Alec McBride, one-time famous syndicated columnist who had, over a year before, disappeared from Chicago. McBride had actually taken some pride in forming and moulding the identity of the quiet man known as Max Alexander. He'd even written a character study of the man he had become. He found, by doing this, he could handle any awkward questions that might arise.

Aside from his incursion into fiction McBride was very slowly progressing with his book on the assassination of John F Kennedy, which had now become a large manuscript. The thousand days of the Kennedy presidency, McBride analysed in an attempt to highlight the enemies Kennedy had made and the strength of their animosity. This had required considerable research and accounted for a number of visits to the city libraries at Baton Rouge and, on occasions, New Orleans. The realisation soon came to McBride that he was writing history and, at a certain point, his view of history must merge into supposition. This supposition had to be backed by as many facts as he could unearth.

Progress was slow. He also found it frustrating to see the increasing number of books which appeared questioning the official verdict on the assassination. Many of them covered the same areas as his manuscript and asked the same questions. He could console himself with the belief that his would be the definitive book on the death of the President. He would be including the names of the actual killers. Sandrup, Buncey and Hayward represented his trump card. He would be naming names and, by doing so, he had hopes that the men behind the three names might be forced into the open.

For relief McBride turned to fiction. The Kennedy book, he was aware, had become obsessional. He could also look back over the years and accept the obsessional qualities of his search for Hayward. Writing short stories at first provided a breathing space. And then, more and more, he began to appreciate how, in writing fiction, he was indulging in an exploration of himself, his own psyche. A few years before he would have dismissed this idea as a pretentious pose by novelists, a sop to their literary consciousness. No more. His short stories seemed to illustrate his own obsessions. There was a persistent quality of dread, of pursuit by the unknown that ran through these stories. Some of them were self-indulgent and those were rejected by various magazines. Two more, however, were accepted by *Playboy* and others appeared in various journals. The New York agent suggested a volume of the collected stories but was insistent that the author come to New York and promote the book. McBride refused. Max Alexander was not for publicising.

Except in the village above Baton Rouge. He had gained acceptance and now to this was added a degree of notoriety. To Jeb Mallon and his cronies, Max Alexander was their local literary figure. They would visit him, drink his corn liquor and suggest local stories they felt he might be interested in.

'Gotta understan', Mr Alexander, folk like us, livin' in the Mississippi Delta we're kinda special. We see things different from folks up north,' Jeb expounded one warm summer afternoon in 1976. 'We got our own ways, our own kinda justice. I'm not a killin' man but I been at three lynchin's in my life. And only one of them was a nigra. See, we believes in protecting our own. You ever killed a man, Mr Alexander?'

'No . . . no, I haven't,' McBride replied, finding the lie simple. He had never quite been able to accept the fact of Jepson's death. As if it had happened to someone else. Also he was uncertain as to how the conversation had taken its homicidal turn.

'I was jest readin' in the paper there about one of them gangsters bein' found murdered in Miami. Now that's something don't bother me. The death of a rat is the death of a rat. No call for folks to be gettin' worked up 'bout that.'

Jeb had just delivered the groceries to Max Alexander and with them the daily paper. He now indicated a story on the corner of the front page. McBride glanced at it. A name caught his eye. He felt ice cold.

'MAFIA LEADER FOUND IN OIL DRUM IN MIAMI BAY'

'ROSELLI MURDERED BEFORE TESTIFYING TO SENATE COMMITTEE.'

The grey-haired man who believed he was untouchable was dead. McBride remembered the calm assurance of the man in the Italian restaurant. It had happened to Giancana but it couldn't happen to him. And now it had. Another witness would not appear before another Senate committee. Jeb Mallon noted his interest. 'They say it was a Mafia killin'. I say the rats kill the rats, let 'em.'

Too easy, McBride thought. The death of a man by violence couldn't be dismissed so easily. And McBride had found a certain attraction in the personality of John Roselli. To end, dead in an oil drum with his legs sawn off, was another nightmare to add to the Kennedy affair.

Mallon looked at him with curiosity. McBride's interest was ill-concealed.

'That newspaper story . . . got to you, didn't it?' he said perceptively.

McBride looked up from the paper. 'It's just . . . that's no way for any man to die.' Again the lie came easily.

'Neither's lynchin'. But I seen it as needful when I seen it.'

The conversation ended. No way to argue with

Mallon. The values he held were simple and deadly. But the character of Max Alexander could not afford to antagonise by disagreeing with the local viewpoint. There was no purpose to be served.

Mallon took his leave affably.

Time passed.

Passed quickly, despite solitude and celibacy. For McBride there was work and his occasional visits to Baton Rouge and New Orleans. The delta was a mixture of the old south – the south of the Creole, of jazz, and of ornate politeness – combined with the new south, with its futuristic landscapes of oil refineries and chemical plants, of pipelines twisting across the countryside curling into storage tanks, creating industrial ugliness in the midst of the old and quaint architecture of other eras.

Time passed as the culmination of nightmares approached; Alec McBride sensed this with a foresight he could not explain. It brought him nightmares in the darkness of the cabin, distorted, unreal dreams he could not define. There was no definition for abstract fear. Only the knowledge that the climax was coming.

Towards the end of 1978 it began.

The book was nearing completion. But McBride began to realise that the names, Sandrup, Buncey and Hayward were not enough. The only background he had on Sandrup was through his now dead sister. And who was Orrin Buncey, reputed to have been killed, according to Sandrup? Was he really dead? Was he too a Dallas man? And there was Bunker Hayward. The dark shadow over fifteen years.

To finish his book McBride would have to return to Dallas. End where he began, he told himself. It was inevitable but he did not look forward to it. Several times he postponed his departure date.

Then winter came. And the weekly visit from Jeb Mallon.

'You got enemies, Mr Alexander?'

'Enemies?'

'Men. Lookin' for you. Well, mebbe you. Somebody like you. Came up river from Baton looking for someone. Guy called McBride.'

The cold in the bone marrow, suddenly there. And then adrenalin in the blood stream. Trembling, unnoticed except to himself.

'Everybody's got enemies, I suppose,' McBride said. 'But I can't think of anybody that would find looking for Max Alexander worthwhile.'

"Taint the law, I made sure of that,' Mallon went on. "Cos eff it were the law I wouldn't be holding back. But I made sure it weren't. See, eff you was a criminal on the run, I would tell them fellers. You'd have taken us in and I wouldn't like that. Wouldn't take kindly to it. But I don't reckon you have. I reckon mebbe it's jest about the alimony.'

'Thanks for that.'

Mallon suddenly chuckled. 'Now a woman, eff it were a woman I would sure understand you running. Wouldn't mind that. But there is something, ain't there?'

'There's something, Jeb. It's not against the law . . .' Easily forgetting the body in the Mississippi. But then Mallon would have understood that. 'Maybe it's the opposite. On the side of the law. There are people would like to do me damage. Because they're afraid of things I know. I can't tell you what they are. If I did I might endanger you. But I haven't taken you people in, not in any way.'

The clock above the open fireplace ticked loudly throughout the pause. The sound seemed to fill the cabin.

After a moment Mallon spoke again. 'Reckon I was

220

right. You're okay, Alexander . . . or whatever your name is. That's my judgement and I always believed I was a purty good judge. Anyway we told these fellers there was no stranger livin' around here. Now, that'll hold them for a time but they jest might hear from somebody else 'bout you livin' here. I can't do anything about that 'cept warn you. That's what I'm doin' now.'

'Appreciated.' A pause. 'I might just have to go away for a while. But I don't want to give up the cabin. Want to leave a lot of my things here.'

'I'll keep an eye on them. You'll be back?'

'Some time. If . . .'

'I'll forget the if. Jest take it you'll be back.'

McBride started out on the drive to Dallas the next day.

Night roads. A shining grey ribbon in the rain, surrounded by darkness. And, with the rain, a coldness pervading the atmosphere. Only the headlights, the road and the cold. In the daylight the lushness of Louisiana broken only by the towns and the used car lots which surrounded the towns. With night the towns became clusters of lights coming and going, clapboard shacks glimpsed in brief spasms of light, main street concrete lit in the rain by lamps which seemed to bleed their illumination.

The radio on for the news broadcast. The grey vast Mississippi threatened to overflow its banks, flood the delta and lands north. In Guyana a US congressman investigating the People's Temple cult has been shot dead. In Tehran there were riots.

McBride was not driving directly to Dallas. He told himself, in the event that he was being followed he would detour and turn back on his own tracks, move fast and then slow, confuse any follower, cover his own tracks. Up into Arkansas and through a town called

221

Delight; then over to Lockesburg and into Oklahoma. Nights in motels that looked as if they were designed after the hotel in *Psycho*. And with a number of Norman Bates's in charge.

He could have reached Dallas in a day. Instead he took a week. From Lockesburg he phoned Dallas. The newspaper office.

A quick conversation. 'Is Charlie Neaman there?'

A female Texas drawl. 'Mr Neaman's been retired for two, three years.'

'Is Harry Schuyler still on crime?'

'Hold on. I'll put you through.'

His voice had grown more tired in fifteen years. 'Schuyler here. Who's that?'

'Alec McBride. Remember?'

'For the love o'God, McBride! What in hell happened to you?'

'What should have happened to me, Harry?'

'Well . . . one minute the big-time columnist, the next minute, disappeared. The word was you crossed some big-time hood and ended up in Lake Michigan in a cement overcoat.'

'You read too many gangster stories . . .'

'Hell, I try to live them. What can I do for you?'

'Three names, Harry. Want you to find out anything about them. Whether they've got any relatives alive, friends, wives anything.'

'Gimme the names.'

'Billy Sandrup . . .'

'Aw, come on, Alec, you were lookin' for his people fifteen years ago.'

'So I'm still looking. Orrin Buncey and Bunker Hayward. They may be from Dallas, they may not but I think they were all from Texas.'

'Christ, what do I do? Advertise?'

'Ask around. Buncey, like Sandrup is almost certainly

222

dead. Look up hatches, matches and dispatches. Anything. Be more careful with Hayward.'

'What's this all about?'

'Research. For a book. The three Texan musketeers. Or whatever. You'll get paid. Anything you get, hold on to. I'll be in Dallas in a few days.'

'If I'm getting paid, you're the boss. See you when I see you.'

Driving again. Oklahoma territory. Wasn't that the name of a movie? Before it was a state. Beginning of oil country. Which meant poverty next to wealth.

Then it was late at night and McBride booked into another of the Norman Bates chain of motels in a small town. A very small town. Main street and anything beyond was suburbia. The youth behind the motel reception desk, fighting a losing battle with acne, was taciturn.

'Sure, we got a room.'

'I'll take it. How about something to eat? You have a cafe?'

'No cafe. No food. No cooking in the rooms. And payment in advance.'

McBride paid. 'Is there anywhere I can get something to eat?'

'Main Street. Two blocks down. Open to midnight.'

Parking his car, McBride examined the room. The television set didn't work and the shower leaked. It would have to do. He decided to walk the two blocks to the eating place.

The blocks were dark, the sidewalk rutted with holes in what passed for concrete. From Norman Bates and *Psycho* his mind wandered to another movie image: *Easy Rider*. Hicksville. For all the oil wealth of Oklahoma, this town had been bypassed. Two old men rocked the evening away outside a dark barber's shop, waiting for rain. A group of youths in tattered jeans stood around two giggling girls in cotton dresses. Who was going to

223

be lucky tonight? Which youths would they give out to? Or would they take them all on? A young negro walked quickly by, and spat with meticulous aim at McBride's feet. Keep moving, ignore the gesture. He was only trying to overcome.

McBride thought, time I went home. America was becoming like phlegm at the back of his throat. Part excitement, part nausea. Perhaps, fifteen years ago, he should have gone to the British consul in Dallas, told him Billy Sandrup's story and then forgotten it. Instead of allowing himself a fifteen-year-long obsession. That word again. Obsessed by an obsession. He walked on. Trapped by himself.

The cafe was a hash joint. Tables were decorated with chequered cloths. The stains on the cloths were a menu in themselves. The waitress was fourteen made up to look fifty. She should have been chewing gum but, thank God, wasn't. McBride ordered a steak with french fries. At least in cattle country you could always get a decent steak. He followed it with coffee. The coffee was black and almost solid.

An hour later he was walking back to the motel.

Nighttown USA. Darkness broken by pools of light. Nightmares come to reality. Footsteps echoing against themselves. Like he was walking a long tunnel arched by a black sky; had been walking that same tunnel ever since that night in Dallas. Underfoot, pitted sidewalks, cratered by time. McBride walking and waiting always for something to happen.

They came out of the alley in a flurry of silent movement. There were two of them.

McBride's first thought was that they'd caught up with him. After fifteen years, this time they'd sent two to make sure. And this time they would kill him. They started by hitting him on the back of the neck with something solid, a piece of pipe or a cosh. He fell forward, hands only stopping his face from striking

224

the sidewalk. For a moment blackness descended, then became flashing lights before his eyes.

He could hear them.

'Come on, come on!'

Hands moving on his jacket, fumbling over the pockets.

'What's he got on him?'

'Gimme time, gimme time . . .'

His wallet was extracted.

'There's only about ten bucks here.'

The sense of relief flooded over him. No assassins, no emissaries from Hayward. Small town muggers. That was it. The big city syndrome spread to the small town. They wanted his money, nothing more. But the bulk of his money was locked in his case back at the motel. And the voices were getting angry.

'Should have more than that. Big car, big city dude. More'n ten bucks . . .'

'All there is.'

'Lemme see.'

Irony. If he was to be killed for ten dollars. After the fifteen-year long, dark tunnel.

More hands fumbling. 'A bum in a big car and only ten dollars.'

A hand grabbed his shoulder and pulled him around until he was staring up at the pale shapes of two faces, moving, grimacing, ugly in their frustration.

'Come on, sucker, where's the real dough? Where's the pot of gold, rainbow boy?'

He tried to speak but couldn't. He moved his lips but no sound came.

Desperate now, the voices: 'Where the greenbacks, mister?'

'Wouldn't want to hold out on a coupla nice country boys?'

'Where's the big bank roll?'

Third rate gangster movie dialogue. McBride tried to smile and was kicked in the ribs.

'What you wanna kick him fur?'

'Encourage him . . .'

Then somewhere a shout. Distant. And running footsteps.

'Hey, it's the pigs!' The two faces disappeared. More running. Reverberating on the sidewalk, sending stabs of pain through McBride's body. Then he was raised up gently. A broad-brimmed stetson shaded the face that looked down at him.

'You all right, mister?'

'In parts,' McBride replied, pleased to have found his voice. 'In other parts, not so good.'

'They roll you?'

The sheriff had a deputy with him. They helped him to his feet. He was pleased to find he could stand, however unsteadily.

'They rolled me. Didn't get much, though.'

'Looked like the Kramer kid. And that goddamn Polack.'

'Bastard! We know 'em, mister. We pull 'em in, you identify 'em.'

And waste time. When he should be on the way to Dallas now. Two kids. And they only get locked up for a few days. Stupid and futile.

'Sorry. Didn't see their faces.' The easy way out.

The sheriff nodded. Glum disappointment. 'You want a doctor?'

'Just want out of your little town.'

The deputy spoke. 'We're not all thugs and muggers, mister. This is a decent town.'

'Isn't everywhere? Just the twentieth century sickness, sheriff.'

Like Dallas in 1963, like Vietnam, like America today. Maybe like the world. 'Sorry I can't help,' McBride said.

226

His ribs ached and his neck pained him. Beyond that he was standing erect now and steady.

The next morning he left for Dallas. Aching but unbowed, he told himself. And he told himself he might ache, even bleed, before the thing was finished.

Whatever the thing was.

14

Harry Schuyler said, 'The prodigal returns. Welcome back to Dallas. Or are you just slumming?'

They were in a bar in the Hyatt Regency.

'Why did you quit the paper in Chi'?' Schuyler went on. 'You had it made.'

'It's a long story. Tell you sometime,' McBride replied. 'Did you find anything?'

'Not much. Sandrup had a sister but she died.'

'I knew that. Anything else there?'

Schuyler shook his head. 'Not there. Buncey, Orrin. Small town boy. From near San Anton . . . Funny thing. Supposed to have been killed after being discharged from the marines in '59.'

'I know that too.'

'Body found in the desert in '64. It had papers on it which showed it might have been Buncey. The man who died twice. We did a piece on it after you left for Chicago. Only living relative was his mother. She came out and actually identified a ring and some photographs. Might have been a big question mark but . . .' Schuyler shrugged.

'But what? Didn't the mother identify the body?'

'That's the point. You find a body that's been in the desert a year or more, what you got? Bones. A few bones. Mother couldn't identify anything.'

'What about marine corps records? Dental chart, any broken bones?'

'Marines said Buncey was dead. Wouldn't release any documents. Something about them being missing. Official story was the guy had probably stolen things from Buncey years before. All sounded crazy and improbable but who cared. The story died. Either way your Mr Buncey was dead.'

So Sandrup had been right. They'd disposed of Buncey. Elimination with due dispatch.

'What about Buncey's mother?'

'She was killed in a street accident in 1965.'

'I could have told you something like that would have happened.'

Harry Schuyler shrugged. 'It's the Kennedy assassination, isn't it? You're still on that?'

'I haven't denied it.'

'For Christ sake, Alec, it's fifteen years.'

'With Richard the Third it's about five hundred years but they're still asking questions about the princes in the tower, Harry.'

'That's in England. This is Texas. We don't go further back than the Alamo.'

'Was that before or after Kennedy?'

McBride ordered another round of drinks. It was difficult. The bar was packed with twenty billion dollars worth of oil.

'I'm glad I'm not staying here,' McBride said.

'Where are you staying?' Schuyler said without interest.

'Remember that hotel Sandrup made me stay at? The Prairie Traveller.'

'You're not staying there?'

'I thought of it. But no. Be carrying nostalgia too far. Also I'm vulnerable to bullets in the head. I'm at the Hilton. Less oil. More cattle.'

The drinks arrived. Schuyler ordered another round at once. It saved time. 'About Hayward,' he said. 'You haven't asked about Hayward.'

'I was getting to it. He's the dangerous one. He's still alive.'

Schuyler smiled. It was a weary smile. The man had been around for a long time.

'I know. I met him.' Even now his timing was perfect. McBride felt cold. 'Say it again,' he said.

'Four days ago. This guy came to the office. Asking for you. Said his name was Hayward. Bunker Hayward. Big guy. Fair hair. Shoulders like Paul Newman. Only taller. Did you know Paul Newman was pretty small?'

'You saw him? You spoke to Hayward?'

'I saw him. He seemed to know you were coming here.'

'And you told him I was.'

Schuyler shook his head. 'I don't tell nobody nothing. Especially when it's for an old pal. Anyway he said he wanted to talk to you. Wanted a word before the senate committee convened. I didn't like the look of him. I don't know why. He seemed okay and yet . . . I don't know . . .'

The next round of drinks arrived. A tall man in a large stetson was calling loudly for the waiter.

'That,' said Schuyler. 'Is the voice of Standard Oil. What is it with this Hayward guy?'

McBride ordered yet another round of drinks. When the waiter moved away he said, 'He kills people.'

Later they drove to the Hilton in a cab.

McBride was suddenly puzzled. 'Back there you mentioned Hayward said something about a senate committee. What senate committee?'

Schuyler showed no sign of alcoholic intake. 'Where have you been living. Don't you read newspapers any more?'

'I've been living in the outback. The papers are kind of local. If the world ended it would be reported on the back page under the local dog show report. So what have I missed?'

'What you've been waiting for. The senate have convened a committee to investigate further the death of John F Kennedy. It's scheduled to convene next year.'

McBride's head was hazed with alcohol. As if he could only dimly perceive the implications of what Schuyler had been saying. After so many years. After the long obsession. No wonder Hayward was looking for him. Was still looking for him. Here. In Dallas.

'Is he still in Dallas?'

Schuyler stared at him. 'Who?'

'Hayward, of course.'

Schuyler shrugged. 'Don't know. Just said he'd be around for a day or so. To tell you he'd be around.'

The nightmare goes on, McBride thought.

The evening of the next day found McBride alone in Dallas. He'd insisted to Schuyler that he should be alone. As if he should challenge the nightmare. If Hayward was still in Dallas, somehow he would know McBride was alone. And perhaps he would show himself. The man he had never seen but felt he knew better than anyone else.

In the afternoon he bought himself a gun. A Colt 45. It seemed the right kind of gun for Dallas. Not that McBride knew anything about guns. But he was determined to do the thing properly. The shoulder holster, he felt, was obvious to everyone in the street, but its bulk gave him comfort.

Above and around the city was the darkness. But in the street the neon turned everything to light. Strip neon, flowing neon, multi-coloured bulbs, shop windows ablaze with light, this was Dallas, the millionaire capital of Texas. Not the actual capital, but the centre of money, flowing like oil from oil. And someone somewhere who wanted to kill McBride. For money.

McBride knew where he was going. Not that he

admitted it to himself. Not until he was facing the Prairie Traveller hotel. One bulb was missing from the sign above the entrance. 'Prairie raveller Hotel.' It seemed appropriate. Otherwise the facade had not changed. He entered the reception area, ill-lit as before although it had undergone a facelift. Like an aging hag doing her best to look presentable. The redecoration was early Alamo after the Mexicans had defeated the forces of Bowie, Crockett and all. A mock adobe fireplace housed an electric fire. Two sombreros hung on a wall above a television set. There were benches with cushions instead of armchairs.

Behind the reception desk a long-haired youth wearing tight jeans and a sweat shirt looked up with no interest. Despite the decor the hotel was still on a certain downward path.

'Yeah?' the youth said.

McBride felt light-headed. 'Is this the OK Corral?'

No smile. No reaction. Just a puzzlement. 'Eh?'

'Skip it. I want to see one of the rooms.'

'You want to stay here?'

'Let's not go to extremes. I just want to look at one of the rooms.'

The youth shifted uneasily. 'What's the game. This ain't no museum.'

'You could have fooled me. Let's say I want to see the room out of nostalgia.'

'What's that?'

'Or let's say I'm Philip Marlowe on a case and I need to see one of the rooms.'

McBride laid two ten dollar bills on the desk. The youth stared at them with interest.

'Look, Mr Marlowe, some of our rooms is occupied. But I don't mind showing you one that ain't occupied.'

'How about Room 300?'

The youth went through a large, tattered ledger. 'You're in luck. Guy just moved out.' He selected a key

233

from a row of hooks behind him. Then he looked down at the two ten dollar bills and pocketed them with an air of abstraction.

McBride was surprised. Room 300 looked almost the same as it had done fifteen years before. The same cracks ran across the ceiling. The same window, encrusted with grime on the outside looked onto roof tops and distant neon light. The counterpane was different but fraying as its predecessor had been. The walls had been repainted, but some considerable time before, so that they appeared almost exactly the same but for a slight change of hue.

The youth stood at the door, still puzzled.

'You can leave me alone,' McBride said. 'Twenty dollars buys a few minutes solitary meditation. Okay?'

The youth looked dubious. He scratched his stomach under the Tee-shirt. 'I dunno . . . you could be a thief. No offence.'

'If I was a thief, I wouldn't come here to steal. Even the towels could hardly be called a worthwhile haul.'

The youth frowned, then made a decision with some effort. 'Okay. You lock up and bring the key down.'

He left, still frowning, certain that McBride was contemplating some act of indecency. Still $20 was worth any solitary indecent act the youth could comprehend.

McBride himself did not know why he had asked to see the room. Except perhaps that it was here, over the body of Sandrup that the obsession had been born. Staring at the bed, he could conjure up the body of the Texan lying bloody and holed with bullets. Sandrup, who knew he was to die, talking to a stranger in a bar. Why? McBride had rarely asked himself why Sandrup had talked, confessed to him. An act of contrition. God and the world, forgive me for what I have done. Grant me absolution from murder of the leaders of men. Somehow McBride doubted the Texan had a conscience.

234

No, he'd talked for another reason. For two other reasons. One, the least, to show off. The need for a small man to be a big man. Look what I did, mister, I killed one of the emperors of the world. Certainly that, but the other reason was more compelling. Sandrup knew they wouldn't let him live. They hadn't let Orrin Buncey live so why let Billy Sandrup who talked too much stay alive? But Billy Sandrup could talk just a little more before they killed him. He could pass on the knowledge of what he had done, of what Hayward and Buncey had done. It would have been a kind of revenge on those who would kill him to keep silent. And Alec McBride had been there, handy, the useful confessor.

And it had dominated fifteen years of his life. God rot Billy Sandrup.

Now it might be nearly over. A senate committee in Washington could have the story. And then there would be no need to keep running, no need to fear for his life.

The telephone in the room rang. McBride stared at it for a moment then lifted the receiver.

'Mr Marlowe, there's a guy on the phone asked to be connected to Room 300. Told him there was nobody there but he said he wanted to speak to a Mr McBride.'

'Connect him.' Calmly spoken. But the cold was again in McBride's bones.

The connection was made. The voice was monotonous, 'Mr McBride?'

'Speaking.'

'I thought it was only the assassin who returned to the scene of the crime. Not one of the victims.'

'Who is this speaking?'

'I think you know. My name is Bunker Hayward. Now, listen, please. Go back to where you've been hiding. We might just leave you alone. If you contemplate going to Washington, forget it. Washington spells only one thing for you. Another hotel room and another body. Yours.'

'You're a very melodramatic character, Hayward. Like a bad Hollywood B picture.'

A break in the monotone. A slight laugh. 'I was brought up on B pictures. You'll do what I say?'

'How did you know I was here at the Prairie Traveller?'

'We picked you up the minute you came into Dallas. Up till then you were good. We didn't know where the hell you were. Now do as I say.'

'Fuck off, Hayward.'

A pause. 'Don't like bad language. Go back where you've been hiding and we might let you live. Otherwise . . . I'll see you.'

The receiver was replaced at the other end of the line. McBride replaced his. He thought, either way, they'll kill me. They've been trying to over the years. Why should they stop now, even if he didn't go to Washington? Either way, the phone call was a form of psychological warfare.

McBride knew he must go to Washington.

Back in the reception area he returned the key to the youth.

'Everything okay, Mr Marlowe?'

'Okay. And from now on you can call me Sam Spade.'

Back in his own hotel room McBride brought out a map and started to plan his route to Washington. He would use the same technique as he had coming to Dallas. Diversion. Head south. make sure he had shaken off all pursuers then turn back and move north to Washington. Move slowly but not too slowly. Meanwhile find out who was setting up the senate committee. A phone call to the Capitol Building would tell him that.

And then there was a form of insurance he could take out. He phoned his old newspaper in Chicago.

'Newsroom here,' The voice sounded familiar. Then he recognised it.

'Is that Bill Senior?'

A pleasant, affable character five years ago. And a good newspaperman.

'This is Alec McBride.'

Senior was genuinely surprised. 'Well, for Pete's sake, Alec. How have you been? It's been a long time.'

'Long enough, Bill.'

'Column's never been the same since you left. Even Marinker had to admit he was sorry he let you go. Anyway, you're okay?'

'I'm okay. And I'm glad I got hold of you. I want you to do me a favour.'

'Anything I can,' Senior said cheerfully.

'I'm sending you . . . you, Bill, not the paper, a copy of a manuscript and a letter explaining the background to it. Now, listen, Bill, if anything happens to me I want you to try and get it published. You'll find it interesting but I'd rather you didn't read it unless . . . well . . . unless something terminal happens to me. Okay?'

'Okay. But what the hell can happen?'

'Don't ask. Just be my insurance. And don't tell anybody you have the manuscript. That could be dangerous.' As he spoke he wondered whether he could trust Senior or not. A decent, ordinary man, not a close friend. Perhaps he was the best person to hold the copy. And there would be no reason for anyone to suspect Bill Senior.

'I'll do as you ask, Alec,' Senior said. 'But I'm damned curious.'

'If everything works out okay, I'll tell you about it,' McBride replied. 'You'll be the first to read the manuscript. Either way.'

'I'll look forward to hearing you tell it, man.'

'By the way whatever happened to Clyde Anson?'

'Anson? My God, there's a name from the past.

237

Marinker forced him to quit and the last I heard, he'd left town.'

'Probably went off with his daughter.'

'Sure, I guess that's it. If she was his daughter.'

'What do you mean?' McBride felt uneasy.

'You were kind of shacking up with her at one time. Well, we all thought we should say something to you. But then, it wasn't our business.'

'Say what to me?' His hand holding the phone started to tremble.

'Well, her being his daughter. You see, until you came along, we'd never heard Anson had a daughter. If she was his daughter. I mean, we'd all worked with him for years and he'd always denied he'd ever been married. Not that that would preclude a daughter. But we'd never heard of her. Not until you came along, like I said. And then the broad . . . the daughter turns up. Then you take off and they both disappear.'

A long pause. McBride was searching for words, something to say. 'Nobody . . . nobody'd ever seen or heard of her before?'

'Nobody. That is . . .'

'What? Tell me.'

'Crowd of us. Saw you with her in a bar once. We had this guy with us from the *Washington Post*. He said . . . he said she looked familiar. Like some dame he'd come across in Washington. Said it couldn't be the same one but it sure reminded him of her.'

'Why couldn't it have been the same one?'

'She looked different in some ways. Did her hair different. Different color. And anyway this broad he knew in Washington, she worked for one of the agencies . . .'

'What agency?'

'Not sure. One of the internal intelligence agencies. I think that's what he said. Yeah, one of the intelligence agencies . . .'

238

15

1979

It was coming back easily now. Everything that night falling into place. He settled back in the armchair. It was going to be easy. No, not easy, but easier. The fair-haired man was listening, making an occasional note on a sheet of paper within the now-open file. It was going to be all right, McBride told himself.

Of course it took all day. He was, after all, talking about sixteen years of his life. And he found he had total recall. Or so it seemed. But then writing the book had helped, brought everything into focus over the last years. In the middle of his narration they paused and the fair-haired man ordered coffee and rolls which were duly delivered. They ate in comparative silence. There was nothing else to say. McBride's narrative was all. After they'd eaten they continued.

The fair-haired man, the interrogator, McBride mentally dubbed him, was polite but completely imper-sonal. As if he saw himself as merely a channel through which information could be funnelled. And yet McBride began to feel an affinity. It seemed during the passage of hours that he was being drawn towards the man, as if they had known each other for a long time; not simply the time it took to tell the story but the years it had taken to live it.

McBride had read of this. Those under interrogation formed a link with their interrogator. In espionage cases it was how a good interrogator manipulated his suspect.

Not that McBride felt in any way under suspicion. The interrogator was closer to a father confessor. And telling his story to authority was, in itself a massive relief.

Finally they came to the end.

'And so you made your way to Washington?'

McBride nodded. He was tired but content.

'And you contacted Senator Newberry by phone?'

'I was told that he might be chairing the committee. If not chairing it, then closely involved. He made this appointment with you for me.'

The interrogator nodded. A pause. A moment of relief.

'Did you try and contact anyone else?'

McBride said 'Yes. I had a thought. Dorfmann had always insisted that Mr Sullivan of the FBI was investigating the death of Kennedy. That he too had doubts.'

'But over the years you had little encouragement from the FBI?'

'I'd never actually got to speak to Sullivan. I thought, in the end that might not have been Sullivan's fault. So I tried to contact him once again.'

'Why did you do that?'

'Something I came across in some Senate documents. I was doing research in the library in Baton Rouge. And there it was. Apparently in 1975 Sullivan was asked if there was any connection between the CIA and Lee Harvey Oswald. He'd said, no, he'd never seen anything like that, not that he could remember. Then he added "but it rings a bell in my head".'

'You couldn't contact Sullivan?'

'No. I phoned. There was a delay and then they started demanding to know who I was. I'm afraid I panicked and hung up.'

The interrogator frowned. 'Of course you've been rather out of touch, haven't you? Apart from your library researches. You wouldn't know about Mr Sullivan?'

'What about him?'

'He was due to testify before a senate committee last year. But before he could do so, he was found . . . shot dead.'

Outside there was the distant sound of Washington traffic. The day and the light were dying.

McBride said, 'Another one. Everyone who doubted the Oswald story dies. Is killed.'

'Not you, Mr McBride.'

'Not yet. And not for want of trying.'

The interrogator smiled reassuringly. 'Now you've reached us. You've told your story. You should be all right. And we have your story.' The fair hair fell across his forehead giving him a boyish look. But his expression denied the appearance of youth.

'Unfortunately,' he went on. 'Sullivan's death proves nothing. Officially it was a hunting accident. It even may have been a hunting accident.'

McBride took this sourly. 'And Dorfmann was a suicide. And Mrs Raymond and her husband were blown up by accident. And all the others . . .'

The interrogator nodded. 'Statistically improbable. Now, to our next move.'

'The senate committee?'

'The Senator first. Senator Newberry must hear your story. Oh, he'll have my report but he'll want to hear it himself.'

'How long? The longer I'm in Washington the more dangerous it is.' McBride shrugged wryly. 'And I've grown into quite a coward where my life is concerned.'

The interrogator nodded. 'We take your point. Mr McBride. So to expedite the whole thing you should see the Senator at once. How would this evening suit you?'

McBride grinned. Thank God, he thought, no red tape. When these people go to work, they move fast.

'Where are you staying in Washington?' the interrogator asked.

'Connecticut Avenue. The Holiday Inn. I'm not using my own name. Call myself Marinker, this time.'

'Very wise. But I don't think we'll set up our meeting at the Holiday Inn. Not quite right. Look, the Senator has an office and an apartment in the Watergate Building. You haven't been so far out of touch you haven't heard of the Watergate?'

The man had a sense of humour, however mild. McBride appreciated that. Never trust a man without a sense of humour. He nodded his assent enthusiastically.

'Good. Watergate. Senator Newberry's apartment, eight o'clock. I think when the Senator hears your story he'll move fast to bring you before the committee. And, if necessary, take a few precautions to ensure you're protected.' The fair-haired man glanced at his watch. 'Five o'clock now. I'll lay on a car to take you to your hotel, you can freshen up and . . . yes, I'll lay on transport to take you to the Watergate Building.'

'I have my own car at the hotel . . .'

'Leave it there. Driving in Washington is an expedition on its own.'

'I'll take your word for it.'

'Ask the porter at Watergate for Senator Newberry's apartment,' The interrogator smiled slightly. 'Don't be late or we'll worry.'

McBride rose to his feet. 'I won't be late. And there'll be no hunting accidents.'

The interrogator opened the door, his smile broadening. 'Good. And thank you for coming, Mr McBride. In case you don't appreciate it, I class you as a very important witness.'

'Thank you for listening. I feel as if, after sixteen years, I've just received absolution.'

'Save that until you meet the Senator. They're the absolution boys. The cardinals of the USA, and Newberry's one of the good guys.'

242

It was raining when McBride left the building. The official transport, a black Cadillac driven by a silent black driver, took him straight to the Holiday Inn, weaving expertly through the crush of Washington traffic. McBride caught a glimpse of the White House, floodlit in the rain, looking like a small damp wedding cake. The driver only broke his silence when McBride climbed out of the car.

'I'll be here at seven thirty, sir.'

McBride lay for half an hour in a hot bath. He was completely relaxed, as if for the first time since that night in Dallas. He had shifted the burden of knowledge to other shoulders. The meeting with the Senator would only be a formality. At last, McBride thought, he could see light at the end of the tunnel.

At seven-thirty he was waiting in the hotel foyer.

The black driver in the black Cadillac appeared a moment later and at ten minutes to eight the dark oblong of the Watergate building loomed out of the blackness, dark areas interspersed with light blazing from the occasional broad window.

'Have a good evening,' the black driver said as McBride stepped from the car.

Another black face, a security guard, greeted him in the foyer.

'Can I help you, mister?' Events of some years before had increased security consciousness, McBride presumed.

'I'm looking for Senator Newberry's apartment.'

'Sixth floor, room sixty three. Mr Hayward's just gone up. And the Senator's already there.'

Fear. Simple, cold fear. Gripping McBride as he moved forward to the elevator. He moved automatically. He should be running, he told himself, from the building, from the city; away anywhere. Back to Baton Rouge, to the heart of the country. To where he could disappear. Keep running, as he had been running for the last years.

He was tired of running. It was his only motivation for moving forward, for standing alone in the elevator, for getting out on the sixth floor. And Newberry was already there, the security guard had said it. The Senator would be his insurance.

He knocked on the door of room sixty-three.

The interrogator opened the door. A small, benign, middle-aged man was sitting behind a large desk. He rose as McBride entered.

'Newberry,' he said, the neatly manicured hand outstretched.

McBride shook the hand, aware of his own palms damp with perspiration. He looked around. The room was simply if stylishly furnished. In front of the desk were two deep leather armchairs. A filing cabinet stood in a corner to the right of the large window, the glass lined on the outside with rivulets of falling rain. A side table held bottles, glasses and a decanter. Beside the table was a door leading to the other rooms in the apartment.

There were only three of them in the room. The Senator, McBride and the fair-haired interrogator.

'I'm glad to meet you, Mr McBride,' the Senator said. 'Been looking forward to it.'

McBride nodded. 'For how long, Senator?'

Newberry looked puzzled. 'Ever since I heard your story.'

'Longer than that, surely, Senator.'

Silence. From beyond the window, no sound, no traffic. A sound-proof room.

The interrogator broke the silence. 'Something's happened, Mr McBride?'

McBride stared at him. Tall, fair, immaculately dressed. Brooks Brothers. What the average Wash-

ington executive should be wearing. What was it Harry
Schuyler had said?

'. . . this guy came to the office. Said his name was
Hayward. Big guy. Fair hair. Shoulders like Paul
Newman. Only taller . . .'

And further back. In Nam. Turvey, in that bar. 'Big
guy, fair-haired . . .'

Then the voice on the telephone in the Prairie Traveller. 'Go back where you've been hiding . . . we might
let you live . . .'

The Senator was pouring drinks now. 'Bourbon, Mr
McBride.'

McBride nodded. Did Newberry know? Was he part
of it? McBride accepted the drink and sipped it.
Newberry handed a drink to the fair-haired man and
then poured one for himself.

'Something's bothering you, McBride,' the Senator
said. 'Don't be afraid to tell us. You're among friends.'

'Am I?' He couldn't resist the question. The two men
looked at each other.

'I think he knows,' the fair-haired interrogator who
was Bunker Hayward said. 'But I'm not sure how.'

McBride said, 'The security guard downstairs. Mr
Hayward has just gone up to the Senator's apartment.'

Hayward grinned. 'Always something you miss in
this kind of work. Some little unforeseen slip. Not that
it matters now.'

The Senator's face was expressionless. 'As Hayward
says, you can't take everything into account. Still, it
makes things easier, tidier, I suppose.'

McBride faced Hayward. A good-looking man. Fair
hair with touches of grey now. Ice blue eyes.

'Who are you, Hayward?' he asked. 'Who do you
work for?'

The Senator replied. 'At this time Mr Hayward works
for me.'

Hayward shrugged. 'I've worked for a lot of people.

245

For the marines, the army, the Department of Justice . . .'

'And the CIA,' McBride suggested.

'And the CIA.'

McBride took a gulp of whisky. He was surprised now at his own calmness. The feeling that nothing more could surprise him. Nothing more could happen. Except for one thing. And he wasn't willing to consider that yet.

'Of course I've always worked within the US government service, McBride.' Hayward added. It seemed to be some kind of justification.

'In Dealey Plaza, with Sandrup and Buncey, were you working for the US government?'

Hayward's lips twisted. It was his version of a smile.

'Yes, sure,' he said. 'For various agencies of that government.'

'Assassinating the head of the government?'

The small, neat Senator replied. 'Mr McBride, government in this country is a hydra-headed monster. The Presidency is a temporary appointment, remember that. The executive arm of government changes every four years. But other arms, security etc., . . . these go on. And other institutions, as important to the country as government. Certain areas of business . . .'

'What's good for General Motors is good for the USA. Somebody said that . . .' Hayward added, the smile fixed, unalterable.

'Oh, for Christ's sake!' McBride burst out.

'For the sake of the sovereign state and its way of life,' Newberry cut in. 'You see, sometimes even the President of the USA can become a threat to the health of the country.'

'The country, Senator, or merely a number of vested interests?'

'It can be the same thing, McBride. One President knew that when he said the business of the United

246

States is business. John F Kennedy, a charming man himself, became a threat to many of us. You see, as a man with an excess of money himself, he saw no need to protect the wealth of others. He had ideas about new societies, about raising up that vast pool of labour we call the poor. Oh, very commendable, but not practical. He wanted to change the system. That would have been too painful for many of us. Anti-trust laws are highly untrustworthy.'

'You killed him to protect your own vested interests?'

'Not just mine. Others much bigger than a mere senator. And not only management. He was a threat to certain unions. Bobby Kennedy's vendetta with the Teamsters, for example. Oh, Kennedy had courage. We respected his stand on the missile crisis against Khrushchev and Cuba. But after that . . . he became a handicap. One that so many of us could not afford.'

McBride throat was dry. He felt as if he was choking. He gulped more whisky. 'But you . . . Senator Newberry, you're on the committee questioning the Oswald version of the assassination?'

'Of course,' the Senator waved an urbane hand in the air. 'The Oswald story is no longer tenable. Another story will take its place. Not yours, I'm afraid, McBride. But something suitable. Not that it matters. It's all history now anyway. Nobody really cares. Not even the Kennedy family. They don't want applecarts upset. Especially if and when Teddy Kennedy makes his bid for the White House. If he ever does. And when he does, he will know better than his brother.'

The Senator suddenly laid his glass on the desk and stared up at McBride.

'And now, Mr McBride, I have to leave you with Mr Hayward. Doubtless, you two have much to talk over. After all, I gather it's as if you'd known each other for sixteen years without actually meeting. Anyway, I'll say good night.'

'Getting out before the violence, Senator?' McBride said hoarsely.

'Of course. I am a member of the United States Senate, McBride. I have my job to do. Mr Hayward has . . . another occupation. He has his job. He's very experienced as you know, and his is a highly paid, greatly trusted, profession. We never interfere in each other's work.' Newberry turned to Hayward. 'You will of course keep this apartment tidy, Mr Hayward. Remove everything awkward. Wouldn't want another Watergate scandal.'

The Senator left.

Hayward looked after him. 'One of the good guys, I told you. For me, I meant. Knows what to do and when to do it. Democrat, you know. One of Kennedy's party. But when it came to the crunch, he knew what had to be done.'

'You work for him, then?' McBride asked.

'No. He's a kind of go-between. A big guy but not as big as the others. The ones that keep out of government but run the country.'

'Like General Motors, eh?'

'Sure, like them. Not GM itself. They kept out of trouble like this. But others . . .' Hayward shrugged, the fixed smile still in place. 'Anyway now we've got together. You see, in the end you had to come to me, McBride.'

'Like a nightmare.'

'More a controlled exercise. Your luck had to run out, McBride. Dorfmann protected you for years, God knows why. He had scruples about too much killing, you could say. But when he had to be taken out, it was only a matter of time until we got to you.'

'Dorfmann was a weak sister, eh?'

'Exactly right. Went in with the big boys but was too small to play with them, really.'

'Not you, though, Hayward. You weren't a weak sister.'

Hayward ran his hands through his fair hair. 'You got it wrong there. I'm only an employee.'

'Murder for money, eh?' McBride felt the bile rise in the back of his throat. The image of the bright, middle aged, young civil servant was there. Underneath the killer. Veins without blood. Pure ice.

'Sure,' the iceman said. 'Maybe a little more. I always thought the President was like the old Greek king in the grove at Nemi. The king who must die. In order to encourage the harvest. That was Kennedy. He threatened too many big multi-nationals. His death ensured the harvest.'

'All this and a classical education. And what about the others? All the witnesses who were killed. The Richmonds, Sonia Sandrup, Sullivan?'

'They were in the wrong place at the wrong time. Or like yourself, they heard what they shouldn't have heard. If they could be . . . contained . . . fine. Otherwise . . .' Hayward shrugged. 'Incidentally Clyde Anson's still alive.'

'But then he was working for you, wasn't he?'

Hayward raised his eyebrows. 'You cottoned on to that, did you? Perceptive.'

'Only when he disappeared. Not until then. You see, he did save my life when the bomb was planted in my apartment in Chicago.'

The thin lipped smile again. 'I always thought he was trying to save himself just then. Of course he might have weakened. Not one of our better people.'

'Not like his daughter.'

'She wasn't, you know, his daughter. But she helped to contain you. At Dorfmann's insistence. Don't kill him, contain him. A mistake in the long run. I tried to make up for it in Nam. Nearly got you. Always uncertain, a personnel mine. Dorrie's all right, you

249

know. Still with me. Useful backup, especially a woman.'

He swung round on the balls of his feet and stared at the door leading to the other parts of the apartment. 'Dorrie!' he said quietly.

She came into the room silently, her face impassive. To McBride she seemed to have aged more than the years that had passed since they'd last met. The dark hair was streaked with grey, not evenly, not applied in an attempt at style. The eyes were underlined, tired, one flecked and bloodshot. The mouth was tight, a line imitating Hayward's mouth, tiny lines running from the upper lip.

'Hello, Dorrie,' McBride said.

She nodded, her eyes moving around him, not looking directly at him.

'I don't think he understands, Dorrie,' Hayward said. 'How you could be with him, make love to him and be working for me.'

She said nothing but went over and poured herself a drink. She wasn't a happy lady.

Hayward went on, 'You see, Dorrie's a professional lady. But getting on. Too many younger ones coming along. A competitive industry, prostitution. Free enterprise. But tougher and tougher as time passes. So Dorrie welcomed the job of working for me. Well paid. Even pensionable. That can be arranged. Not a lot of job satisfaction, mind you.'

'You're a bastard, Hayward.' It was the only thing McBride could think of saying.

'I think Mrs Macklin would agree with you. But I am needed, sir. Governments always need people like me and Sandrup and Buncey.'

'And when they cease to need you, they dispose of you. Your turn'll come, Hayward.'

Hayward lit a cigarette, then as an afterthought

offered one to McBride who refused. He didn't bother to offer one to Dorrie.

'No, not me. You see, when we were in the marines, I recruited Sandrup and Buncey. I was in charge. Even my idea to arrange for them to appear to be dead. But they couldn't keep up. They visited relatives, they talked too much. Their one asset was their ability with rifles. But when the job was done, they became a handicap. No . . . no vision. Otherwise they could have had a career, like me.'

Another long silence. Dorrie Macklin sat in one of the armchairs nursing her drink. She still did not look at McBride. Even when he broke the silence.

'And now, what happens?'

'First of all I take that cannon away from you. The one you bought. In Dallas, was it? Oh, don't try and reach for it. This PK Walther is much more efficient.' The gun appeared in Hayward's hand. 'Such a melodramatic business we're in.'

'You're going to use that here?' McBride managed somehow to sound casual. He didn't feel casual. He was feeling even sicker than before. But he summoned up enough self-control to feel some kind of pride.

'Oh, not here. We don't want another Watergate scandal. In a short while we'll go for a drive.'

'Not much desert around Washington.'

'Plenty of arable land. Easy to dig. You won't be found, McBride. And anyway you disappeared a few years ago. Who's going to look for you? Incidentally we intercepted that package you sent to Chicago. 'Fraid your book won't get published, not even posthumously. Sorry. I would like you to understand this, though. I'm an instrument. That's all. No guilt. That resides with the others. My employers. So you see, all this is nothing personal.'

'My imminent death is rather personal to me. But I get your drift.'

251

Hayward took a pace towards him. 'I'll take that cannon from you now.'

Perhaps it was carelessness. Perhaps, after all the years, Hayward expected resignation from McBride. Or perhaps, simply, it had always been too easy for him. Or maybe McBride had gained experience when he had killed Jepson in the south a time ago. He told himself he knew how to kill now.

Hayward reached out, pushing aside the lapel of McBride's jacket, fingers feeling for the butt of the Colt. The Walther PK was in his left hand. McBride suddenly slumped forward, the weight of his body pushing the Walther aside, deflecting the barrel away from him. Hayward sensed too late what McBride was doing. He tried to pull back but McBride brought his knee up sharply, digging into the fair-haired man's groin.

Hayward doubled up, jackknifed, permitting himself no sound of pain but a low grunt. McBride slammed his hand down on Hayward's wrist and the Walther fell to the floor.

It was at Dorrie Macklin's feet. She stared at it dully but did not move. It was a break, McBride told himself. If she picked up the weapon he was finished.

Hayward's fingers, away from the butt of the Colt, clutched at McBride's lapel. McBride knocked the hand away and brought out the Colt.

It was an unwieldy gun, heavy and awkward and inaccurate at a distance. But at close range it was devastating. Hayward knew this and he knew he'd been careless. Bent double, he was still able to kick out effectively at McBride's knee. The pain was excruciating. McBride fell to one knee agony stabbing through his leg and spine. But his right hand was free and he brought the Colt around towards Hayward.

The explosion was deafening. The bullet took Hayward in his shoulder twisting him around and throwing him to the floor. He rolled over, leaving blood and fragments of bone on the carpet, his face distorted with pain, his shirt and jacket coloured by a spreading rosy stain.

McBride grabbed the arm of one of the chairs to support him. His kneecap was agonisingly painful but he reckoned unbroken. He swung the revolver around towards Dorrie Macklin. It was not needed. She sat immobile, eyes wide open, staring at Hayward. She was somewhere else, in memory or in shock. McBride turned again towards Hayward.

The man stared up at him now, eyes narrowed, but an expression of surprise on his face.

Finally he managed to speak. 'Doesn't . . . matter . . . about me. No point in killing me . . . . They'll send someone else . . . always someone else.'

The pain was easing from McBride's leg. He forced a smile. 'Maybe,' he said. 'But you've been after me a long time. I've had nightmares about Bunker Hayward. I'd like to be rid of them. And anyway I can't kill you, Hayward. You're already dead. In 1959, remember.'

'You'll be found.'

'Sure. But not by you. Not now. No more people found by you, Hayward. One professional less is . . . just that. One less.'

More blood was staining more carpet. Hayward was lying prone now, weakened, weakening more and more. Unto death, McBride thought. But he had to be sure. Had to . . .

Hayward coughed blood. The bullet had touched the lung. With difficulty he spoke again.

'You can't kill me. Haven't the nerve. Not professional. Not used to it. Not able . . .'

'You taught me to be able. A man called Jepson, you or your people sent. I killed him. With difficulty. But I learned how. This is much easier.'

He fired again. One shot. The top of Hayward's head disappeared in a red mist. His body shuddered once

253

and was still. McBride put the Colt back in its holster and buttoned his jacket. He tested his leg and found it supported him. He turned again to Dorrie Macklin.

Her face was still expressionless. But she spoke now, for the first time. 'He's right, you know. They will send someone else.'

'He'll have to find me first.'

She took a gulp of whisky and stared at Hayward's body. 'Am I next?'

'No.'

A pause. 'It was a job of work, McBride. Living with you. Everything. But I was getting to like it. That's why they made me go away.'

'Okay. I believe you. Better for my ego to believe you.'

'Yes, I suppose so. You'll be going now?'

He nodded.

'Where can you go? Hayward was very precise. They're big people. They'll send someone all right. What will you do? How will you live?'

'I'll live,' McBride said. 'How? Somehow. Different names. Different places. Invisible man. No light. No light at the end of the tunnel. But they won't be able to see either. And I might be able to do something. Publish my book. Show people a part of them.'

'They won't like that.'

'Good.'